SLABSCAPE:RESET

S.Spencer Baker

www.BlipBooks.com

First published in the UK in 2010 by Blip Books

British Library Cataloguing in Publication Data.
A catalogue record for this book is available from the British Library

ISBN 978-0-9567387-0-7

Typeset in Courier and Times New Roman

Printed and bound in the UK by CPI Mackays, Chatham ME5 8TD

Edited by Nick Coldicott

First edition
13579108642

www.BlipBooks.com

for S.

From paperback to webback.

The slabscape is littered with ideas, words and technologies that haven't been invented yet[1]. Some of these need a little explaining[2].

I loathe footnotes[3]. Every time I turn the page and see a footnote, that's the first thing I read. Glossaries are even worse; all that page turning and place losing – it dices your head.

www.slabscapedia.com acts as a backup to the slabscape series and was originally intended to be a repository for explanations, back-stories and definitions. Unfortunately, it's got a bit out of hand.

SSB, Tokyo, September 2010

---

[1] *we can only hope*
[2] *and some need a lot*
[3] *this is patently untrue*

Asynchronology: $^{\delta t}SS^{ES}$

one

He was falling.

For a long, long time, this was the only thing he knew.

two

three

There was no wind against his face, no sound of rushing air and no clue from the featureless white fog that surrounded him.

Still, he knew he was falling. With accelerating certainty, he knew he was getting ever closer to something. Closer to something unknown and further away from something comfortable and safe.

Reference points. Reference points. He needed something to latch on to. Where was he falling from?

He thought back.

There was no back.

OK, OK, he thought. How about: *Who am I?* That should be easy enough.

Nothing.

Not even a hint. A blank surrounded by a void.

All he knew was that he was falling.

He felt sick.

Now he knew two things: he was falling and he felt sick.

Oh well, he thought, I suppose that's progress.

four

Falling. White. Sick.

Something was niggling him. A thought was scratching around in the back of his head.

His subconscious was trying to force some key detail into his conscious mind. It seemed important. He tried to focus and squeeze the message out. It was like trying to remember someone's name and just as the word was about to form … forgetting it again. He hated it when that happened. It was a kind of mental stuttering that stopped him from remembering. Stopped him from …

Stopping was something to do with …

Oh shit!

Falling was a finite process. He was going to have to stop falling at some point. Maybe soon. Something told him that stopping falling might not be the type of experience that a non-falling person would volunteer for. Then he was sure of it. He was not going to want to stop falling anywhere around here anytime soon.

No.

No way.

He screamed.

No sound. Or maybe he was making a sound but couldn't hear it. He felt like he was screaming. He tried to reason with himself but that didn't help so he abandoned reason and became mindlessly lost in fear and panic. Then he gnawed desperately at reality by trying to make himself believe he wasn't really experiencing any of this and it was all a dream. If it was a dream, then he couldn't be in any real danger. Or if he really was in danger, it was probably nothing to do with his dream and he couldn't even know about it because if he was dreaming, he must be asleep or maybe he really was in danger but as he was asleep, he couldn't do anything about it anyway so he might as well stop freaking out and calm down.

Just like that, he calmed down.

He re-evaluated his circumstances.

No significant change.

White blur, still falling, feeling sick (although that seemed to be fading). Maybe his mind had been playing tricks on him. Maybe falling was a natural state for someone like him. Not that he knew what that was or if there was anyone but him in the realm of existence. So far, all the evidence available to him suggested that he was alone.

For ever.

Maybe, he thought, I'll just have to get used to it.

He slammed into the ground.

five

His body convulsed in the recovery frame.

'… and we have re-entry. Mark inception.'

He gasped for breath and realised, as he felt the air rush into his raw lungs, that he hadn't been breathing until that exact moment. Funny that he hadn't noticed it before. He must be dead of course, because no-one could have survived an impact like that. But then if he was dead he wouldn't be gulping in air for dear life. And someone had said something about re-entry. He'd entered something. Again. And in the process he had screwed up, crashed horribly and destroyed his body. Odd thing though: He felt no pain. No physical pain that is – his *mind* was turning itself inside out.

A soft gauze was taken from his eyes. He tried to focus on the vague blur in front of him. It was a face. It moved. It was the face of a strange and wonderful being, with wide, crystal-clear eyes.

As he gazed, breathless, into what he knew was the face of the most beautiful woman he had seen in his entire thirty-second life, her full lips parted slightly and she too, took a brief intake of breath. Her gorgeous, dark eyes focussed fractionally and captured the moment. Then she smiled and he was falling again.

Her face was surrounded by a white, helmet-like cap. She reached up with white-gloved hands to remove something warm and comfortable from the side of his head and expose him to the larger sounds of the white, featureless room.

'Hello, can you hear me?'

'Uuuhhhhhhgghhh.'

'Good. Now, can you understand what I'm saying to you?'

'Wehramhaigh'

'Hmmm?'

'Where … am … I?'

'Oh good. You can speak. Excellent. Well done! That will save us a lot of work!'

'Of course I can speak, I'm … er …' He still had no memory of anything before the fall, and even that was fading out like a dream. What was fading in was a profound sense of irritation.

'What the hell has just happened to me?' he demanded. 'Where the hell am I? Who am I? And who the … are you?'

Waking from a long period of zerosleep has been described as rather like having your toes sucked – through your ears. His facial muscles contracted around his perfectly formed nose.

'Yes, I was warned you might be a tiny bit tetchy. Never mind; apparently it's quite normal.' She smiled winningly. 'OK. First off, you are in a re-familiarisation ward of the cryonic suspension unit in the Vincent Van Cloud biological repair centre, Seacombe SideUp. You are a reset and because you are a reset, you don't have a name yet, dear, just a numerical signifier. I've been calling you Dielle because you were stored in Level Three, Row D, Column L. See? D, L: Dielle. I thought it was clever.'

Patient facial response; imperceptible.

'You can choose your own name before you leave if you like.' She was disappointed. She'd been using the name while he'd been thawing out and had grown fond of it. 'I am Nurse Kioki Sypher-Marie Pundechan and I'm in charge of your rehabilitation training. You can call me Kiki.'

She was focussing her attention on something behind his head that he couldn't turn to see. He couldn't move anything else either. Every part of him seemed to be rigid.

'Why can't I move? What's wrong with me? Am I a prisoner?'

'A what? No! Of course not!' She looked horrified. 'You can't move because, even though your muscles have been artificially stimulated to keep them viable, they haven't actually been doing anything useful for a very long time. Also, the terms of your regen contract stipulated that you were to be a lot taller than you were before, which means you are going to have to re-learn how to do basic things like walk and feed yourself and so on. To help you do that, you are connected to an automated external skeleton which will control your limbs and balance your body while you practise moving around. You'll like it, it's very strong.'

Dielle started to feel his mind reeling again. This was just a bit too much for someone who had only just been born.

'Uh, how long have I been in this place?'

'Well, *you* are a reset which means that *you* have only been here for about ten minutes. Today is your birthday – type of. Happy birthday dear.'

'But you said my muscles hadn't been used for a long time. How long?' At this point he wasn't really interested in the niceties of resetiquette, he was desperate for some bottom line facts to anchor into some hard-core reality.

'Well, let's see …' She did something with the panel behind his head. 'You were in regen for just over three hundred and twenty-five body years. We can't regenerate bodies in real time, it takes over six years in regen to get a year younger, you see?'

'I've been here three hundred and twenty-five years? Nurse … how old am I?'

'Oh, you have the body of a perfectly healthy twenty-seven-year-old male. Rather a nice one too, I think you'll find. We've made quite a few improvements during the regen. All as per contract – except for one thing which unfortunately hasn't become possible, but there you go, no-one could have predicted we wouldn't have solved that one in a kilocyke. Lookadat! Anyway, RegenInc disclaims all liability as per the technology-not-yet-invented waiver. Hang on.'

Kiki's face momentarily changed. He couldn't describe it as a blank look, but for a fraction of a second he thought she was looking at something slightly in front of him that he couldn't see.

'You were officially declared *born* four hundred and forty Earth years ago.'

'Shit!'

'We don't use that word anymore dear, you'll have to learn some new ones. I'm going to crank up your neutragens now and leave you to rest a while, then I'll be back to start your physicals after lunch.'

'One more thing,' said Dielle wearily as his brain began to vibrate. 'Why am I here?'

'Oh, you'll have to ask yourself that question dear, I'm sure I don't know.' She smiled cheerfully as she turned on her heel and walked through a wall.

Ask myself? Ask myself? What the hell does she mean? he thought.

He dreamed of white osmotic walls and Kiki Pundechan.

six

He had no idea how long he'd slept, but at least he woke without having to go through the whole hitting-the-ground-at-high-speed thing again. This time it was weird. In his dream, Kiki had been floating around the white room, bobbing about like a balloon on the end of a string. One moment, she would be face to face with him, her eyes radiant behind the visor of her nurse's helmet, then she would slowly drift away again until she seemed to blend into the wall, her uniform accentuating curves and proportions which appealed to him in ways he couldn't fully understand. Cute, he thought. Cute? he thought. What does that mean?

But as his dream faded out and reality faded in, the only thing that changed was his equilibrium because when he opened his eyes, there she was, exactly as he had been dreaming.

She floated closer, smiled into his eyes, said 'Hello dear. Did you have a nice rest?' and started to recede again.

'What's happening?' he asked, feeling spacey and on the verge of losing his lunch, except he hadn't had any lunch for over 325 years so that wasn't an option. 'Would you mind just keeping still for a minute, please? I'm feeling a little nauseous.'

'I am still, dear, it's you who's moving. Look.' He found himself looking at his feet. Sure enough, they were moving underneath him, but they looked to be a lot further away than he thought they should be.

'How did you do that?' he demanded, as Kiki came back into view.

'I'm controlling your recovery frame, dear. We're going to have to teach your muscles how to work again. Don't fret now, I kept you asleep for all the boring stuff and it won't take long to get the hang of the rest. Do you remember what music is?'

'Yes of course I remember what music is. I …' he was about to say something else when he realised that although he knew what music was, he couldn't actually recall any. How very odd, he thought.

'Well, we're going to play you some music while you do your exercises. You'll find your brain rewires much quicker if you move around to a rhythm, so I'm going to transfer the frame control to Sister and she'll play you some music. If you want something different, just call out.' She turned and walked through a wall again. It bothered him when she did that, but he really liked the shape her body made when she turned, he just couldn't figure out why.

Rhythmic music filled the room – a gentle, repetitive beat interwoven with something that sounded like a human voice, but wasn't. It was much richer, with a range of tones that made his scalp tingle with pleasure. Yes! he thought, as his adrenaline levels elevated and the recovery frame responded to the beat. He could sense the blood pumping in his veins. He was not the only one.

'Louder!' he shouted, and the music instantly ramped up in volume. He was really going to enjoy music, he thought, as the delicate articulated frame danced him around the white room. The bass rhythms resonated through his body as something deep in him stirred. When the first piece came to an end it was immediately followed by a different piece, this time with people singing together, hundreds of people, singing in a language he didn't understand. It was wonderful and uplifting. He knew it was uplifting and didn't give a damn why.

An hour later he was physically exhausted but mentally elated. Pulmonary emties administered drugs to combat muscle fatigue and calm his brain, then the frame placed him in a comfortable resting posture. He fell asleep instantly and dreamed of Kiki again, but this time they were dancing. She was a pretty good dancer too.

She came to wake him after the prescribed dream time had elapsed, and checked the status panel behind his head.

'Hello dear, did you enjoy your dance?' His warm smile answered her question.

'You must pay attention to what I'm about to tell you, dear. Are you properly awake?'

'Hmm?'

She looked slightly blank again for a split second, then he instantly felt more alert – almost excited.

'OK.' Kiki took a breath. 'Everything that happens in here is recorded and you have total control over its eventual exploitation. The cryo unit will take a standard admin percentage of 10% of gross after excessive taxes and data storage charges. In the event that any of the recorded material features me, I will receive a standard non-background participatory fee equivalent to 50% of your net receipts pro-rated. These rates are applicable for initial sumes only I'm afraid, and reduce to the standard 5% of net thereafter. Which I think is a bit mean, don't you?'

'Huh?'

'It's all right dear, I just have to tell you all this now so you can agree to a pre-consultation agency fee and appoint a proxy to act on your behalf until you're in a better state to negotiate full I.P. exploitation, endorsements and representation deals.'

'What the fuck are you talking about?'

'There is something I have to ask you though. While the sellouts will be fine and should make you enough to keep you going for a good while, there's a SlabWide sumecaster that's interested in putting you out live, no edit, sensurround constant feed. What do you think?'

'Everything is being recorded?'

'I really can't formally advise you … not yet anyway, but there's a lot of people interested in your re-fam experience. They want to sume it live and as we never do any original resets these days, you're a bit of a celebrity already. It's terribly intrusive though. You don't want to do it, do you?' The way she asked made him think that *yes* would have been the wrong answer.

He thought about this while he looked her in the eyes. He wondered how many other people there were in the world he had just been born into. He wondered whether Nurse Pundechan loved him as much as he loved her. He wondered what taxes were. He instinctively didn't like the sound of the word. He wondered what percentage meant and if someone was trying to con him, a mere twenty-seven-years-and-three-hours-old man.

'No I don't,' he said with a lot more conviction than he felt.

'That's good dear,' she said cheerily. 'We'll get a much better deal if we play hard to get. Let them see some of the really good stuff first, sucker them in, then screw them on the affiliations, sub-licenses, merch and stimsellthrus and keep a hundred percent of the residuals! Can I assume you're happy to let me have your proxy until you decide otherwise? You can always re-negotiate at a cycle's notice and you really do need someone who cares about your welfare acting in your best interests.'

'Nurse,' he said. 'I have no idea what all that meant, but I'm with you all the way!' He was definitely warming to Kiki Pundechan. Didn't she just say she cared about his welfare? He thought he remembered what a celebrity was too.

{[to mygroupname inisumecast :: reset incept date 1039:96:4:22:15 affirmative decline live feed. All enquiries to official proxy negotiator and current agent kiki tiger@Pundechan Media. Start high guys, this one's a cutie!]}

[[••]]

{[Note: reset incept date 1039:96:4:22:15 doName

Dielle UFN. Tx agent proxy to self along with SWAMPI-4 pre-consult fee. Standard T and C, 1 cyke reneg]}

[[••]]

'OK – let's see how you're doing. I'm going to release your right hand.' She pointed; 'This is your right, by the way. You are genetically right-handed so this should be the quickest to retrain. Don't try anything too complicated. Can you lift your hand up to your face and touch your nose?'

He thought about where his hand was and where his face was. While he knew both these things, he found it difficult to transfer the knowledge to his arm muscles. Nothing happened.

'Any hints?'

Kiki reached into her pocket and brought out a stick with a fluffy, pink end. She reached up and tickled his nose with it. His hand flew up to his face with amazing speed.

'Ow!' he yelped. Kiki's stick had a small sponge on the other end which she used to wipe away the tears.

'Very good, dear,' she said. 'Right on target. Let's try it again with a little less enthusiasm, shall we?'

Extremity awareness training took several hours and required so much concentration that he found it difficult to talk at the same time. Kiki helped him find his various body parts with a variety of things on sticks and an easy laugh. Finally she let him have another dance before steering him back to the sleep field.

'Sleep well, Dielle dear, tomorrow's going to be your last day on the frame and you'll need lots of energy for the back flips,' she said, adjusting something on his panel. She called out 'Nighty night!' and disappeared through the wall.

Shit! he thought, I keep forgetting to ask her how she does that.

The next day turned out to be different from the first, primarily because he now had a memory of a day before. There was a lot more dancing, co-ordination work and complicated balancing, frequently accompanied by elaborate falling over which could have been prevented by the recovery frame, but wasn't. After a break and more sleep, Kiki disconnected the entire upper body section of the frame. The golden skeleton was stark against the white background and far more fragile than he had imagined, especially for something powerful enough to make him perform back flips. Kiki hadn't been joking, he'd had so much fun doing those, they had to stop several times to catch his breath because he was laughing so hard. The panel fascinated him because it had lots of colours and lines and lights and weird symbols. Kiki wouldn't let him touch it.

During a rest period, they sat together on the sleep field which shimmered in mid-air. Kiki massaged his hands.

'You see,' she said, 'while you were in Regen, we grew you an extra forty-five centimetres in height, so we had to make sure everything grew in proportion, like your arms, hands, chest and well, just about everything really, and your contract had some specific body requirements too that had to be tweaked and adjusted. That's why you might feel a few tingling sensations in your hands.'

He already knew about tingling sensations. He reached up with his free hand and cupped it round Kiki's left breast. Now that's what I call a tingling sensation, he thought. Kiki stopped massaging and studied his face.

'Why did you do that, Dielle?' She spoke softly but deliberately, as though the answer were important.

'Because I … like it?' he said, feeling very unsure of himself.

She looked at a couple of coloured symbols on his panel. 'Hmm,' she said. 'That's quite interesting.' She waited. Dielle did nothing. There didn't seem anything for him to do. Something had happened but he didn't know what.

'Now, dear,' she said slowly after a few minutes. 'Why did you touch my breast just then?'

'I don't know,' he said. 'I think I thought I liked it, but I have no idea why now.'

'That's fine, dear,' she said, getting up briskly. 'We'll get to all that soon enough after your contemporary morality update. But don't worry, it'll be lookadat fine!'

Dielle suddenly felt very alone and vulnerable. 'This is a very strange place, Kiki,' he said. 'You will look after me, won't you?'

{[to glibGirl :: Gabs! Just a day old and he's 20 points hot already. Told you these oldies were goodies! You free dindins ToNight SideUp? Have sumes!]}

[[••]]

'Of course I'll look after you dear, that's what I'm here for. Shall we try some hand-eye stuff? You won't believe how often it'll come in handy.'

Most of the rest of the day involved Dielle having a lot of fun trying to catch balls and throw them back. It was hard at first, but he was a quick learner. He discovered he could make Kiki jump up to catch his throws in a way that made him feel happy and he could tell she was having as much fun as he was.

'I like this body, Kiki,' he said, a little breathlessly.

'Me too darling,' she said, red faced. 'Better get some rest now though, so it can recover and your brain can process everything you've been learning. You're doing very well dear, I'm proud of you. And tomorrow you're going to get a new eye!'

She was gone before he could react. What? A new eye? What was wrong with the ones he'd already got? And what was it with all this walking through walls stuff? Dammit, he must try to remember to ask that one.

seven

He woke from pleasant, manipulated dreams into the cool reality of his white room. His lazy reverie crumbled when he remembered something was going to happen to his eyes. He looked around the room for anything he could use as a weapon. There was nothing. Just white, featureless walls. There was also a white, featureless ceiling and a white, featureless floor. He jumped off the sleep field and shuffled toward what he guessed was the nearest wall. If Nurse Pundechan could walk through it, maybe he could.

'Dammit!' That was the second time he'd hurt his nose. He wondered why his eyes were leaking again. Maybe they were faulty. Maybe they were the only part of him they couldn't regenerate. What had she said on that first day? Something about not being able to do something? He put his finger in his right eye and rediscovered, with a shocking immediacy, something he thought he *should have fucking well remembered in the first place*. He decided that no-one was going to get anywhere near his eyes – not if he could help it. Not ever. He backed up against a corner and rolled himself up into a ball, feeling vulnerable. He wished Kiki was there. A deep instinct made him want to put his thumb in his mouth but he decided it would not only be stupid, but pointless. He did it anyway.

'Ohio to you, my new old friend,' said a peculiar male voice close to his right ear.

Dielle flinched. He hadn't heard anyone come into the room. 'Keep away from me!'

'Don't tell me. Paranoid regression to foetal position in the face of an unrecognised threat. Had two resets just like you this cycle already. Don't be frightened. There's absolutely nothing to worry about. Been sucking your thumb, too?'

'No! Where's Nurse Pundechan?' His voice was muffled, but that could have been because his knees were covering his ears.

'She'll be right down after I've insinuated the new eye. She said to say hello.'

Insinuated? He definitely didn't like the sound of that. Of the thousands of things he was prepared to accept as a new experience that morning, he thought, insinuatedation was definitely not on the bloody list.

'Who the fuck are you and why don't you fuck right off?'

'My name is Plurethaby Triathelon Dempster; you can call me PT. I'm a neural implant technician and I'm not going to go away because unless you have a functioning, legal and updated N.I., you won't ever be allowed to leave this room. So you'd better extract your head from your arse pronto, Tonto, 'cos I charge by the deciday and the clock started running before I left home.'

'What the hell is an N eye?' Dielle asked, staying foetal.

'An N.I. is a neural implant. An interface between you and System, or Sis, or Big Sister, Mum, Mother or any damn thing you want to call the thing that controls everything that surrounds you, protects you, feeds you, informs you, entertains you, deals with your garbage and keeps you alive. Believe me, primitive man, you would rather be blind than not have an eye.'

'Look, I've only been here a couple of days. I'm finding it a bit difficult to keep up with all this stuff. It's all a bit … and who the fuck are you calling primitive?' He jerked open and was confronted by five sets of dark, round lenses peering at him from five different directions. He was just about to re-curl when he realised they were all attached to a cloth-covered helmet worn by someone with a limited social life. All of his clothing – even his footwear – was made from the same coarse, brown fabric. Everywhere Dielle looked there was a pocket with something in it or a fastening with something hanging off it. Now he didn't feel frightened; just offended. He moved threateningly toward the intruder who wanted to steal his eyes.

The festooned form jumped back in alarm. 'Whoa now! Don't take offence. Primitive is a term of endearment around here these days. You're something of a celebrity, you know. I've never even met a reset who wasn't born here.'

He remembered. Yes, he was a celebrity, and he was being recorded too. He straightened up and attempted to look dignified. Good job he'd not sucked his thumb, he thought.

'An interface between me and what? How does it work?'

'Simple. It's a meta-pico network made up of several hundred million nano devices which link the neural impulses of selected parts of your brain, nominally the medium level functions of language and numeracy, aural processing and visual perception along with knowledge-base search and acquisition functions to the system interface that is ubiquitously embedded into the infrastructure of this environment. In order for you to interact with any technology, from a shower to a fivedee sensurround sexinema, you have to have one.' He turned to the large silver trunk which Dielle had only just noticed was behind him. It transformed into a floating bench covered with delicate looking tools.

'Sexinema?'

'Yeah, how old are you?'

'Twenty-seven.'

'And how many days?'

'Two. I think.'

'Sex is in a couple of days. You'll like it'

'So you don't touch my eyes then?'

'Nope, not directly. Just the standard focus-aware, augmentation and image-capture stuff, although we've been working on some pretty cool total visual displacers that I might be able to let you have on a reduced fee, seeing as they're still in alpha.'

Dielle ignored this last comment. He was quickly getting used to ignoring things this strange person said. 'So what do you do to give me a new eye? Is it painful?'

'Nopey dokey, doc. You won't feel a thing. In fact the interior of the brain doesn't have any pain receptors at all – not like your nose, eh?' he pointed at Dielle's face.

'How'd you know about that?' he asked.

'Here's a tip: You can always tell a man who's walked into a locked transvex by the tiny trickle of blood from the nostril.' He moved his multi-eyed helmet up to Dielle's face. 'Smarts, don't it?'

Blood? He wiped his nose with the back of his finger and looked down. The smear of crimson red liquid on it looked amazing. Wow! he thought, red is such a fantastic colour. He stood and studied it for a while, taking in the richness of the scarlet stain, slowly turning brown against the white background of his world. After some time he realised the guy with the glasses had assembled something that looked like a multi-legged mechanical web.

'Now, if you'd just like to put this on your head, we'll be through in a jiffety whiff.'

'You can't seriously expect me to put my head in that thing, can you? What the hell is it?'

'It's a neural implant manipulator – it telefuses the N.I. into exactly the right synapses of your brain. It has to be accurate to within a nanometer so it needs to be pretty firmly attached to your old nodle. See?' he said, holding up the glistening implement proudly. 'Look, these things zero in on your frontal lobe and scan the interior of your brain to tune into the parts of the cortex that link to the interlingual conduits; these are remote probes that specialise in the math processors and these little fellas at the back fuse into the visual and aural pathways to enhance the standard but sorrowfully inadequate input interfaces you inherited from some extinct simian millions of years ago.'

'You are not exactly filling me with confidence.'

'Look, it's no problem, really. Tell you what, I'll just semi-fuse the aural one in and you can see how it feels, if you don't like it, I'll take it right out again, no charge.'

'If it hurts me, I'll pound on your nose with my hands really hard.'

'No need for that,' he said brightly. 'You won't feel a thing. Just put this over your head – it auto-locates to your specific internal brain topography. There you go, spiky ones at the front.'

Dielle gingerly lifted the brain spider over his head. It immediately came alive in his hands, grabbed the top of his head and went through a vibrating dance before clamping itself tightly to his cranium. 'Get it off me!' he screamed, trying in vain to pry it from his skull. The harder he tore at it, the more it held on.

[['Hello Dielle,']] said a voice somewhere inside his head. [['Calm down dear, I won't let anything bad happen to you.']] It was Kiki.

'Hello?' said Dielle out loud. 'Where are you?'

[['Cool, isn't it?']] said Kiki in his head.

Dielle snarled at the N.I. technician who he thought was looking very smug for a ten-eyed lying bastard who was liable to get his nose rearranged at any moment.

'You said this wouldn't hurt,' he complained. 'This bloody thing's crushing my head in!'

'Look, if you don't jerk around so much, it won't have to clamp itself so firmly. This is very, very accurate implant location, you know. Now relax, I've got to locate your other centres. Think of a number.'

'Seven,' he said, impatiently.

'I said think of a number, not say it. And can't you think

of a more original number? Like something with several digits?'

Dielle thought of a number and scowled. He was getting good at scowling.

'OK,' said the techie. 'I'm getting something. Keep concentrating on the number … OK … hang on … first digit: eight … then I've got five, four, seven, another eight – this is coming in fine now … two, two, seven, six. OK, you can stop now. You're tuned to the numerics. The implant is transfused into the right cortex numerical processor. Got that? The right side.'

'Right, right.'

'Yes, I'm one of the best in the business, you know. Trained in the original Implant Development Centre. One of my professors had done this stuff by micro surgery. Can you imagine?'

He couldn't imagine, so he shook his head. That was a mistake; the spider clamped harder.

A shower of highly animated, brightly coloured dots suddenly filled the room. Dielle's eyes tried to follow everything at once, but the more he tried, the less he saw. Every time he focussed on a dot, it disappeared. Within a few seconds, they had all gone.

'Right, that's image capture sorted. OK, be very still now, this takes concentration. Language. Think of a phrase that is simple and direct. Try to imagine that you're giving me an instruction to do something, very precisely. Hear the words in your head, but don't vocalise them. Form them as if I can hear them.'

Dielle did as he was told.

'Hmm,' said PT. 'Just keep going. The spider's searching for the pattern. It'll be around here somewhere.'

As far as Dielle was concerned, nothing was happening. The technician was immobile. 'How are you doing this?' he asked.

'Oh blocks! I almost had it then.' He fidgeted irritably.

'I'm using my own highly tuned and specialist eye to listen to your neural impulses, now kindly shut the dice up and put out that phrase again.'

Dielle settled down and thought about a specific instruction.

'OK, now be silent for a second, I mean stop thinking the phrase so we can eliminate the rebound from the synapses … OK, that's good. Now think it again … Good … got it!' he looked triumphant. 'OK, hang on a moment.'

{[sys i/f N.I.logon for reset incept date 1039:96:4:22:15 basic level i/f standard security level 3. Accept. Confirm to self, authorisation Bravo 23 Alpha dot two dot zero]}

[[Hi PT. Got him. What? Just the basic? You slipping?]]

{[Yeah, and Seacombe UpSide's gonna win the SlabSeries by 50 clear]}

'Now think of a question; something you couldn't possibly know the answer to,' he said, removing the now limp mechanical spider from Dielle's skull. 'Think it deliberately as if you were saying it out loud in your head.'

Dielle tried to think of a question. Sod it, he thought, why is it whenever someone asks you to think of something spontaneously you can never do it?

[[Because spontaneity is not something that can be summoned on demand, it is something that happens without premeditation]]

'WOW! WOW! FUCKING WOW!' said Dielle. 'Did I just remember that or did you just do something?'

'Now try asking where you are, and just think *stop* when you've had enough.'

Dielle did as he was told.

[[Your centre of mass +251252.59:+35987.33:-5928.89 metres relative to Slab datum/re-fam ward, cryonic suspension unit/level 192, Vincent Van Cloud Bio repair centre/Day section 1(aka Seacombe)/Joint Earth Council Space Vehicle Galactic Conveyor (ISS.001.000.0001 uka

Slab)/ 2.53951x10^17Km from galactic centre, bearing - 173.245646, mark +89.359 (SlabRelative data convention version 19.3.112rev9 as defined Spda)/Galaxy position relative data 9.256x10^]]

{[STOP!]} thought Dielle loudly.

He sucked in two lungfulls of air through his nose while his eyes tried to escape their sockets. The answer to just one simple question had blown a hole in his head so wide that he felt as though one side of his brain had just had a major disagreement with the other, declared war, inserted a strategic nuclear device and triggered a pre-emptive strike. He grabbed hold of one of PT's weird appendages for balance.

[[Do you want to know what universe we are in?]]

{[NO!]} Dielle's eyes crossed.

'Lesson number one,' laughed PT. 'Be specific with your questions until you've set your preferences. Best to do that roughly straight away. Just think *use average prefs for info update* and you'll get what most people use for the region you are in. You can always request more levels of data and Sis will stop when she thinks it's too deep, or if you try to go down an enquiry thread that you aren't ready for.'

'Not ready for? I've just been told I'm in some sort of space vehicle and you're telling me it won't let me know stuff I'm not ready for? If this is the shallow end, how deep does it get?' Shallow end? thought Dielle, what the hell is a shallow end? He held his head and tried to think straight.

'Look, just do the preferences, will you? Think *use average prefs for info updates*. I'd do it for you but from here on I can't get to your stuff. That's something very important you need to be aware of: What's in your head is private and no-one can get at it. Do not believe all those windfarmers who tell you Sis is leaky. She's not. I can platinum guarantee it. No-one has infiltrated Big Sister ever – not even once. That's for latenight fivedees and something you tell kids to get them to do their asking work.'

'OK.'

{[Use average prefs for info updates]} thought Dielle.

[[••]] Two reassuring sensations of compliance.

'I've done it. Now what?'

'Ask where you are again.'

Instantly he was aware of the answer:

[[Van Cloud's re-fam ward]]

OK, he thought. I knew that. That's fine. He started to breath easier.

'Next you learn some basics. Try thinking *time exact*.'

He tried it.

[[1039:98:4:09:20.625341]] streamed into his head.

'You get a string of digits, right? They all mean something, cycles, days, hours etcetera – but who cares? You just want to know the time. So just think *time* and you'll get the standard preference setting which is much more suitable. Try it.'

He did:

[[Ten past four]]

'Cool!'

'See? Much easier. Now all that info is received into the interlingual conduits through the N.I. It's not a real memory, so if you want to remember it you have to put effort into storing it into the biological memory areas of your brain. Just like you're doing now with the information I'm telling you. The numbers come up in the right side of your brain – remember that, it's important. When you hear sound, it's raw audio that's straightjacked into your aural nerve conduits. You control it through the eye; just *sound on/off/up/down*. You can't transmit voice internally with your current setup because you have the basic package which is free and gratis, except of course for my fee for installation and training which is what I'm doing now. The eye will function to a distance of up to a hundred klicks from anywhere and everywhere onSlab except where some clowns have deliberately installed multi-phasic shielding.

You won't believe how many jokers there are in this wonderful transcultural agglomerate we call home who think it's a cool idea to log-off Sis. That's what most people call the SlabWide Integrated System you're now linked to. Everyone seemed to be happier conceptualising it as a she – you can look up why later. When you do that, you can find an enquiry thread that will lead to the biggest scam of the last few millennia, but I'll let you discover that little doozy all by yourself. There's an automated training programme I'd advise you to go through. It will familiarise you with what Sis can do for you – and what she won't. Don't go into the enquiry threads for too long at a time because until you get used to it, your brain will feel like it's going to seep out of your ears. There is a natural tendency for the bio side of your brain to try to absorb all the information you get, but after a while you'll learn not to bother remembering stuff you can get through your I.O.D. package – that's Information On Demand – it's a basic level package that everyone has and comes along with the standard N.I. set.'

Dielle was surprised that he seemed to be following PT quite easily, it felt as though he already knew most of what he was saying.

'Now, as I said, I can fit you with a sub-vocaliser so you can send voice as well as info but let me advise you: Don't bother. It doesn't use your individual voice sound, it's generic and can't handle inflections properly or accents at all. On top of that almost everyone has voice-receive filtered out at all levels except for very close personal friends and Sis-override emergency messages which are broadcast through all media lines anyway. If you really want to send voice you can use any standard sound transducer embedded into system while using your eye to direct the recording.'

That must be how I heard Kiki earlier, he thought. Obvious really.

'The eye is powered by Nole, which is, for all intents

and purposes, non-degrading and will function for a lot longer than you will, unless you reset again, in which case don't come looking for me, fella, 'cos I'll be back in the atomic soup long before you wake up. The mere thought makes me shudder,' he shuddered.

'Anyway, as I was saying, the power supplies were implanted with each separate interface and use standard Noles. You can look that up later, too. We call it looking up when you ask Sis for information. Don't ask me why. If you'd like I can fit you with our latest in visual implants. It does colours and some textures and is OK for relaxing and tuning out. We've given up development on the full resolution visual interface. Not because it can't be done; nothing's impossible right? It's just there's a general anti-tech thing going on at the moment and a whole group of people who think it'll stop us from being human. Personally I think that's a complete load of blocks but you can look that thread up later, too. Anyway, if you want the visual implant I can do that for a fifteen percent discount if I do it at the same time as the stim unit which I already know you are gonna want. Look up *additional implant options – Mega Stim-o-Rama* – they're our speciality.'

'Hang on a minute.' Dielle had spotted something. 'Installation fee? Fifteen percent discount? I'm not aware of having any, er ...'

{[How do I pay for stuff?]}

[[Trading carried out by exchanging SlabWide economic units currently known by 2,452 different names starting in order of common usage; credits, money, bucks, slugs, dosh, moolah ...]]

{[Stop]}

'I mean, I don't think I have any credits.'

'Oh sure you do. You just haven't found out about it yet. You'll have to wait until you tell yourself the access codes, but you can be absolutely sure that even if you used to be broke, you either have credits already or you will have.

You're a celebrity, you know. It's impossible for you not to make serious wonga outta that.' PT lowered his voice. 'In fact, if you want a little help on the fivedee deals and such, I know a very good agent. You don't wanna let cute little nursie get her hands on all those residuals.'

Dielle still didn't know what PT was talking about, but he sure understood what was going on. He was being hustled. And worse, this creep was insulting the woman he loved. 'What did you call that stim thing? A stimo-what?'

[[Ext srce Spda:3rdEye Implant Corp. ::The latest in the Triathelon range of major pleasure area Neural Implants, the Mega Stim-o-Rama (V.16.3.2) is the best sensual stimulator within a thousand parsecs. Guaranteed to stim all pleasure centres from the low-level de-stress/relax reflex all the way up to the high-level ecstasy receptors (subject to personal licensed usage). With full-band, multi-phasic, multi-channel simul-feedback this unit will happily interface to all the latest stimcasts, simulations and private channels and has the widest and wildest range of configurable options available on the market. Price 9,300 credits including ExTax, fitting and Sislink tuning. Keywords: [test] for free trial; [more] for further information; [upgrade] for latest version which fixes the feedback loop error in V. 16.3.1]]

'No thank you,' said Dielle.

'What? Don't be a cake! This is ultragoodstuff – the latest in N.I. stims – it's what it's all about – you gotta be crazy not to want a stim unit! What you gonna do for fun? Read a book? You gotta tryout the latest stim titles – and then of course there's the private channels – oh yeah, you're not old enough for that yet. Look, why don't you just take a trial shot and I guarantee you'll be begging me for the whole package.'

'No.'

'What?'

'No.'

'You don't want a stim unit? What did little nursie tell you about them, eh? It's not true that they're addictive. I'll bet a cutie like her uses her stim unit every night!'

'Would you like to know how a primitive like me reacts to what you've just said?' said Dielle with barely masked menace.

'Sure. How?' said PT who, naively, had not seen it coming.

'It does smart doesn't it?'

The senior implant salesman for 3rdEye Implant Corporation briskly packed his equipment while mopping his bleeding nose with a dirty rag.

'I hate working with primitives,' he snivelled. 'Why in Dice's name we bother defrosting you lot is beyond me.'

'Here's a couple of tips for you,' said Dielle to the departing figure. 'Don't call me primitive, don't insult beautiful women and think of a better name for the dope you're trying to peddle than Mega Stim-o-fucking-Rama.'

On the floor, a line of glistening dark red spots ended abruptly at the wall.

'Hmm,' said Dielle, following the dotted line. 'I'd have thought we'd have been free of assholes like him in the future.' He stopped at the white wall and put out his hand. It was solid. How come ten-eyes could walk through it? he wondered.

[[This is a transvex wall. It will only allow individuals through under specific circumstances]]

Oh right, he could just ask now.

{[OK, tell me how I can get through this wall, and while you're at it, tell me why that rude little bastard wanted to sell me a stim unit so badly]]

[[Subject transvex wall is under sub-system control of this cryogen facility. It is currently restricted by system to lockout reset incept date 1039:96:4:22:15 until such time as re-fam has been completed and contractual obligations met. Said little bastard only earns commission if he sells you an extra implant. It is the right of every citizen to have the standard set at no charge]]

{[What is reset incept date 1039:96:4:22:15?]}

[[You are]]

{[Huh?]}

[[You are a reset and experienced re-entry at 22 minutes and fifteen seconds past 4 on the 96th day of cycle 1039. Kioki Sypher-Marie Pundechan has registered a personal doName for you of *Dielle* – do you want to adopt that as your doName main?]]

{[Yeah, whatever]}

[[••]]

He was becoming accustomed to it anyway – it reminded him of ...

'Oops,' said Kiki as she walked into his outstretched hand. 'Mr Dempster wasn't very complimentary about you. Did you really hit him?'

'He was being very rude about you.'

'Oh, how gallant! My hero!' said Kiki feigning adulation and batting her eyes at him. He was quite a bit taller than her and had to look down into her face. He had a strange urge to put his arms around her. 'I'm sure he wasn't rude at all, PT is a complete professional. Did you get a stim unit?'

'No I didn't – although I must admit it did sound attractive. He was just trying too damn hard to persuade me to have it, so I automatically turned him down, even though I actually wanted one. Don't know why.' He was constantly being surprised by his own impulses. Well, he thought, that'll probably go away soon.

[[No, it won't, sorry]]

{[That was a private thought]}

[[Suggest expedite N.I. training routine]]

{[OK, OK, later]}

'That's good. You can get one anytime you want. But some people do find them a bit habit forming. You might want to test your addiction tendencies if you're worried. I can do it for you if you like.'

'Maybe later,' Dielle rubbed his head. 'I've got about a million questions to um … look up before that.'

'OK dear, but don't overdo it on your first day. I'll set your monitor to put you into a mediate brain processing state after half an hour – that's fifty minutes – OK? You'll want to see stuff, too, so here's a nice comfortable seat for you.' She pointed behind him. In the middle of the white room there was a large, black padded chair.

Wow! he thought. Where did that come from?

[[Emtied from central store]]

He sat down hard. 'Hell, have I got a lot of questions to ask!'

Kiki gave him a gentle peck on the cheek. 'Alright dear, have fun! I'll drop in after your nap.' She turned to leave. The kiss on the cheek had made him feel tingly again and it seemed that the simple curve of her body was able to make him feel good.

Nice ass, he thought.

[[Yeah, not bad]]

{[Hey, that was private! Start that training routine]}

Fifty minutes later, after having mastered most of the basic levels of the eye, he fell into yet another state of vivid dreaming. Sis had been carefully steering him around practice loops and hadn't given him much opportunity to ask questions. At least he'd learned how to keep his thoughts private. He suspected that was going to be useful.

eight

By the time Kiki entered the room he'd already been awake for a while and felt more relaxed than he'd been since his …

{[What was it called?]

[[~?]]

{[What does that mean?]}

[[••]] Two tiny pings, like getting a nod with an invisible smile.

{[That, er … Oh, I get it.]} The answer to the question was in the question to the answer.

{[You need more specifics]}

[[••]]

{[What's the name for the process I went through to get here?]}

[[Re-entry]] Yes, that was it, re-entry. He was more grounded now. He thought he knew where he was, he had a name and he felt safe – something he realised he hadn't felt before. Maybe that's what having a big sister does for you, he thought, privately.

'OK, dear,' said Kiki brightly. 'Sis tells me you're ready to graduate re-fam. Well done! I'm really proud of you, my darling.'

Dielle had a spontaneous desire to kiss Kiki on the cheek. He missed. Kiki seemed to have managed to avoid him by smiling. That was confusing. Perhaps, he thought, a little too loudly, there was more to this than was apparent.

[[You're not kidding]]

'Now, before you're allowed to leave the room, you have to agree to what is called a Life Disclaimer. It's a list of things that everyone takes as common sense but it's very important that you formally accept it.'

'Why is it so important? he asked. 'Is something bad going to happen to me?'

'No, of course not. Not unless you want it to. But it's a rule that goes back a long time – maybe even as far as origin. It's all about lawyers and stupidity.'

'Lawyers?'

'Used to be they didn't just make laws, they also made fortunes by exploiting the complications of the laws they had helped to shape. They made so much money through the suing of businesses and individuals that it forced everything anyone ever did, made or said to be covered by unbelievably expensive liability insurances and those costs had to be passed on to the consumers. It was a sickness that very nearly ruined several national economies as well as preventing people from doing almost anything because they were so paranoid.'

'And they were allowed to get away with this?'

'Well, the only way they could be stopped was by using the law – and that required lawyers.'

'Oh, right.'

'So you have to agree to the Life Disclaimer. Sorry, it's rather long but you have to be recorded listening to it and saying *I agree* at the end.'

'I can get out of this room after that?'

'You can go anywhere you like.'

'Bring it on.'

Immediately a dark, flat rectangle appeared in front of him, just beyond his reach, extending from his eye level down to the ground.

'What's that for?' he asked.

'It's for the text dear, symbols that join together to make words. But nobody uses text these days, it's just for traditionalists and naturalists,' she frowned slightly as she said the *n* word. 'But you do come across it sometimes when something old happens and this Life Disclaimer is as old as Slab itself. Anyway, it's only a silly formal thing, dear. Just listen to the voice and I'll be your witness.'

As she said this, a loud, deep and angry voice interrupted them with a cough.

'READY?'

Kiki jumped. 'Oh yes, sorry. Please proceed.' She looked at Dielle, bit her lip, raised her eyebrows and forced a smile. He thought how pretty and full of life she looked.

'STATE YOUR NAME,' boomed the voice.

'Dielle,' said Dielle, looking around and wondering where the voice was coming from.

'D.L? WHAT KIND OF A NAME IS THAT? ARE YOU NOT RESET INCEPT DATE 1039:96:4:22:15? AM I IN THE RIGHT PLACE?'

'I am the same person. Dielle is my doName main.' He felt like standing up straighter but decided to slump a bit instead.

'I donated that name to him, your internship,' said Kiki. Her voice seemed higher and a little choked. 'He's adopted it as his main for the time being.'

'WHY WASN'T I INFORMED? HOLD.' There was the briefest of pauses, then: 'ALRIGHT, LET'S GET ON WITH IT. RESET INCEPT DATE 1039:96:4:22:15.'

'Dielle,' said Dielle.

'QUIET. YOU ARE REQUIRED TO LISTEN TO THIS LIFE DISCLAIMER WHICH IS CURRENT AS OF THIS MARK 1039:98:7:95:23 AND IS VERSION 9199.12.SUB2R AS AUTHORITATIVELY PUBLISHED IN SLABSCAPEDIA. AT THE END OF IT YOU WILL SAY *I AGREE* AND THAT IS ALL.'

'I agree,' said Dielle.

'QUIET!'

Interns have very little sense of humour. He cleared his throat with a wet, explosive sound that made Dielle want to duck, and started: 'I HEREBY DECLARE THAT I KNOW LIFE IS INHERENTLY RISKY AND IT IS UP TO ME TO

DEAL WITH THE RISKS WITHOUT TRYING TO
BLAME OTHER PEOPLE. I AM RESPONSIBLE FOR
MY OWN STUPIDITY AND OTHERS ARE
RESPONSIBLE FOR THEIRS. SOME THINGS DO NOT
WORK, AND SOME THINGS WORK AT SOME TIMES
BUT NOT AT OTHERS FOR NO APPARENT REASON.
THAT IS JUST THE WAY IT IS. HOT COFFEE IS HOT.
IT WILL SCALD ME IF I SPILL IT ON MYSELF. THE
SAME GOES FOR HOT TEA, HOT SOUP, HOT
CHOCOLATE AND IN FACT ANY HOT BEVERAGES
THAT ARE USUALLY SERVED HOT. I DO NOT HAVE
TO BE TOLD IT IS HOT TO KNOW THAT IT IS
PROBABLY HOT AND I DO NOT NEED ANY SIGNS
TELLING ME IT IS HOT. RUNNING INTO SOLID
WALLS, UNAUTHORISED TRANSVEX DOORS AND
WINDOWS WILL HARM ME AND IT IS MY FAULT IF
I DO SO. LIKEWISE FALLING FROM HEIGHTS,
HITTING MYSELF WITH HEAVY IMPLEMENTS, OR
GETTING IN THE WAY OF FAST MOVING, DENSE
OBJECTS IS ENTIRELY MY RESPONSIBILITY. IF I
EAT TOO MANY HIGH-FAT FOODS OR INTAKE
MORE ENERGY FROM FOOD THAN I EXPEND, I
WILL PUT ON WEIGHT WHICH WILL AFFECT MY
HEALTH AND THE PROVIDERS OF THE FOOD ARE
NOT TO BLAME. ENTERTAINMENT IS USUALLY
FICTIONAL AND I DO NOT HAVE TO BELIEVE IT OR
CARRY OUT THE THINGS I SEE OR EXPERIENCE
WHILE BEING ENTERTAINED. SPECIFICALLY, I
PROBABLY DO NOT HAVE SUPERPOWERS AND
WILL DAMAGE MYSELF IF I BEHAVE AS THOUGH I
DO. I DO NOT HAVE TO BELIEVE EVERYTHING I AM
TOLD, OVERHEAR OR IMAGINE. BUT IF I DO, IT IS
MY RESPONSIBILITY TO FIND OUT IF IT IS TRUE OR
NOT.

Dielle was getting bored. He had never heard so many
inane and obvious things. I might not remember anything

from my former life, he thought, but even I know about all this crap, and even if I didn't, I could have figured it out in a micro-second. He discovered that if he concentrated on the text that floated across the display, words and meanings came to him. He could read. That might come in handy, he thought. Pity this disclaimer nonsense wasn't worth the effort.

His attention started to wander. He looked over at Kiki who was trying to encourage him with a broad smile. But then, thought Dielle, she was always happy. He supposed that this must be a pretty good place if someone like Kiki was so consistently happy here.

'… THINGS WITH OR WITHOUT PROTECTIVE CLOTHING, SAFETY-NETS AND/OR QUALIFIED SUPERVISORS …'

He does go on a bit, thought Dielle.

{[Who is this guy?]}

[[Intern 001.434.0955]]

{[Is that a real person?]}

[[He is a real person but as an intern his physical body is wired and held in storage while he carries out his internship. As such he is part of the SlabWide human contiguation known as SlabCouncil]]

'… I DO NOT NEED HUGE WARNINGS ON THE PACKAGING TO REMIND ME ABOUT THIS …'

{[Council huh? Sounds important]}

[[Well, that's a matter of debate really; do you want to know more about that debate? It's been going on a long time.]]

{[Later Sis, sounds like he's winding down]}

'… AND RESULT IN PERSONAL INJURY ESPECIALLY, BUT NOT EXCLUSIVELY, IF THE ACCUSATIONS ARE TRUE. DO YOU AGREE?'

'I agree, and may I say it's been a ple…' there was a loud click. Simultaneously, the black screen and white walls disappeared and Sis informed him that he'd had

Contemporary   Morality   Update   1039:85Rev1.02 (SlabWide version) installed in shell but he didn't get a chance to query this because Kiki flung herself at him. He caught her lithe body easily as she wrapped her arms around his neck.

'You can kiss me now,' she instructed. He was surprised to find her open lips against his. He experimented with a bit of sucking and blowing, then Kiki put the tip of her tongue into his mouth which felt very good so he tried to do the same to her. He was enjoying this a lot but had to stop for air.

'You mean I had to agree to all that before we could do this?' He looked around: more white walls and white corridors, only further away and far less claustrophobic.

'Yeah,' she said, kissing his face enthusiastically. 'You can catch all sorts of stuff from kissing, you know. It's a legal thing.'

'Is it dangerous?'

'Oh, I hope so!' she laughed. 'Come on, let's go outside!'

'Outside? On a spaceship? Are you crazy?'

Dielle followed her down the white corridor. He'd been noticing some discrepancies with his comprehension. He had no memories of anything that had happened to him before his body came back to life two days ago. He had no conscious knowledge of anything he might have done or learned before, but somehow he knew you didn't just go outside when you lived in a spaceship. It was as though he knew the meaning of the words but nothing more. There was something else, too. Something to do with words, or rather *a* word, that had a meaning he thought he understood, but the word and the meaning seemed to have gone away and left a gap, something he couldn't quite put his finger on, something missing. He was trying to search his memory when Kiki reached the end of the corridor and stopped.

'See this light blue panel? It's an unrestricted transvex to the outside. Anyone can use it without clearance from Sis. The darker blue ones usually require clearance of some sort. I'll show you those later – they're fun. Come on!' Kiki walked through the light blue panel and disappeared. Dielle stopped short, he wasn't so sure about this. Was this some sort of trick? A test? Was he being watched? He looked around and could see nothing that might indicate that he was, but then hadn't Kiki told him he was being recorded in the re-fam area? There'd been no sign of any recording device in there either. He stuck his hand out cautiously. It went straight through with a faint tingle. Like an osmotic membrane, thought Dielle. What the hell, he wondered, was an osmotic membrane? He was just about to ask Sis when something grabbed his hand and tugged. He took a deep breath and closed his eyes.

'Come on silly,' Kiki laughed at him. 'You're going to love this.'

Dielle opened his eyelids a fraction, kidding himself that if something horrible was about to happen, he could avoid it by snapping them shut again. His pupils contracted in the bright light and darted from side to side, taking in details that his brain found almost impossible to process. Gradually, he allowed his eyes to widen as Sis compensated for the adrenaline rush and stabilised his cortisol levels. They were standing in bright daylight on a recreation platform scattered with morph-frames, floatshades and variable tables. Everywhere he looked, he saw buildings and platforms; gigantic, slender towers of tessellated mirrors hundreds of stories high, smaller structures with surfaces that swallowed light or modified it in brain-tickling ways and slender tendrils which joined the towering spires or curved into the hazy distance. Their platform was edged with shimmerail, a chest-high barrier which transformed from its barely visible default state into an opaque, solid wall as he approached it. He looked down over the edge.

Below them was a three-dimensional matrix of buildings, walkways and public spaces, all of them lit by the ubiquitous sunlight that seemed to cast no shadows. It was a vast, sprawling metropolis, filled with light and space and teaming with people. And as far as Dielle could tell, every building, bridge and platform was floating. Hanging in the air. Impossibly so. He started to laugh. Kiki, who had been studying his face, laughed along gaily.

'It's a joke. Very funny. You really had me going there.'

'Which part, darling?'

'The whole thing! The spaceship thing, the reset thing, the four-hundred-and-forty-years-old thing, even the information-in-my-head thing. Come on! You don't expect me to believe,' he cast his arm in a broad sweep across the incredible vista, 'this?'

'Believe what, dear?' asked Kiki, puzzled.

'A floating city in a landscape on a spaceship.'

'It's not a landscape, silly. This is Slab. It's a Slabscape, and we're not on it, we're inside it.'

'Right! OK, keep it up. How big is this so-called spaceship supposed to be then?'

Kiki was offended. 'I don't remember,' she semi-lied. 'Why don't you ask Sis?'

{[Slab dimensions?]}

[[Current overall Slab dimensions (external rounded) length: 1024 kilometres; width: 455 kilometres; height: 114 kilometres [more]]]

'What?'

{[More]}

[[Slab is comprised of eight main sections: two permaday, two permanight, two variable day/night, a rear environmental/supply section and a frontal buffer/mass-conversion section. Total habitable volume: approximately 2.2 million cubic kilometres with another 2 million about to come online when AllWeather opens [more]]]

A nearby morph-frame configured into a lounge chair as Dielle sat down, holding his head.

{[OK, I know I'm going to regret this, but how many people live in it?]}

[[Current live human population: 31,873,998. Breakdown: Male 42.24%, Female 42.95%, Non-gender 5.23%, Bi-gender 8.56%, Transitional 1.01%.]]

Dielle's head reeled as he tried to take in what he was being told. He looked up at Kiki, who was watching him with concern.

'You alright, dear?'

{[Verification required]}

A torrent of minutely detailed temporary data flooded his head. Dielle closed his eyes and soaked it up until Sis was sure he was convinced, then she rested his brain as he moved into a new reality. After a few seconds, the data cascade faded away like half-chased memories, leaving him with a deeper understanding and an infinitely bigger world to play in.

He took a couple of deep breaths and walked over to take her hand. They turned to gaze at the Slabscape. 'So I'm on a thousand-kilometres-long spaceship together with nearly thirty-two million people who live in floating buildings?'

Kiki nodded enthusiastically.

'Hell ... why not?' he said with a grin. 'Any other surprises?'

'Look up dear.'

The buildings overhead channelled the light from the sky through to their bases, making them appear hollow. Far above them he could make out thousands of buildings linked by causeways.

'A mirrored sky. That's a nice idea. I guess it would be weird to see a ceiling.'

'No dear, that's not a mirror. That's UpSideDown.'

He looked closer. The city above wasn't quite the same

as the one that surrounded them. It was subtly darker, spikier and more industrial looking. There were fewer connecting tendrils and he thought he could see hills and rivers in the distance. His eyes opened wide as he began to get a proper understanding of the scale of the place. He swallowed hard and his right eye started to twitch. Sis emtied a couple of milligrams of a muscle relaxant into his bloodstream.

[[You're gorping]]

{[Sorry]} Dielle turned to Kiki for help.

'We're in DownSideUp. For us, down is this way,' she pointed to the floor. 'But for everyone in UpSide, it's that way,' she pointed to the sky. 'See? Their up is our down and vice versa. There's a boundary layer in the middle called the interface where we have all sorts of fun messing around with ups and downs and so on. I'll take you there soon.'

Dielle looked up at the city and wondered if there was someone up there looking down – or up – at him.

'You know what, Kiki?' he said, rubbing his neck as she looked at him with beautiful raised eyebrows. 'I'm hungry.'

'Yes, you should be. You haven't eaten anything for around three hundred and sixty years and now you're out of re-fam, it's up to you to sort out your own nutrient intake. I want to take you to my favourite bistro. It's authentic French from France, Earth. Oh, do you speak French?'

'I don't know. Hang on.'

{[Do I speak French?]}

[[Not according to records, however pre-departure data veracity cannot be guaranteed]] 'Naturellement! Bien sur! Let's avant. J'ai famished!'

'Well, never mind, dear, you'll have plenty of time to learn. Come on. We'll take the tube.' She turned on her heels and disappeared through the transvex. Dielle followed.

{[Tube?]}

[[SlabWide transportation system. Ref: katabatic peristalsis [more]]]

'Now this is really fun,' she said, walking back down the re-fam corridor. 'All you do is tell Sis where you want to go and she'll let you through the tube's vex and take you there. Most people use a privacy shield while they're travelling, but it's much more interesting if you freetube it. Wherever you see a dark blue vex, that's a tube access. Just about every building in Seacombe has at least one on every level and Saint Vincent's has loads of them.' She rounded a corner and stopped. 'Here's one.'

'And they go everywhere in this Slab? How do I find them?'

'You just ask Sis and she'll hilight the way to the nearest one. It's handy for exploring and only you can see the hilights. Keeps everything nice and tidy. Now, this *can* be a bit scary at first but don't be frightened, Sis is in control and nothing bad can happen. Tell Sis you want to go to *Aux Renoir 92*, walk through the vex and she'll get you there toutes suite. I'll be right behind you.'

'But what happens if it goes wrong? What do I do?'

'Don't worry dear, it'll only go wrong if it's supposed to. You shouldn't take that whole Life Disclaimer thing too seriously. Sis will take care of you.' She nudged him toward the blue panel. 'Go on. I thought you said you were hungry.'

'Well, OK then. It's not like anything unusual has happened today.'

{[Oh Renwa 92]}

[[••]]

He walked through and started falling. Falling and screaming. Falling, screaming and trying to grab onto the smooth sides of a white tube with rapidly accelerating blue panels. 'SHIIIIT!'

'I told you we don't use that word anymore, dear,' said Kiki. He looked up and there she was, falling with him, smiling calmly. 'See? I told you it was fun, didn't I?'

They were moving so fast that the panels blurred, but there was no wind. He looked down and saw the end of the tube rushing up at him. He figured they only had a few seconds before impact.

'Don't worry, dear,' called out Kiki. 'We'll be going UpSlab in a moment.'

Dielle closed his eyes. He wanted to believe that Kiki hadn't sent them both to a messy death. He tried to tell his screaming nerves to calm down. Be cool, he said to himself, pull yourself together. That made him feel worse so Sis helped out a little.

When he opened his eyes, Kiki was by his side and they were speeding along a broad, roofless causeway that curved through the floating city. They flew through the windless air alongside scores of other travellers and a jumble of colourfully animated globes hurtling along the wide thoroughfare. A constant stream of bubbles and people joined or left the flow through overhead funnels, side feeders and plunging sinkholes. A shimmering buffer zone separated them from a similar variegated mass flashing past in the opposite direction.

'What do you think, darling?' said Kiki. 'It's called Sixth Avenue and it's a main intersection surge. Saint Vincent's is usually directly above it. Very convenient'.

'Brilliant!' said Dielle, 'How does it work?'

'It's all to do with mass and gravity manipulation and inertia stuff. It's the same technology that makes the buildings float and powers the space-drives. Ask Sis.'

He made a mental note to find out later.

[[••]]

{[Huh?]}

[[All mental notes are held in system memory and will be re-prompted during perceived idle time]]

{[Erm … ••]}

He was too interested in the scenery to delve into the

technology. Slab was filled with people. Busy people. Dielle was fascinated. He had never seen so many people and they were of all shapes, sizes, colours and styles. That should keep things interesting, he thought.

'Darling, it's considered rude to stare at other people in the tube.'

'Sorry,' he said to no-one in particular. 'Is it OK to check out the bubbles?'

'Yes, that's expected really – they're privacy fields. There are people inside them who either don't want to be seen or have things to do while they're travelling. The images on the outsides are softAds and generate income for the occupiers if you watch them.'

'SoftAds?'

'Non-aware advertising. Just general stuff that isn't targeted to you or anyone else. Helps pay for the cost of the privacy field.'

'Can they see out even though we can't see in?'

'You can set it that way if you want but most people choose solids so they can watch sumes or snooze or whatever.'

Dielle looked down. They were skimming above a billowing, misty surface.

{[What's that?]}

[[Inertia absorption matrix. Protects the biomass in case of catastrophic failure. Instantaneously expands to fill the tubeway in the event of katabatic drive compromise]]

Right, thought Dielle, that would be useful.

The tube curved in the direction of a sky-high, endless wall of apartments and multiplexes.

[[Entering Mitchell]]

As he stared at the millions of windows, balconies and platforms, one of the apartment blocks detached from the wall and fell toward them.

'Look out!' he screamed, flinging himself to protect Kiki. But he couldn't reach her. It was too late. He braced himself for the impact, incredulous that they could let a building fall onto the tube.

The wall passed through him to reveal the interior of a large, tastefully furnished apartment. His point of view spun around the room and then up a wide, spiral staircase to a balcony with a spectacular view of an idyllic pastoral landscape. He heard a voice say: 'Mountain Heights on The Wall, Seacombe side. The best way to end your day.' After another swirling tour, the projection vanished. Kiki was laughing again.

'What the hell was that?' he spluttered.

'I don't know, dear. You should have seen your face! It must have been a hardAd. They're targeted to your profile. I didn't see a thing. What was it?'

'An apartment called Mountain Heights. Looked pretty nice too.'

'Mountain Heights? SideUp?'

'Just said Seacombe.'

'I bet. It's DownSideUp, way down DownSideUp. It's a dump. They're always pushing that graveyard on newbies.'

'Had a nice view.'

'Well of course, darling. You can have whatever view you like but when you go outside you'll find nothing but dreary boxed-in condos and sky-through-cracks. It's strictly low rent. No-one wants to live on The Wall anymore – it's dead. Anyway, you won't be needing a place to live for a while, you're coming home with me.'

He liked the sound of that. They were sucked down into a narrow funnel, then abruptly pulled sideways into a deserted tube at right angles to the direction they'd been travelling before. This one had a dimly lit roof and, with no visual clues, it was easy for Dielle to imagine he was falling again.

'CrosSlab joiner,' said Kiki from behind. 'Almost there now.'

Another fast turn sent them back UpSlab and after less

than a minute they came to a sudden but completely inertia-free stop beside a blue panel.

[[Aux Renoir 92]]

Dielle felt himself being pulled toward the vex and heard Kiki saying something about *getting ready* when he fell onto a soft, dark-red floor. He looked up at a tall, skeletally thin man with a long nose who was peering over the top of a lectern in a professionally disapproving manner.

'Reservation?'

'Hello Makepiece,' said Kiki, walking through the vexit.

'Mam'selle Pundechan, how splendid to see you. Is this gentleman with you?' He said *gentleman* as if trying to remove something stuck between his front teeth with his tongue.

'He's not outsauced, Makepiece, he's a reset. He only just got here.'

The maître d' jerked into action, brushing down Dielle's hospital coveralls with a diaphanous device that had appeared from his sleeve while helping Dielle to his feet. 'It's an honour to meet you, sir! I'm sorry I didn't recognise you. Mr Dielle, isn't it?'

'Do you know me?'

'Only what I've managed to catch on the sumes, sir. Welcome to Aux Renoir quatre-vingt-douze.'

Aux Renoir was designed to impress. The flourishing vine above their heads filtered a summer afternoon sun past luscious bunches of Chardonnay grapes, projecting a mottled pattern that looked random but wasn't, onto the cooled stone slabs. The glass-panelled rosewood door was an exact replica of a six-hundred-year-old door which had been used almost every night for over three years by the eponymous French impressionist painter before he'd had a three-bottle disagreement with a tableful of boisterous dinners, insulted the owner, thrown up over the cat and been physically ejected and barred for life. There wasn't a single customer-facing detail that couldn't be authenticated and historically referenced by Sis if Dielle had thought to ask – which he hadn't.

'Would you like to dress in something a little more suitable for lunch, sir? Mam'selle, I assume a terrace view?' He led Dielle by the arm toward a side vex. 'I think you'll find something to your liking in there, sir.'

Dielle walked through the vex into a standard changing room with a full-wall multimirror, an upholstered bench and a cabinet full of clothes. He chose a tailored black suit over a white sweater that tingled when he touched it. Everything fitted perfectly. He looked up and realised he was looking at four sides of a stranger. He stopped and stared.

'Hello Dielle,' he said aloud. 'You don't look half bad.' He checked his profile and straightened his long, dark hair with his hands. He had big hands; bigger than anyone's he'd seen so far. He was tall, too – not quite as tall as the stick man outside, but tall enough, he thought. Tall enough for what? he wondered. He took another look at himself and smiled. 'Not too shabby,' he said.

Kiki was waiting for him. 'Oh darling, you do look handsome! You are going to be such a big hit!' She gave him a quick peck on the cheek. 'You go along with Makepiece, dear; I'll get a frock from home.' She hurried into the changing room while the maître d' led him through a series of sumptuously carpeted corridors, past some private rooms, to a terrace under another verdant canopy. Beyond the terrace, a broad waterfall plunged down a rock-face, forming a light, prismatic mist around its base. Rich aromas wafted from the kitchens, triggering previously suppressed glandular secretions. Food! he thought, with relish.

The table was laid with sparkling glasses and polished cutlery on a crisp, white cloth. A basket of freshly baked bread was placed by his right hand as the maitre d' gently adjusted Dielle's chair and a waiter poured scintilleau into a tall, iced glass. Not too shabby at all, thought Dielle. He looked round as Kiki walked onto the terrace and his heart skipped two beats then raced to catch up. She was wearing a simple light-blue dress which flowed down almost to the ground and moved to a rhythm of its own. The dress fitted neatly around her firm waist and breasts and left her arms bare all the way up to her delicately sculpted shoulders. A sweeping, broad-rimmed hat shielded her face from the bright light above. Kioki Sypher-Marie Pundechan knew how to make an entrance, especially when she was planning on using the recording later. Dielle sprang out of his chair.

'Are you leaving?' Kiki asked, concerned.

'No, why?'

'Then why are you standing up?'

Dielle looked confused. 'To … er … I don't know.' He sat down quickly. 'Nice dress. So, do you live near here?'

'Oh no, only very wealthy people live around here. It's very exclusive. I live quite near Saint Vincent's actually.'

'But you said you were going to get a dress from home? You've only been a few minutes.'

'Oh I see! No, I said I was going to get it from home, not that I was going home to get it. I just had it emtied here.' Makepiece fussed around Kiki to get her seated and muttered something to her. Dielle was looking confused.

'M.T. means matter transmitter. Don't you remember them? They were invented on Earth before we left.'

There was something about this that started to ring a bell for Dielle but he couldn't pin it down. 'Matter transmitter. Maybe we called them something else? You can send stuff from one place to another, like your dress from home?'

'Yes, or the clothes you're wearing now, for instance. Sis emtied some into the closet as you walked into the changing room. She knows your sizes of course and the location and genre. We use emties for everything. You even have a few dozen of them implanted inside you.'

'I do? Where? What do they do?'

'Just ordinary health stuff mainly. They get rid of stuff you don't need, put in stuff you do, monitor stuff, regulate stuff.'

Food and wine arrived at the table in a flurry of activity that interrupted Dielle's train of thought.

'Now, seeing as this is your first meal in your new life and it's a special day for us,' said Kiki. 'I wanted to make sure you had a special lunch. Everything here is of the highest calibre. Aux Renoir is my favourite French restaurant in Mitchell.' She was holding herself straight as if making a speech. Makepiece was hovering in the background being formal and attentive. Kiki held up her wine glass and the deep red liquid caught a highlight from the waterfall. 'This is real wine made from real grapes, in the Aux Renoir group vineyards in The Valley. It's a '21 vintage.' Dielle lifted his glass and was just about to throw the contents down his neck but Kiki held his arm. 'A toast dear, we must first lightly brush our glasses together and celebrate the moment. It's a tradition. Look at the waterfall, dear, isn't it wonderful?'

Dielle looked at the waterfall, but he didn't have anything to compare it to. Kiki clinked their glasses together and looked at the waterfall too. 'The First!' she said enthusiastically.

'Yeah, and hopefully not the last!' Dielle replied and took his first taste of wine in a very, very long time. Now that, he thought, he did remember. Kiki was laughing again.

'Not the last! That's fantastic!'

Dielle rediscovered the exquisite pleasure of mixing a fine wine with the laughter of a beautiful companion. He smiled inside and out.

'You know, Kiki,' said Dielle as a silent waiter waived something mesmerising under his nose, 'this is one hell of a spaceship you have here.'

The food was, as advertised, spectacularly good. Course

after course was expertly prepared and beautifully presented. Dielle ate it all with gusto. Each new taste was an experience better than the last, every smell and texture a new discovery. Here he was, in a wonderful place with a great menu, a new set of clothes and, most importantly, a charming partner who filled the time with lighthearted chatter about the food, the chef (who she knew well), the history of her dress (an antique), how she acquired it (something to do with a bet that Dielle couldn't understand) and how the dress animation worked (choreographed by a long-dead artist). He hardly had a chance to say anything at all, which was fine by him. The new-born in paradise knew nothing more than this moment and that was enough for him.

As they left the restaurant to much bowing and grovelling from the staff, Dielle asked Kiki if the whole thing was free.

'No dear, the food here is lookadatplus expensive – but don't be concerned, I'll make sure we positivise the transaction. You can keep the suit, too. I think it looks rather good on you.' She took Dielle's hand and pulled him toward the tube vex. 'Come on! Let me take you home. My treat.'

In less than the time it takes to draw breath, Dielle found himself in a dimly lit privacy field with Kiki kissing him passionately. He had no sense of movement but he guessed that they were currently falling at an insane speed.

'You were absolutely great, my darling!' said Kiki, taking off her dress to reveal a form-fitting, black one-piece. 'Ah! That's better. I love that dress, but all that wriggling around is dicing irritating after a while.' She giggled and pushed him over backwards. The privacy field instantly deformed, creating a soft bench that absorbed his fall. She was kissing him again, now sitting on top of him. 'Wow!' he thought. 'This is even better than the food!' He was getting excited, and he didn't need to bother his patchy memory to know what was happening. Kiki moved around a little and her face changed from a happy smile to a wide-eyed look of amazement.

'Oh darling! You *are* advanced! You're not supposed to be ready for *that* yet!'

Dielle looked down and recognised an old friend. 'I think I'm ready now, nurse.'

Ten minutes later, the privacy field dumped two sweaty, naked bodies onto the floor of Kiki's uptown, DownSideUp apartment. Kiki had the body of an athletic young woman. Athletic and loud. If Dielle hadn't had a meal in 360 years, he hadn't had energetic sex in a lot longer than that and his body had been returned to its prime. He relearned the meaning of abandon. Several times.

After an impossible-to-subjectively-measure period, they prised themselves apart and lay on their backs, breathing hard. Dielle looked up. There were two towels on a low chair just within arm's reach. He handed one to Kiki, her glistening breasts rising and falling with the effort of her breathing. The chair silently moved away and defaulted.

'Wow!' gasped Kiki. 'I have never, ever, ever had sex that good with a real man! I knew you'd be great! I just knew it!' She got onto her knees, still panting. 'Come on! The plunge pool's ready.'

Dielle looked around. 'Shit! We left our clothes in the privacy field.'

'No problem. Sis will have emtied them to the wardrobe by now. And we don't use that word anymore, darling.' Her perfectly re-formed bottom disappeared around a corner. 'Come on!'

nine

He woke alone between silky sheets and scented pillows. The shower and plunge pool had led to some fabulous water-enhanced sex, after which they'd passed out exhausted on Kiki's huge bed. A real bed, not a sleep field. He stretched the long muscles of his pleasurably sore back and smiled. Food was great, sex was great, the bed was great and life just kept getting better and better, he thought, curious to see what the new day would bring.

He picked up a navy and burgundy striped robe with deep sleeves from the morfit by the bed.

[[•]]

{[What was that?]}

[[Voice message from Kiki]]

He tried to recall his eye training.

{[Deliver]}

[['Hello darling, I had to go out for a while. Make yourself at home. If you're hungry just ask Sis, or if you want to go and explore the local form, ask Sis where Jenny's is. You'll like it. I'll ping you when I'm coming home. Remember: Sis can tell you anything you want to know. Later darling!']]

He padded into the lounge and absorbed the pervading feeling of peace and understated quality. The dark flooring felt warm and pleasant to his bare feet. In the middle of the large room a semicircle of embedded high-backed couches surrounded an animated floral arrangement on a low, black plinth. Three of the walls were transparent panels revealing, through overhanging leaves, a slatted deck with steps leading down to a large piazza. It was light outside.

{[Time?]}

[[4:35]]

{[Morning or afternoon?]}

[[Those terms are meaningless here. Seacombe has no day/night cycles and therefore no mornings or afternoons. The nearest night section is The Strip which is 90 klicks DownSlab from here. You are now almost halfway through the SlabDay]]

Right, he thought, of course. He had to start asking the right questions – or maybe just talk to Sis and see where a conversation led.

{[I'm thirsty]}

[[Food prep area behind you]]

An opening behind him hilighted. Inside, copper-coloured pans and utensils hung from a canopy above a multiform worksurface that floated in mid-air. Four high-stools sat under the side nearest the door and the wall behind was covered with a patchwork of curved panels and display cabinets. The room was subject to continuous bio-filtering which generated a tongue-tingling sensation of hygiene. If he had had the misfortune to have been a free-floating unicellular organism, he would have been crash-emtied into one of Slab's particle recyclers and separated into his component atoms as he crossed the threshold. Fortunately for him, he had lots of interdependent cells and several billion of them needed re-hydrating.

{[Can I have a cold drink?]}

[[What would you like?]]

He didn't know what anything was called. {[What do you recommend?]}

[[Cooler]]

{[~?]}

[[Cooled MT. Blue light]]

One of the cabinet panels was outlined by pulsating blue light. The panel slid open as he approached it, revealing a tall glass filled with a muddy-looking iced drink.

{[Do you have control over everything in here?]}

[[Define control]]

{[Do you flash the lights and send drinks and so on?]}

[[If you require it, yes, but you ultimately have control over that requirement]]

That's not particularly comforting, thought Dielle, very privately.

{[And can you do that with everyone's apartment throughout the entire spaceship?]}

[[••]]

{[For almost 32 million people? All at the same time?]}

[[••]]

{[And, you do all that and simultaneously control every single tube passenger's movements, all the floating buildings, all the life-support systems and everything else that goes on in this place?]}

[[••]]

He hesitated, staring at the cold mist drifting from the glass and wondered if he should feel scared. Sis was everywhere and controlled everything down to the smallest detail. Sis was inside everyone's head and knew virtually everything about them. Sis had absolute power and Dielle had a bad feeling that absolute power might not be a very good thing. He could easily let paranoia take over. He could feel its dark presence hovering nearby. He shrugged. So far, everything was just fine. He was going to assume that Sis had his best intentions at heart until something convinced him otherwise.

He took a mouthful of the cool liquid, reconsidered his assumption and threw up all over the shiny black counter top.

'What the fu … '

{[What is this?]}

[[You asked me to recommended you a drink. Your current bio-analysis shows fatigue poisons and low electrolytes. This drink will serve to replenish those and add a few extra essential trace elements]]

The morfit hurried through the doorway, deploying an array of telescopic cleaning tools.

{[It tastes bloody awful]}

[[••]]

OK, he thought, he wasn't going to change his assumption. He just needed to learn how to ask better questions.

{[Gimme something that'll do all that and taste great too, something that other people enjoy]}

[[Cooler]]

This time the panel slid open to reveal a glass of sparkling amber liquid filled with citrus fruit and rimmed with a variety of healthy looking edibles. That's more like it, he thought, taking a sip. 'Delicious,' he said, returning to the lounge and the sunken couches.

{[I need some help here]}

[[What do you need?]]

{[I need to find out a load of stuff that I don't know but I don't know what questions to ask]}

[[General subject?]]

{[Well, Slab for a start. Can you tell me about this place and some stuff you think I ought to know?]}

[[Suggest Slab newbie routine, levels one through five. Options [more] and [stop] anytime]]

{[Fine, go ahead]}

[[What?]]

{[Sorry. Proceed]}

The large flower arrangement in the centre vanished and was replaced by an image of a dark obelisk. Brash, orchestral pomp faded in, followed by a smiley mouthed male narration.

'Welcome to Slab, or, as we used to call it, the Joint Earth Council Galactic Conveyor ISS.001.000.0001, the most advanced human-conceived, machine-made, mobile habitat in all the known universes. This tour is designed to familiarise you with your home and many of the facilities that exist within it. Life onSlab is an abundance of fulfilment opportunities tailored precisely to each SlabCitizen's needs. We know you're going to enjoy a long and healthy life exploring the myriad possibilities of our fabulous home, so let's start with some of the basics.'

Over the next few hours he learned of many things. One of the first was that an hour wasn't an hour anymore. As soon as the ship had departed Earth orbit, the media corporations, eager to extend their most profitable prime-time slots, had lobbied hard to have shipboard time decimalised. The SlabDay was altered to ten hours of a hundred minutes each. A minute was comprised of a hundred seconds but because seconds had stayed the same length as Earth seconds (in order to prevent a mass boycott from the physicists), the SlabDay wound up being a little over fifteen percent longer than an Earth day. The length of the working day stayed the same (in order to prevent a mass boycott by everyone else), so all of the extra time was, in media terms, super-prime. Weeks and months were consigned to history. Days were identified by numbers instead of names and a hundred days made a cycle. One Earth year was the equivalent of a fraction over three cycles but despite this, and just because it made everything that bit more complicated, everyone still measured their biological ages in Earth years. An Earth no-one would ever see again.

Slab was on a one-way trip. A trip that was probably going to take over twenty thousand Earth years or sixty-five kilocykes in deciTime. The reason for the voyage was to lodge a formal complaint, in person. Sending a message would have taken almost twice as long and was considered to be a waste of time anyway. It was universally acknowledged that if you really wanted something done, you had to turn up and complain face to face (or whatever the non-corporal equivalent of a face turned out to be). No-one, not even a non-physical collective conscious entity, was going to ignore you if you turned up on its doorstep after a twenty-thousand-light-year journey. Or so it was hoped.

It had also been hoped that the journey wouldn't have taken quite so long, but unfortunately, Slab, which was now travelling at about ninety-five percent of lightspeed, had all but stopped accelerating. This was irritating a lot of people because they had assumed that someone would have figured out faster-than-light transportation by now, but nobody had. The gravity drives had reached maximum thrust hundreds of cykes earlier and it no longer made any difference how much more mass they took on during the journey, the increase in velocity was almost imperceptible.

One school of thought held that the problem was ultimately a question of philosophy rather than physics and that in order to transcend lightspeed, Slab's human cargo would have to believe in concepts involving multi-dimensional, unbelievably small and impossible-to-measure, vibrating filaments of pure energy as the basic building blocks of the universe. No sane person could accept this idea with a straight face, so the speed of light was smugly intransigent. Philosophy, of sorts, was also connected with the reason for the journey in the first place.

They were heading for the MacGoughin Sequester, a dull and somewhat anonymous region of the Milky Way which was, as far as could be ascertained, the origin of the alien consciousness which had infested human minds for eons and was responsible for virtually all of mankind's existential anxieties. Humanity had had enough of the whole 'duality of man' torment and was determined to seek out whatever it was that lived in this Dice-forsaken section of the galaxy and give it a very serious talking to.

Dielle repeatedly asked Sis for more information.

The human consciousness problem had been ignored

for centuries on Earth largely because most of its early history had been dominated by religious organisations who benefited hugely by promoting mysterious explanations over rational ones. No-one, under pain of excommunication, eternal damnation or worse, had been allowed to investigate the truth. However as a more rational, scientific approach gradually displaced superstition and fear, hundreds of experiments were conducted to determine exactly what happened when people died. Eventually, in the mid twenty-first century, it was proved that energy was leaving the physical body at the point of death and heading away from Earth. Years of research coupled with the extraordinary sacrifice of the MacGoughin twins produced telemetric data which confirmed a world-shattering conclusion: every single energy transmission was directed to the same point, a region of space approximately 20,000 light-years nearer the centre of the galaxy.

The media had a field day – in fact, a field year. Headlines proclaimed the discovery of the origin of the soul and the soul planet, which was instantly called *Home*, citing the fact that humanity had never called Earth home, choosing instead to name it after the basic dirt from which it was formed. Pundits were confident that being able to scientifically lay the blame for the struggle between good and evil on an alien infestation heralded the end of virtually all of the world's religions. Many people who had encountered what was termed a *near-death experience* suddenly went public saying that when they had *said* they were travelling down a dark corridor toward a light, what they had actually *meant* was that they had been zooming through empty space toward a brilliantly lit planet. Going toward the light. Going Home. Everything started to make sense.

However, the world's major religions had far too much at stake to take the news kneeling down. Huge resources were diverted into further scientific research aimed at proving human consciousness was separate from the human soul. An entire new industry of theographic P.R. companies sprang up to promote the idea that the newly discovered consciousness energy was measurable proof of the existence of God/Gods/Prophets/Tulkus and/or Divine Instruments (depending on where the research sponsorship came from). Pressure was brought to bear. The scientists who had been measuring the dying energy vectors publicly denied they had ever said human consciousness had anything to do with the soul.

Organised religions became truly organised for the first time. They pragmatically brushed aside millennia's worth of spilled bad blood and joined forces, formed dummy corporations, pooled assets and covertly took control of all of the world's media. The public were deluged with information and bombarded by TV programs, feature films, magazine articles and even comic strips all featuring theo-scientific experts using very long, often completely made-up words targeted at rubbishing the idea of a soul-filled home planet. The public did what the they always did. They got bored.

As soon as the public's attention had been diverted, an expedition was instigated and the interstellar spaceship that was to eventually become Slab sprang from blueprint to orbital construction. Originally, the ship had a drive section, a life support section and one large habitable section stacked as a series of themed floors, like a city-sized skyscraper. The ship used a gravity drive, or more accurately, an anti-gravity/gravity drive and was designed to continually take on mass during the voyage. The theory stated that as the ship became ever more massive, the drives would become more powerful and the acceleration would increase. It worked just as predicted for a couple of hundred years, then it tailed off. As the ship approached the speed of light they had virtually stopped accelerating.

One hundred and twenty cycles ago, it had been decided that after the opening of the new AllWeather section, Slab design would be frozen and the expansion phase would be complete. SlabMedia was referring to this event as coming out of Beta.

Everyone was looking forward to AllWeather opening. The promotional material showed mountain ranges and ski resorts, buildings carved from ice and log cabins laced with snow. There were deserts, rainforests, swamps, safari trails and clear blue seas with long, sun-drenched beaches. Above all there were sunsets. No-one had ever seen a real sunset before. AllWeather was going to have a moving sun simulator which was designed to recreate both dawns and sunsets in a range of sponsored colours.

Each section of Slab had a different climate and character. Dielle was currently in Seacombe, the oldest of the day sections; approximately 355 kilometres wide, 200 kilometres long and 14 kilometres high. Its climate was the one which most people felt was invigorating and positive: early spring. And since it was such a nice day, he thought he should go out and explore a little.

{[Stop. Can you direct me to Jenny's?]}

[[Follow flashing yellow squares]]

A display of aromatic flowers replaced the sume and a small flashing yellow square appeared on the glass panel which opened silently as he walked toward it. About a hundred metres away, hovering above a group of sculpted bushes, was another yellow square.

Jenny's was a single-story building with an elevated view over the local form. Dielle looked up at the jolly sign on its roof.

[[Jenny's]]

{[I know]}

[[Cancelling auto-read for roman characters. Assume you still require auto-translate for non Ænglish?]]

{[••]}

This Jenny's was one of over two thousand almost identical Jenny's restaurants onSlab. The original Jenny, who had insisted on describing herself as *just a waitress*, had been born on Earth and had become stupendously rich simply by being a really, really good waitress.

As he entered the diner, a hyper-attractive, happy young woman floated toward him as if she were on wheels, but as he checked out her smiling face, glossy hair, full breasts, slender waist, tight ass, long legs and delicate feet he realised she wasn't on wheels at all. By this time, however, he'd had such a pleasant experience he'd forgotten why he was looking at her shoes.

'Hi Dielle, how are you today?' she asked, using the mandatory Jenny's patented smile.

'Fine, I guess. How'd you know my name?'

'Well Sis told me, but I knew it already of course! How are you settling in, honey? You want something to eat? Sit over here, it's our best spot.' She guided him, smoothly, to a booth. 'I know you just got here too, so I want to give you a real special welcome to Jenny's,' she purred, using smile number thirty-one, extra sparkle.

'Are you Jenny?' asked Dielle, feeling special already.

'Why no, honey. She went on ahead a long time ago, but I do admire her so. She was my idol when I was just a little girl. I used to tell myself that one day I'd have a Jenny's all of my own and here I am! Little old me!'

Little wasn't the word which had sprung to the front of Dielle's mind.

'You can call me Mary-Belle or Bella, or just plain old Bee.' Plain was another word that hadn't even come close to surfacing in Dielle's thoughts. This was a girl with a lot of valuable personal assets as far as Dielle could tell. Not at all like Kiki, more like a … more like a … what? He couldn't find a word for it.

'So how hungry are you, Dielle honey? You want to tell me what you want, or do you want me to bring you something really good that I just know you're going to enjoy a whole lot?'

Dielle smiled back and tried some serious eye contact. 'Yeah, that sounds good. Whatever you think.'

'Yewgardit!' she said and slid off to greet a pair of customers who had just arrived. Probably a couple of guys, thought Dielle. Or perhaps two women who liked to wear identical serious-looking uniforms which flattened their chests and hid their faces under peaked caps. He couldn't make out what they were saying but Mary-Belle was giving them the full welcome treatment in a language he didn't understand. She seated them, slid off to a rear section of the diner and returned to Dielle's table with a plate of steaming food in less time than it took him to ask Sis what language they were speaking.

[[Modified German]]

'There you go honey, these are what I call Bella's all-day-any-day pancakes. I made them myself to a personal secret recipe.'

He doubted that very much. She couldn't have been out of his sight for more than fifteen seconds, tops. He dug in. They were delicious.

'Ummmm! These are fantastic! I'm never going to eat anywhere else!'

'Well that's great honey, but we'll have to clear that with your agent if that's OK?'

He tried to speak through a mouthful of sweet'n'sticky JennyTang sauce 'Clear what with who?'

'Oh never mind, sugar, we can do that later.' She sat down on the other side of the table and whispered conspiratorially, 'So, have you spoken to yourself yet?'

'Huh?'

'I can only imagine. It must be really weird, yeah?'

'What the hell are you talking about?' he whispered back. He had no idea why he was whispering. Speaking to himself? A very pleasant meal had just turned slightly freaked-out.

'You know, talking to your previous self. Before you reset.'

'I can do that?'

'Why sure. Least, I think so.' She looked uncertain. 'Didn't you know?'

Maybe that was what Kiki had meant when she said he could ask himself why he was here. If he could talk to himself before he reset that could fill in a lot of blanks.

'No. How do I do that?'

'Well, usually any holo-projector will do it, but you'd better ask Sis, maybe ours won't work. You are maybe the oldest ever reset to be re-fammed you know. I don't know if they could do that stuff in those days.'

'I didn't know that either. The oldest, huh? Let me ask Sis.'

'Yewgardit!' Bella said cheerfully as she slid off to attend to her other customers.

{[Can I talk to my previous self?]}

[[Yes]]

{[More]}

[[Your so-called previous self, that is the you before you reset who lived on Earth while Slab was being designed. He, or you, recorded a fully interactive download of his/your personality into a digital storage matrix which was transferred to SlabWide Integrated System and held in trust awaiting your successful re-fam which has now taken place. You are the only person authorised to access this data. Unfortunately, the technology for complete integration of you, or him, had not been invented then so the only way you can communicate with yourself is via voice and visual language. Sorry]]

{[And how do I do that?]}

[[The data is very, very old; it is not compatible with modern onSlab holographic projection systems. You will need to use an old fashioned portable vDek unit]]

{[And how do I get one of those?]} Dielle was getting slightly impatient with all of this, was it him, or was Sis being a little reluctant to tell him something he really thought he should have been made aware of earlier?

[[Your waitress is bringing you a vDek now]]

'Oh, I haven't seen one of these in ages!' said Bella as she placed a small silver cylinder with two opposing vertical slits in the middle of the table. She turned it so that one of the slits faced him.

Dielle peered at it. 'What is it? What does it do?'

'It's a portable holo-projector; people used to use them to have face-to-face conversations. You sit here and you see the person you want to talk to over there.' She nodded toward the opposite side of his table. 'And wherever they are, they can see you the same way. Everything like that is just built-in now. You'll have to log into it using Sis. I already tried, but it's locked to little old you.'

'OK. Thanks a lot,' he said, hoping that Bella would leave him alone. The prospect of meeting himself had unnerved him and didn't need any extra company. Bella got the message.

'Well, I'll leave you to have a chat then. Busy, busy, busy!' she slid off, smoothly. He still couldn't see any wheels, but enjoyed looking anyway.

He took another mouthful of pancakes.

{[Ok, can you connect me with this thing?]}

[[Specify thing]]

{[This vDek thing that you just sent over. I want to talk to my previous self]}

[[Are you sure?]]

{[What th...]}

[[Intern interrupt: 'Dielle, there is free intern advice available for this decision if you wish to accept it.']] This came in the form of a voice, a pleasant and gentle female voice that sounded clear but matriarchal. It was the type of voice that expected to be listened to.

{[OK, I'll listen. What's up?]}

[['Up? Up is up. Do you require information about Slab gravitational orientation?']]

Jeez, he thought. These interns were really pedantic.

{[No, I mean: deliver]}

[['The action you are about to perform will activate a long-dormant interactive personality made by a human entity over 360 Earth years ago using outdated and not fully comprehensive technology. Even though it is flawed in its data integrity, this entity, once activated, will immediately be allowed temporary citizen rights. Although it is currently locked to you, it will have free will and the right to exercise that will. This has already precipitated debate in SlabCouncil as to the validity of the rights so granted.']]

{[And why should I care about that?]}

[['Quite']]

Dielle felt sure he heard a sigh in that word.

[['There is one other thing to consider of a more personal nature; You are, at this moment, for all intents and purposes, like a new-born in a world that is designed to protect and provide for you. You have no encumbrances from the past and are free to explore and discover your new life as an innocent. It is a state that many would envy and some deliberately re-create through voluntary resetting. You may discover much from your past that you would rather not know. The purpose of this intern interrupt is to make you aware of this, as it is possible that you may not have considered this option.']]

Well, thought Dielle, he certainly hadn't considered the possibility that it might be a mistake. He could, he supposed, just walk away from his own past and never look back. Life had been pretty good so far without knowing why he was here.

He wondered why he was here.

{[Yeah, thanks, but I thought about that already]}

[['Are you ABSOLUTELY sure?']]

{[Yeah, and I'm pretty sure that I, that is the I that I used to be, would want to be reactivated, like I would]}

['Admirable rationalisation. Good luck.']]

A smiley male voice cut in. [['This intern interrupt was brought to you free of charge and is a service of SlabCouncil. Thank you for adding your thoughts to the contiguation. Enjoy the moment.']]

Dielle took another mouthful.

{[Sis?]}

[[vDek assigned, loaded and locked. Options start/stop/pause]]

{[vDek:start]}

'Who the fuck are you?'

Dielle jumped. 'Hey! Watch your mouth! Who do you think you're talking too?'

'I just fucking *asked* you that, you fucking moron!'

'Who are you calling a moron?'

'That's exactly what I was trying to find out. Fuckwit.'

Dielle was glaring at a guy sitting opposite who was supposed to be him, but couldn't be. This guy was short, bald and ugly with a huge, bent nose and beady eyes. It couldn't be who he used to be. This guy was a complete asshole.

The old guy looked about him in amazement. 'Hey, where am I? And what the fuck is that?' he asked, pointing at the vDek.

'You're in Jenny's Diner in Seacombe SideUp and that's a vDek, it's a portable holographic projector which must be broken or something.'

'Portable? Fuck me! Portable? They had to construct a whole fucking room around me to get my personality down into that machine. It took ten fucking days! And I'm portable? Fucking A! What's your name, numbnuts?'

'I'm Dielle. Who are you? I was expecting to talk to my previous self.'

'I,' said the projection, proudly, 'am Louie Clinton Drago, self-made business gurulla and semi-retired philanderer. And unless something has gone so woefully wrong that I'm going to have to sue somebody until they bleed, you must be the new, improved version of me. But if you are me, how come you don't remember me?'

'I'm a reset. All my memories have been wiped by the cryo process.'

'Jeez! How long was I in there?'

'Three hundred and sixty years.'

'Sheesh!' Louie was nonplussed, but not for long. 'Hey! Let me look at you! I wanna check the merchandise!' he scrutinised Dielle's face. 'Stand up!'

'Who the fuck?'

'Look, I paid the equivalent of a small African country's Gross Domestic Product to re-make me into you, so the very least I get is to check that the contract was delivered. Right?'

Dielle couldn't argue with that – at least not right away.

'Stand up! turn around!'

Dielle reluctantly stood up and turned half to one side, but that was all he was prepared to do. He sat down again.

'Not too shabby! What are you, six four? Six five? How's it feel?'

{[How tall am I?]}

[[1.97 metres, 6 foot 5 1/2 in imperial units]]

'Yeah, it feels OK.'

'Lemme see your hands.'

Dielle obeyed like a puppet. An angry puppet.

'That's great! Job done, eh? You can play the adrenalin game now! I never stood a chance, but you … you could be a contender!'

'What game?'

'Basketball of course! You have the hands and the reach now – you can play!'

{[What is basketball?]}

[[Ball game played between two genetically-enhanced sides in the twentieth and twenty-first centuries on Earth. Highly specialised physical prowess was required and opposing sides became so evenly matched that games were often decided by less than a 2% margin, which was far smaller than the influence of pure chance. Ultimately this meant that no matter how much effort was invested into improving athletic skills, pure luck would always override it. Exponential audience decline resulted in it being abandoned on Earth October 19th 2099. Never revived onSlab]]

'They don't play it here.'

'What??' said Louie. 'I can't believe it!'

'Too little interest, apparently,' said Dielle with a shark-smile.

'Not interesting?!' Louie was aghast. 'The slam dunk? The craze? The hizzerflop?' He waved his arms about, mimicking moves.

{[What the hell is he talking about?]}

[[No idea. Running data integrity check on his program]]

'The poodly-woodly! The jigger-bite! The grace and beauty! The tension courtside at the top of the fourth!'

[[You may have to consider the possibility that your former self was severely ...]]

'I mean, DeLoitte Spinner for Christ's sake! DEEEE-LOITTE!'

[[DeLoitte Spinner was a Basketball star in the 2020s. That's a relief, I thought I was going to have to take him offline for a millisecond there]]

Louie held his head in his hands, muttering to himself about not letting someone down. He came to a conclusion and looked around, brightening instantly.

'Hey, what is this joint? Looks just like a diner I used to practically live in when I was your age. Nah, that's not possible. Maybe diners never change, eh? One of those constants the white-coats keep boring on about, eh? The Diner Constant – or the Constant Diner, that's even better. Write that down!'

'No way are you me, er, am I you. No way,' said Dielle.

The holo-projection of Louie abruptly disappeared to be replaced by a two dimensional picture of a younger man. Louie's voice continued: 'That's me aged twenty-three. That's about four years younger than you should have been regened back to. Imagine this guy with a smaller nose and, like, a bit taller.'

Dielle had to admit, the picture he was looking at did carry a vague resemblance. 'Shit! How'd you get to be so ugly?'

Louie reappeared, and gave Dielle a piercing look, 'You know, people used to accuse me of being a bit blunt too, but fuck 'em! They're all dead now, right? Listen, I know I may not be the dupest guy in town, but you'd better remember that you're me, and I've got a lot of secrets stashed up here in my head, or better still, somewhere in a triple-encrypted interactive programme loaded into some quadruple-redundant data core somewhere. Sooner or later you're gonna need to know some of the things I do, believe me, would I lie to you? What for? Why would I lie to myself? How could I win? Just think about it. You gotta be as smart as I was when I was your age and I may have gotten old but I never got stupid. Think about it.'

Dielle thought about it. He was right. What possible reason would he have for lying to himself? He'd already realised he was pretty good at lying to others, but to himself? He was still too young and naïve to realise how many people spend the majority of their lives lying to themselves.

Louie launched himself onto his back and lay on the table looking up at Dielle's face. 'Shit! Those bastards! They were sure they'd figure that one out!'

'What's that?'

'Fucking nose hair, that's what! There is no point at all in the little fuckers and they're irritating as hell! Shit! With all this technology,' he said, waving his arms around at nothing resembling technology at all, 'you'd have thought they could have got rid of a few bloody hairs.'

'They don't bother me,' said Dielle.

'No of course they don't bother you *now*,' said Louie, exasperated. 'Just you wait another twenty years or so, then they'll drive you fucking crazy!' He looked as though he was trying to put all his fingers of both hands up his nostrils. 'Goddamn not-yet-invented clauses,' he muttered.

Louie looked around and spotted Mary-Belle, who was over at the table with the military-looking customers. They were all staring in Louie's direction.

'Hey, who's the Barbie?'

'That's Bella, she brings food and stuff and she's a really cute mover – watch.' He waved at Bella who immediately came gliding over.

'Are you going to introduce me to your friend, Dielle?'

'Hi Bella, Louie Drago,' said Louie, extending a hand which disappeared out of the edge of the projection field. He pulled it back in with a shrug. 'How d'you glide like that?'

'Anti-grav stick-ons,' she replied, lifting a foot to reveal thin pads on the souls of her shoes. 'I have them on all my work shoes. You won't believe how much walking you have to do in this job.' Both men looked at Bella's finely shaped calves with a similar intensity. 'So are you really from twenty-first century Earth? What was it like in those days?'

'So far, exactly like this place. I used to breakfast, lunch and dinner in a joint like this one back in the twenties. You're cute! What time you get off work? Maybe I got a few stories you haven't heard?'

'I bet you have!'

'Hey!' said Dielle. 'I think we have some other stuff to talk about and anyway, in case you haven't noticed, you're a projection. You aren't going anywhere without me.'

'Well I'm sure Bella doesn't mind, do you gorgeous?' Louie tried to give Bella his winning smile, but as usual, it came out like a dirty leer from an old man. 'And I don't mind watching.'

{[vDek:stop]}

Louie disappeared. Dielle turned to Bella, his face reddening. 'I'm really sorry. I didn't know I was such a disgusting old man.' He remembered the warning from the intern about discovering aspects of his past he'd rather not know. Maybe he should have listened.

'Oh, don't apologise for him, honey, he's just a holo. All he can do is watch and make noise.'

[[•]]

{[Deliver]}

[['Hello darling! I'm on my way home! I see you're at Jenny's. Shall I meet you there?']]

{[It's OK, I'm just finishing up. I'll come over]}

[['I'll be in the tub – it's nearly ready now.']]

Now that, thought Dielle was the best idea he'd heard all day. He picked up the vDek and put it in his long sleeve. 'Well,' he said, turning to Bella, 'I have to go.'

'Now you come back whenever you want, honey. You'll always find a warm welcome at Jenny's!'

[[Debit 14.35]]

Dielle found his way back to Kiki's place without asking Sis for directions and felt particularly proud of his navigation skills. Despite passing a few low buildings set discreetly into the landscaped platform, he saw no-one. As he entered the apartment a fine mist formed outside like a cloud descending.

{[What's happening?]}

[[Routine cleaning and static biomass maintenance]]

Dielle was glad not to have got wet until he heard Kiki call from the tub and the idea took on a sudden appeal. What a fine place this is, he thought. What a very, very fine place.

Later, in the lounge, while drinking a large *Generous Peasant*, a refreshing, fruit-filled drink with light sparkles and level 2 regulated alcohol which Kiki said couldn't get him drunk, no matter how many he drank, Dielle started to tell her about his day. When he got to the part about the two people he saw in Jenny's wearing uniforms, Kiki sat up.

'That's reminded me, I overheard something earlier. Something happened today.' She pulled her robe over her bare shoulders and turned to the flower display. 'Let's check on the war.'

The flowers vanished and a fivedee projection of a firework display filled the space.

'Dice!' shouted Kiki. 'That was a galactic-class destroyer. One of ours!'

Dielle had a sinking sensation. He knew everything had been just a little too good so far. 'We're at war? Those people in Jenny's – they were soldiers or something?'

A flotilla of heavily armoured battle cruisers bristling with spines and antennae ploughed through the remnants of the annihilated spaceship. Lines of incandescent light shot out from the fleet in seemingly random directions. Small explosions flowered into a semicircular shell surrounding the scene.

'Yeah, of course,' said Kiki, getting excited. 'All those spiky ones are ours, the enemy are in cloaked mode so we can't see them, but they can see us.' As she spoke a line of light originated from the top right corner of the display area and ten ships instantly targeted the point of origin. Nothing happened. Kiki slammed her fist into the couch. 'Missed! Lookadat!' The display cut to a full-length picture of a handsome middle-aged man in a similar uniform to the ones Dielle had seen earlier. 'Oh, it's Admiral Massive!' said Kiki.

Behind the admiral was a jumble of displays filled with flashing graphics and information he didn't understand and military types doing incomprehensible things.

'They let you see what's happening on the warships?'

'They're not on the warships, silly!' Kiki without take her eyes from the scene. 'They're here onSlab. Most high-ranking officers will co-ordinate from one of the local command centres, but the marines and pilots usually fight from home. Admiral Massive lives quite near here. I've met his wife a couple of times. She's nice.'

'So who's on the warships and who are we fighting?'

'No-one's on the warships!' Kiki was shocked. 'People would get killed! How horrible!' She shuddered. Dielle thought that killing people was probably one of the main tactics of war, but didn't feel secure enough to say it. 'And we're fighting *the enemy* of course.'

'So the ships are run by remote control or something?'

'Well of course! You wouldn't send actual living people into a war zone, would you?' she looked at Dielle suspiciously. He felt his next answer might be strategically important.

'No, of course, it's just that … where is this war taking place anyway? Are we in danger?'

'It's a couple of million klicks behind us at the moment, so no, we're not actually in any danger. But if they get any closer we might be. It's really crucial we figure out a way to detect them through their cloaking device and fast. They've advanced almost thirty thousand klicks since they got this new technology and that's in just three cycles.'

'Shit!'

'Exactly!' Kiki was excited. 'That's more than they've gained since the quantum collapse over five hundred cykes ago and we were nearly invaded then! I can still remember the crisis over that, even though I was just a little girl. Everyone freaked out when they got to within two hundred thousand klicks. Oh, and we don't use that word anymore, dear.'

The display cut back to the battle as a cloud of small fighter craft exited one of the spiky ships, all heading in the same direction – toward nothing that could be seen. Kiki became even more excited, 'Oh! Maybe they've figured something out! Hang on ...' She paused briefly while she checked with Sis. 'No.' She said, deflated. 'Just a trial sortie apparently. More of a training run. They're not going to make a big offensive until the new gigaplat arrives. It should get there the day after tomorrow. I've heard a very reliable rumour that it's got some really cool stuff in it, too.'

The point of view pulled away from the main area of conflict as sporadic fire fizzled down to a few dying explosions.

'That must be it for today,' said Kiki. 'The enemy must have disengaged. Yes. Same time tomorrow for the next skirmish.'

'They tell you when they're going to fight next? Who are these people?'

'Yes – and we tell them – it's a kind of convention.' Kiki smiled innocently. 'We don't actually know where they came from or what they look like because there's no-one on their ships either. We've never even seen one. The rumour is that they are just like us though, because of the way they fight and the type of weapons they use. There's a theory about parallel humanform development which states that any life-form capable of being in the same time and place as us and having similar technology to us must therefore look and behave like us. I think it's a load of blocks, but I suppose it could just about be true.'

'Why don't we attack their planet or wherever they come from?'

'No-one knows where it is, dear. But you can bet there's a lot of effort going into finding out. If you're interested, there are loads of sumes about it.'

Dielle took another drink, wishing it was stronger. 'So we're at war with an alien life-form we've never met and no-one ever gets hurt?'

'Yes! It's terribly exciting at the moment, too!'

'How long has this been going on?'

'Ages! Must be at least five hundred and sixty cykes by now – ask Sis.'

Dielle suddenly felt very tired. 'I guess I'll look it up later. But first I have to ask you something. Something a bit, well, weird.' Kiki looked concerned and the display changed into a brilliant arrangement of variegated penRoses, bringing a fresh fragrance to the room. 'You know how you don't use the word shit any more here?'

'No dear, we don't.'

'Why is that? I mean I've type of noticed something about myself. That is something I haven't done, or even needed to do. It's a bit … delicate.'

'We don't use the word shit, dear, because we don't shit, dear. That is, all of us non-naturalists don't.' She wrinkled her nose. That *n* word again. 'You, like all of us *civilised* people, have emties installed in our digestive tracts and urinary systems which extract all of our body's waste products after we've finally squeezed everything we need from our food and drink, and send it for recycling. It's all completely automatic and you don't even know it's happening. Nice and clean.'

Well, he thought, that explains that nagging feeling he'd been having and why they don't use the word anymore – no-one here has ever seen the stuff. 'Very efficient,' he said, draining his glass.

'Yes, the toilet paper manufacturers didn't half kick up a stink about it though.'

'No shit!' said Dielle and they laughed.

Wars, lost souls and useless assholes. Dielle thought it sounded like the name of a song.

'Kiki, it's sure felt like a long day,' he sighed. He hadn't got around to telling her about Louie yet. That could wait until the right moment. He needed to have a few words with himself before he let those two meet.

He wondered for a moment about the integrity of hiding what was an important part of his past from the woman he loved. Then he looked at Kiki happily sipping her Generous Peasant, giving him sexy come-hither looks.

'Let's go to bed,' he said.

ten

Kiki was missing again when he woke up. She'd left a voice message to tell him they'd been invited to a NewCycle party and that she'd be back around seven to get ready. She sounded excited. But then, he thought, it wasn't too hard to get Kiki excited. He liked that about her.

He had a conversation with Sis about clothes and learned he could select anything he wanted from a seemingly endless sume catalogue. He settled on a simple green tunic with knee-length baggy pants. He'd been wearing the same shoes he'd been given at Aux Renoir and couldn't see a reason to change them, so he grabbed the vDek from the pile of clothes he'd discarded the night before and headed for Kiki's transvex tube portal.

[[State destination]]

{[I don't really know. Can I just explore?]}

[[I can randomise you a selection of public portals or offer you one of 78.9 million personal tour recommendations]]

{[Does Kiki have a personal tour recommendation?]}

[[402 currently registered]]

{[Then select one of those which starts with a quiet and stress-free place to eat]}

[[••]]

Dielle took a breath, stepped through the transvex and had to fight hard to control his rising panic as he plummeted down the narrow shaft. This was going to take a lot of getting used to, he thought.

He hurtled into a wide, gracefully curving inter-section surge which was filled with hundreds of animated bubbles. All of the privacy fields were showing softAds. As one shot by, he heard the sound of clinking glasses and a familiar voice saying 'Aux Renoir is my favourite French restaurant in Mitchell' and thought that he saw … nah, he thought, it couldn't be. Another one sped passed him then slowed down before careering up toward an approaching funnel. It was showing the same softAd; a view of him smiling out at himself, sitting next to Kiki with Makepiece proudly bowing to camera in the distance. He looked around to check if all the other privacy shields were showing the same softAd and noticed a few of the other freetubers watching him with undisguised amusement.

{[Can I have a privacy bubble please?]}

It appeared instantly.

[[Debit 26]]

A support surface rose up as he sat down.

{[Sis, I just saw a softAd that looked like it featured me and Kiki]}

[[••]]

{[What can you tell me about this?]}

[[More precision required. What do you want to know about? Options: projection system/content creation/purchased media and market penetration/related affiliates/revenue streams/brokers/syndication]]

Dielle interrupted.

{[Who authorised this?]}

[[Your agent]]

{[Who?]} He remembered Bella had said something about an agent too.

[[Kioki Sypher-Marie Pundechan of Pundechan Media Corporation]]

Dielle became quiet and thought for a while. {[Do I get paid anything from the use of my image in this way?]}

[[Do you want details?]]

{[Deliver]}

[[Your standard trading account is currently being credited at an average rate of 0.78 bucks per second, however there was a peak of 343.37 bps last night during the live sume cast of the copulation event which momentarily reached the top thirty of SlabNow mostSumed (54plus rating)]]

'What?!' Dielle said out-loud.

{[What?]}`

[[~~?]]

{[People were watching us have sex last night? How?]}

[[Normal sumecast subscription service syndicated by Pundechan Media]]

{[I earn money from this? How many credits do I have at this moment?]}

[[At this moment you have 524,345 credits after exTax]]

{[Is that a lot?]}

[[That depends on your point of view]]

{[I don't have a point of view]}

[[Comparisons indicate your median bps income since re-entry is approximately 120.34 times that of the average SlabCitizen which would infer that most people would consider you to be doing very well. Does that help?]]

{[I guess it does. If Kiki is my agent, I assume she is making credits out of this too?]}

[[Of course. Pundechan Media has significant interests in the exploitation of your intellectual property]]

{[How much?]}

[[Private information; not authorised for your access. You will have to ask her]]

{[That, I will do]} Not authorised, thought Dielle, why is that the only piece of information which doesn't surprise me?

[[Round Park Plaza level 521. Debit 45.23. Watch your step]]

Dielle stumbled out into a bright, sunshiny day and a panorama of meadows and low, rolling hills. He walked toward the grass, looked down and froze in his tracks. The pavement between the tube portal and the park was transparent and more than a mile above the ground. Dielle threw himself onto the metre-thick invisipane and started hyperventilating. Sis emtied 2µg of Karmdown into his adrenal gland, then the equivalent of a rat 3 gin and tonic into his bloodstream and some reassuring information into his cognitive centres while the other two took effect.

Round Park Plaza was a folly of magnificent proportions and the winning entry in the 'Mess with a Megatonne' competition that had been held subsequent to the capture of interstellar mass $BJ^{sus}89654$ in the early fourth century PD. It was a seven-kilometre-wide disk of pastoral peace floating two and a half kilometres above the Slabscape. A hundred translucent tubes spiralled down from a tranilinium perimeter to converge at a mobile interchange which tracked the park on its journey around the forests, plains and lakes of Mitchell SideUp. Daylight repeaters on the park's underside meant that from below it looked like a gigantic jellyfish – which was exactly what the artist had intended. Visitors to the plaza were distributed around the park according to a personal-space optimisation algorithm and this, along with the low pressure, hyperoxygenated atmosphere made it a popular destination for wandering poets, strolling lovers and claustrophobic anti-socialites.

After a few minutes Dielle felt confident enough to open his eyes and crawl, slowly, to the grass verge. He stood up gingerly and backed away from the edge checking to see if he'd been spotted doing his bug-against-the-windscreen impression. There was no-one around. There was also nothing remotely resembling a restaurant within sight but he could see the top of a copse half-hidden in a nearby hollow so he decided to explore.

As he walked, the grass flattened before him, sensing his path and adapting to his speed. He tried walking faster but the grass was always a step ahead of him. It whispered as he moved. When he sped up, it hissed. The air was cool and invigorating and made him want to take huge gulps of it and run. He ran.

Beneath the trees was a sheltered clearing with wooden tables and benches but nothing that looked like a building or a machine that might dispense food. Hunger overrode his desire to figure it out for himself.

{[Where do I get something to eat?]}

[[What do you want?]]

{[What do you recommend? No, scratch that. What do most people eat around here?]}

[[Popular foods after an extended sleep period include: full Ænglish breakfast/fresh fruit and yoghurt/muesli/miso soup and desiccated fish/sugar cakes and chocolate drink/coffee, croissants and marmalade/cold cuts …]]

{[Stop]} Dielle had a feeling the list might be a long one.

{[The first one]} He had no idea what he had just ordered.

[[kTable to your left, flashing green]]

One of the tables had a flashing green square above it which disappeared when he looked away. He sat down in the dappled sunlight and waited. After a few minutes, the central panel of the catering table slid open and one of the finest hand-cooked breakfasts onSlab rose to the surface. The sausages were sizzling, the bacon pink, firm and giving off a smell that made his saliva glands gush. The egg yokes were brilliant yellow, the tomatoes lush, the mushrooms steaming and juicy, the devilled kidneys plump and glistening. A stack of inch-thick brown toast oozed golden butter, and a large glass of freshly emtied orange juice sparkled with beads of condensation. The Seville orange marmalade fought the steaming coffee for olfactory dominance. The coffee won.

[[debit 124.86]]

'Not too shabby!' said Dielle, pulling the plates toward him. He grabbed the hyperceramic cutlery and attacked the feast. After he'd taken the edge off his hunger, he wiped the grease from his chin and slowed down to savour each of the tastes. The combination of tomatoes with bacon triggered a deep and pleasant association that he couldn't isolate, but the effort to delve into his past reminded him of the vDek in his pocket. He took it out and, with a sigh, asked Sis to activate it.

'Hey! What the fuck? You turned me off! Who do you think you are?'

'Don't start that again. I'm having an absolutely fantastic breakfast and I'd quite enjoy turning you off again.' He meant it.

Louie took stock of their surroundings. 'The fuck? We're on a planet now?'

'Nope. We're still onSlab. This is a floating park in Mitchell SideUp and we're alone because I need to talk to you.'

'Your jerking my chain! This ain't no spaceship.' He looked up. 'I can see the sky! Hey, what's that?' he said, pointing upward.

'That's UpSideDown. Look, can't you just ask Sis all this stuff?'

'Who's Sis?'

'You know, the system, the thing that runs everything.'

'Well you show her to me and I'll fuckin' ask it, OK? I don't see no Sis.'

'You just think to it through your neural interface. There's nothing to see.'

'Listen, the only interface I have is the one you're listening to now,' he said, pointing at his mouth.

'Great,' said Dielle. 'So I have to explain everything to you?'

'Yeah, right. Think of it as a public service,' said Louie. 'What the hell is wrong with you? I'm the guy who put you here in the first place. You don't have the time to tell me what's going on?'

'Would you want to spend time talking to a three hundred and sixty-year-old projection of your former self that behaves like an animal and gives you shit?'

'Good point! You *do* remind me of me a bit – only I was never such a creep!' He looked down at Dielle's plate. 'How's the food?'

'Pretty great,' said Dielle, through a mouthful of toast.

'You should try mixing the tomato with the bacon – it's a winner.'

'Yeah, right. I need you to tell me how to eat.'

'Look, kid, I was eighty years old when they popped me in the freezer. You don't think I know stuff that's valuable? I was a business man. I made a shitload of money. Enough to put me, that is you, into space on a luxury liner the size of a fucking country!' Louie waved his arms toward the horizon and UpSide. He waved his arms a lot. Perhaps, thought Dielle, that was because they were so short.

'I reckon I can get by without you. I don't care what you know. That was a long time ago. You're out of date.'

'Yeah, I was always an independent son of a bitch too. Well, I thought of that.' Louie tapped his nose as if he had some secret to tell.

'What?'

'I told you I was rich, right? Well I was still rich even after I'd paid those money-grubbing bastards for my cryo and our ticket out of there. If you want to know how rich, just ask your new *sister* about IRAK and how much it was worth when I cashed in my chips. I have a lot of moulah stashed away that only I know the access codes to, seeing as you can't remember anything!' He had a hands-around-the-testicles-and-ready-to-squeeze look on his face.

'So you've got money – I have money too. I'm a star here. I'm making money just by sitting here.' A thought crossed his mind. He put up his finger to silence Louie.

{[Is all this being recorded?]}

[[Of course, everything in range onSlab is recorded]]

{[Can you make this private?]}

[[••]]

'What was that?' said Louie. 'You went all far-sighted on me. You talking to Sis?'

'Yeah, I was just making sure this conversation wasn't being broadcast.'

'OK. Good point. Yeah, I would have thought of that if you'd let me know it was fucking possible!'

'You just don't get it, do you? You're a fossil. I don't need your money and you can't even communicate with Sis.'

'So what did you activate me for then?' asked Louie.

'Well I just wanted to ask you a couple of questions. Personal stuff. You know.'

Louie wasn't paying attention, he was staring over Dielle's shoulder. Across the clearing, a beanpole of a man attired in top hat and tails was striding toward them.

The man stopped and bowed slightly, removing his hat in a formal salutation.

'Jeez!' said Louie. 'It's Abraham fucking Lincoln!'

'I'm very sorry for disturbing your repast,' said the man in a slow, deliberate tone. 'Please allow me to introduce myself. I am system admin representative 001.735.3160. However, you can call me Erik. I wonder if I could have a few moments of your time?'

'Well, I suppose so,' said Dielle. 'You're a system representative? You mean *Sis*?'

'Precisely sir. May I sit?'

It looked as though the old man needed to. Dielle moved over.

'Why did you come to talk to me?' he said. 'Surely Sis can talk to me anytime without sending someone?'

'Of course, sir. It isn't you we need to speak with, sir, it's your holo.'

'Fuckin' A!' said Louie giving Dielle a triumphant look. 'I need to have a few words with you, too.'

'We have a …' he paused, uncertain for a second, 'situation.' He was clearly unhappy about having to use this word. He turned to Louie. 'Something has happened that we need your help with, something of the utmost secrecy and importance.'

He turned back to Dielle looking grave. 'We're sorry, but we have to ask if you would mind turning yourself, your previous self, over to us for a while until we can get this little difficulty sorted out.'

'Do I mind?' said Dielle. 'You can keep him.'

'Little difficulty?' said Louie. 'You said it was of the utmost importance, and then that it was just a little difficulty. Which is it?'

'Well it is both, Mr Drago, both. However it won't do to spread alarm. And Dielle, sir, we'd be grateful if you kept this to yourself.'

'No problem. In fact I'd already made sure the recording of this was private, so you're fine here.'

Erik was mildly amused. 'Oh no sir, this isn't being recorded.'

'What's in it for me?' asked Louie.

'I am authorised to certain limits, Mr Drago. What is it you want?'

'Well, I want a long list of things but the first is complete autonomy from him!' he said, pointing at Dielle.

'Of course, Mr Drago. That is effective immediately.'

'Call me Louie,' said Louie with a smile, putting out his hand. Erik reached over and shook it. 'Wow!' said Louie excitedly, 'I felt that! How'd you do that?'

'I am a NAH, sir. Sometimes physical, but more often closer to your state of being.'

'Nar?' said Dielle. 'What's that?'

Erik looked him steadily in the eyes. 'Not Actually Human, sir.'

Dielle shivered.

'I'm sorry to be insistent but do you accept this requisition of your vDek, sir? We are in something of a hurry you see.'

'Please, take it,' said Dielle. And fuck off, he thought, loudly.

[[~?]]

{[Not meant for you, sorry]}

Erik stood up, doffed his hat and collected the vDek. Louie floated in mid-air.

Dielle grinned. 'You're legless!' he laughed, pointing at Louie's lower body as it faded out to nothing.

'Yeah, well, I didn't think I'd be needing them did I?'

'Good day, sir' said Erik, bowing slightly.

Good riddance, thought Dielle. Then he wondered how he was going to find the answers to the things he wanted to know now that Louie was no longer under his control. Well at least he wasn't going to have to introduce him to Kiki. That was a bonus. Then he thought about Kiki. Now *that* was going to be an interesting conversation.

eleven

Erik asked Louie if he would like to take a private tour to see 'how magnificent their conveyance was'.

'You said you were in a hurry,' said Louie.

'Yes sir,' Erik smiled like he had an ulcer. 'I was in a hurry to remove you from your own presence.'

'You're the man!' said Louie. 'Lead on. You know, I can't understand it, I wasn't a jerk like that when I was his age. Something's happened to me.'

As they strolled through the park, Erik greeted everyone by name, usually with a deferential touch to the brim of his hat. Occasionally he would say something relevant or personal, as though they were old friends. Erik introduced Louie as a new arrival onSlab and the SlabCitizens treated them both with respect. No-one seemed bothered by Louie's semi-corporal manifestation.

'Nice people,' said Louie after a typically pleasant encounter with a young couple who'd been playing Frisbee with an eye-controlled manoeuvrable disk. 'You know everyone, huh?'

'I have never met these citizens before. Of the current 31,878,256 living humans onSlab I have personally met less than 0.223 percent.' He looked at Louie soberly, 'I don't get out much.'

'They seemed to know you.'

'By convention, all system avatars are called Erik and all Eriks have access to every level of Slabdata on the biomass and therefore know more about each individual than do their closest friends.'

'What's the biomass?'

'It's a friendly term we use to refer to our honoured guests to whom we are merely protectors and servants.

Humans make up the vast majority of the sentient biological mass onSlab.'

'I guess that excludes me then,' said Louie.

'Have no fear, sir, we NAHs respect all manifestations of intelligence.' He paused. 'And humans too.'

Louie figured he was being given a none-too-subtle message and winked at Erik, who responded with a barely perceptible nod. Well, thought Louie, we're all lads together here, aren't we?

'I have to warn you, sir, that my task is to introduce you to SlabCouncil and that has the potential to be a rather perplexing experience.'

'How so?'

'Council is a combination of NAHs working in conjunction with the SlabWide Integrated System alongside a statutory number of interns who are non-corporal human consciousnesses. It was mandated in the Initial Design that humans must play a significant role in all decision making, strategic planning and philosophical debate.'

'Causes problems, huh?'

'Usually, sir,' said Erik gravely, 'it's a total bloody disaster.'

'I bet. We had a lot of that type of thing in my day, you know. You should have witnessed the negotiations between us and the U.S. and Mexican governments when they tried to claim territorial rights over Arizona Bay.'

'I was reading up on the transcripts, sir. You are somewhat of a legend in our little group.'

'Oh yeah?' said Louie, preening. 'That's dupe. It's nice to know I'm remembered so many years after I turned into a popsicle. What type of group is it?'

'Many of us are students of the century prior to Slab's departure. You were privileged to have lived through the most rapidly occurring scientific advances and cultural changes ever recorded in human history. The social disruptions brought about by technological developments were wide-ranging and traumatic. Absolutely fascinating. In fact there are some who suggest that *you* were a significant influence upon that most turbulent of times.'

'Well, we did some stuff!' beamed Louie, trying, and failing, to be modest.

'Indeed you did, sir.' They walked onto the perimeter invispane and Louie looked down at the lush countryside far below.

'Wow!' said Louie, impressed. 'Anti-grav, right?'

'Correct, sir.'

'We invented that, you know.'

'Yes, sir, although there is some debate in our circle about the use of the word *invent* when it comes to a lot of the claimed intellectual property of your corporation.'

'I'm not surprised,' said Louie with a grin, 'Milus Blondel was the biggest bullshitter I've ever met – and I've met more than a few, I can tell you. He was also the luckiest son-of-a-bitch. All that matter-transmission stuff was a total accident you know.'

'Yes sir, the irony of him meeting his end in the California Disappearance did not escape us. We would be honoured if you would come and talk to us about your experiences and would happily reimburse you for your time. Perhaps we could even provide valuable information in return? A bargain could be struck!' Erik looked mischievous and Louie knew he'd just been thrown some bait. What he didn't know yet was just how delicious that bait might be, but he was pretty sure that he, Louis Clinton Drago, business gurulla, would be able to leverage it for all it was worth.

'Sure, no problem,' he said enthusiastically. 'I can talk for days. How many people in this group of yours?'

'As of this moment, 34,542 sir.' It was Erik's turn to feign modesty. He walked through the transvex portal giving Louie a brief moment of panic which he dismissed when he remembered he was a holographic projection and couldn't be hurt. Or so he thought.

'Peristaltic gravity propulsion, sir,' said Erik calmly as they hurtled to the floor at barely subsonic speeds. 'A network of a hundred and twenty million kilometres of multilevel interconnected tubes and causeways which serve as SlabWide transportation. Each individual is delivered to their chosen destination via routes determined by traffic flow and tube capacity. Momentum compensators absorb the accelerations.'

'Another one of ours,' said Louie. He looked around at the crowds of people and animated bubbles. 'Though I don't think we got it working this well.'

'We have made some improvements to the original design, I believe. Of course, as neither you nor I are subject to momentum restrictions, we can move around at considerably faster speeds if we need to.' As he said this, they rose into a space above the travelling throng and accelerated to a speed that turned everything around them into a blur. 'I want to show you the mass input and conversion zone before we arrive at Council. It might help you get a valuable perspective on our world and, in any case, they are currently debating the interpretation of the record of the last meeting and that could take hours. Days even.' He sighed wearily. 'I suspect you would rather walk back to Brooklyn than be involved in all that.'

'Yeah, sounds about right,' said Louie. Some things never change, he thought. 'Hey, how is my old home town these days? Are you still in touch?'

'Unfortunately not, the telepaths lost touch with Earth about eighty of your years post-departure. The time-dilation effect made it unworkable. We were sending messages as normal but the gaps between sending and receiving made the information irrelevant. Although telepathic communication is instantaneous, they would take hours to respond and those hours turned into days at our end. We would read back the message for confirmation and they would have forgotten all about us.' Louie nodded. He had no idea what Erik was talking about. 'We used to intercept some very outdated narrowcasts too, sir, but after we changed course, even those stopped.'

'Changed course?'

'Nothing sinister about it, sir. Just more accurate information came in about our destination and we altered course accordingly. Don't believe what you'll hear in the scandals.' Erik looked bored. 'It will be several minutes before we are there, sir. Would you like a brief audio-visual overview of our environment?'

'Sure,' said Louie. A privacy field surrounded them, the lights dimmed and a holographic image of Slab started playing.

'Welcome to Slab,' said an irritating male voice, over music that reminded Louie of cheap hotels. He watched, spellbound. By the time the pair arrived at their destination Louie had gained a general overview of Slab and its systems. The privacy shield dropped to reveal a side-on view of a blue-shifted galactic core.

'Woah!' said Louie. 'Are we in space? Like outside?'

'Yes, sir. Welcome to the leading edge.'

Louie stared ahead. He'd just learned that they were travelling at incredible speeds, but he couldn't see anything that supported this. Before them lay a seemingly stationary panorama of the Milky Way and the Universe beyond. It was orders of magnitude more impressive than the Hubbles he had pored over as a child. If he had still been able to breathe, the view would have taken his breath away. Of course, he thought, if I could still breathe, I'd be dead. Dead, irradiated and frozen solid. For all of its magnificent grandeur, the environment he was floating in was the most hostile to life in the known universe.

He looked back. All he could see was black, impenetrable darkness. A flash of light caught his eye. 'What was that?' he asked, pointing to the fading embers of a violent explosion in the centre of the Slabface.

'That's the focus of the gravnet funnel, sir. What you saw was some small mass being steered into the central collector and accelerated to Slabspeed. We project gravity fields which divert anything within a million kilometres down into the gravity well on the Slabface. As you are aware, Slab uses gravity drives both fore and aft. The aft ones are anti-grav thrusters and the forward ones, here, are enhanced gravitational attractors which are currently tuned to the central mass of the galaxy. You will no doubt recall that the gravity drive equations relate power to mass so that the ship's acceleration is proportional to mass accretion. Basically, the more mass we capture along the way, the faster we should go. We have increased Slabmass by over twenty times since we departed Earth orbit and have attained a speed that is now within five percent of light-speed. But there's a problem.'

Louie was used to problems. He'd spent his entire life overcoming problems, especially the type of problems other people had told him were impossible. He really liked those kinds of problems. He suspected, though, that Erik was about to describe a problem he couldn't even begin to solve.

'Our current status,' said Erik, as a stray speck of interstellar dust streaked toward the mass collector interface and disintegrated, 'is that we've virtually stopped accelerating. The drive techs can't figure out why but we seem to have hit a curve of diminishing returns. It's looking like the light-speed barrier is impenetrable after all. Of course, the Rellies are driving us crazy about this.'

'I think there's been a bit of a mistake,' said Louie. 'I know we invented this anti-gravity tech, but I was the money guy. I was the one who exploited our I.P. and handled negotiations and licensing arrangements. I know zip about the science. I barely understood what the hell I was making the deals about.'

'That's not why I brought you here, sir. We know who you are.'

Uh-oh, thought Louie.

'I'm sure we'll solve that problem eventually. It is just science after all,' said Erik. 'We have a much bigger problem we're hoping you might help us with.' He moved them away from the mass collector and its silent, spasmodic explosions.

They sped across the face, beyond the edge and away from Slab. Behind them, two parallel lines defined a perfectly flat sidewall that stretched back for more than a thousand kilometres. It shimmered blackly, against the blackness of receding space. Louie hoped that whatever technology was holding them in place was fool-proof, or better still, genius-proof.

'Look towards our destination, sir, if you please,' said Erik, pointing forwards. 'Can you see a dark spot in front of us?'

Louie looked at the concentration of stars ahead. He raised his hand instinctively to shield his eyes from the glare of the galactic core, then realised what he was doing and sheepishly dropped his arm. 'Holographic hands,' he muttered. He *could* make out a shape. A dark shape. An angular dark shape. It looked just like …

'What the fuck?' he said, turning to the forlorn facsimile of a long-dead president floating in space.

Erik nodded grimly.

'But it … it can't be … it's not …' Louie was unaccustomed to being flustered. He couldn't remember the last time anything had happened to surprise him enough to make him miss a beat. Even when most of the State of California and almost all of his company's assets and executives had disappeared in one cataclysmic instant and the Pacific Ocean had rolled into the newly formed Arizona Bay, all he had done was smile. Smile and triple-check that the transactions divesting himself of his major shareholding in IRAK had cleared the week before.

But this was something that had definitely renewed his respect in the ability of the universe to throw curve balls.

'Is it?'

'I'm afraid it is, sir. It's an artefact identical to this one.' Erik swept his hand over the 53 million cubic kilometres of Slab pushing the barriers of the space-time continuum silently behind them. 'As far as we can ascertain it's another spaceship, directly ahead of us, matching our course and speed and it is exactly …' Erik paused for effect and repeated the word, '*exactly* the same as this one. It is the same size in every dimension, has the same external detailing, the same material structure, the same configuration of drives, the same communication arrays and the same insignia. Our probes cannot get within 1000 klicks of it before they are vaporised by the shield defences, but then our own Slab has exactly the same defence capability and barriers. However, there have been no communications emanating from it, no responses to any of our hails. In fact, with the exception of the automated defence attacks on our probes, it appears to be completely oblivious to our presence.'

Louie looked at the dark shape ahead. Now that he knew what it was, he could clearly make out the Slablike geometric outline silhouetted against the stars.

'Every remote test we have been able to carry out indicates it is inert. There is no measurable heat radiation and no vibrational signature which would be typical of an inhabited ship. Therefore, we speculate, it is abandoned, empty and lifeless. A veritable Mary Celeste. We have only two possible explanations: either, it is a replica of our own Slab made by some other civilisation – an alien species far more technically advanced than our own who decided to build a copy of Slab and manoeuvre it into a precise matching course ahead of us, perhaps to provoke us into paranoia or possibly even as a form of *joke*.'

'Or?' Louie was clearly not buying that option.

'It *is* Slab.'

'That's impossible.'

'Quite so sir; as you say sir. Absolutely impossible. But there's going to be a bit of a flap about this if it ever gets out. Which is why I have been authorised to tell you that if you utter one word about this to anyone outside Council, your communications facility will be shut down before you have formed the shape of your second syllable. Sorry, but we can confidently predict that the mere knowledge of its existence among the biomass would spark a widespread panic at the very least.'

'You'd better take me to meet this council of yours Erik,' said Louie seriously. Jeez! he thought, first they tell me there's no basketball and now this.

They hurtled back to a tiny square of blue on the Slabface. Despite the bizarre news, he had enjoyed his first EVA. It was so much easier to be disembodied, he thought. Hard vacuum was a piece of … .

'Hey,' he said, turning back to Erik. 'How come I can hear you speak?'

'How do you mean, sir?'

'Well, you know, sound, air, in space no-one can hear you sneeze, that type of thing.'

'You are presuming, sir, that you have normally functioning ears.'

'Ah,' said Louie. 'Good point.'

As they entered the portal and went transonic, Sis emtied six million tonnes of lead shielding into the tube behind them.

twelve

Dielle spent most of his day following one of Kiki's recommended routes. He bounded through a forest of hundred-meter-tall zigzag trees in Mitchell SideUp. High above, a canopy of white wingleaves beat lazily against the local one-sixth gravity. The leaves held the slender trees upright and made them tremble like taut springs. Ranks of right-angled trunks quivered in sympathy, creating interference patterns that rippled into the distance.

He tumbled down white-water rapids inside a privacy field that absorbed every blow as he bounced off the mirrorrock canyon walls like a pachinko ball in a race to the sink-hole.

The contextureality corridor was mind-blowing. Literally. It was a 300Km long, full-scale representation of the history of humankind – in context. The context was provide by Sis who fed him intensive data cascades that blew away his recently gained concept of reality and replaced it with a detailed understanding of the technology and circumstances of the moment in history he'd been transported to – in his case, Kiki's itinerary took him to mid-fifteenth-century Germany. He was awed by the implications of the invention of hand-cast moveable type. He realised that information which had previously been the exclusive domain of the church and state would become available to everyone. Barely educated people would learn to read. Everything would change. As the temporary reality faded from his brain, Dielle re-remembered that nobody bothered reading the printed word anymore and learned a very important point: context is everything.

But when it came to being impressed, as far as Dielle was concerned, nothing compared to the Allways Falls, a fifty-kilometre-wide curved curtain of water that plunged thousands of feet into a churning lake. The noise was deafening and there was an energy in the air that exhilarated him. Lightning flashed between erupting spumes of mist and hundreds of rainbows flickered in and out of existence, forming corridors of parallel arches between the lake and the falls. Dielle queried where all the water came from, so Sis manoeuvred his privacy field further along the arc to where the water surged upwards. White-walled spirals formed at the turbulent interface between the opposing torrents, curling into tight whirlpools that span away across the face of the water like angry sprites.

He'd met a few people and found that the best thing to do was nod and not get too close. He got the feeling that privacy was important because everyone seemed to know who he was, but no-one approached him. He didn't have a problem with that. He had Sis to talk to.

Eventually, his brain struggled to take in anything new so he tubed it back to Seacombe for a few glasses of rat 3 red wine at an award-winning café overlooking a jogging park. He watched people exercising and felt happily absent for a while. The light was warm on his face and everything was fine.

Nothing here felt out of place to him. Including himself. Social customs were easy to get along with and everything seemed to be geared toward making life easy. People were friendly but unintrusive, styles and fashions were subdued and comfortable. Everything seemed normal. But as he had no memories to compare anything to, he realised that even if something extraordinary had already happened, he would probably still have accepted it as normal. He wondered if something extraordinary had already happened. It didn't feel as though it had, but how would he know? He decided not to worry about it. Life, after all, was just fine. More rat 3 please.

Knowledge is a valuable thing. Knowledge, reasoning and experience are the three key ingredients of wisdom. However, the real wisdom is in knowing what questions to ask and how to ask them. If he had thought to ask Sis why he felt so relaxed and unfazed by such a barrage of new experiences, he would have discovered that he had been continually monitored for signs of anxiety or panic since he had started re-entry. Sis had been regularly administering a cocktail of calming drugs directly into his bloodstream via miniature intravenous emties. It was all part of the standard re-fam procedure. Of course, Dielle didn't know that because it hadn't occurred to him to ask what the standard re-fam procedure entailed. And the reason he hadn't thought to ask what the standard re-fam procedure entailed, was because of the cocktail of calming drugs in his bloodstream.

There is a popular saying onSlab: It isn't knowing what you know, or knowing what you don't know, it's knowing what you don't know you don't know that matters.

[[•]]

{[Hmm?]}

['Darling!'] Kiki. ['Come home! I need to talk to you about tonight']

Yeah, he thought, I need to talk to you too. {[On my way]}

He told Sis to take him home in privacy and dived into the nearest portal. Two days ago, he'd been terrified of the tube. Now he felt completely accustomed to it. He tried to see if his ass could hit the floor before the bubble grew a bench. It couldn't.

{[Can you show me the broadcast of me and Kiki from yesterday? The copulation scene]}

[[Debit fee 25 credits; acknowledge approval]]

{[I have to pay to watch myself?]}

[[This sume is licensed via Pundechan Media and distributed through five wholesale aggregators to fifty-eight SlabWide sumecasters, all of whom own a micro portion of the income stream. As a performer, you will, of course, have your share of the fee instantly credited back into your account. Acknowledge approval]]

{[How much do I get?]}

[[The figure is a variable depending on provider, sume times, regions, media space prominence, side endorsements by market faction and cumulative escalators. Acknowledge approval]]

{[What the fuck does all that mean? Can't you tell me how much I get from paying 25 credits to watch my own stuff?]}

[[In this particular instance the amount will be a little under 2 bucks after ExTax. Acknowledge approval]]

{[Two bucks! Is that all?]}

[[Note: The sume in question is just under 15 minutes edited duration and you are now 4.56 minutes from your destination. Do you still wish to view the material? Pundechan Media takes no responsibility for refunding fees for any part of the sume that is not sumed. Acknowledge approval]]

{[Alright! Alright! I approve. Show me the ...]} A close-up of his buttocks filled the screen.

I don't fucking approve at all, thought Dielle. Decent ass though.

He stumbled into the apartment four and a half minutes later with a raging erection. Kiki was catching up on the latest war news but didn't mind being distracted by Dielle lifting her up and turning her over. It didn't take long.

'Hmmm, that was nice,' purred Kiki.

'Yeah, a bit quick though. I bet I won't make a buck a sume out of that one.'

'Ah.'

Dielle looked into her dark, stunning eyes. 'Yes,' he said. 'Ah.'

Kiki rearranged her house-robe and sat up. 'You don't like the percentage?'

'No, I don't like the percentage! And I don't like having my ass broadcast all over Slab without my permission and I don't like being lied to!' Dielle was trying to get angry about this but finding it very hard work. He wanted to give Kiki a hard time. After all, this was the woman he loved, who had betrayed him and exploited him. But somehow, every time he got angry, he felt fine about it.

'I never lied to you!'

'Nurse Pundechan? Is that Nurse Pundechan of Pundechan Media then? Do media enterprises here have many on-staff medical professionals?'

'I am a nurse! I took a course! I have a certificate on file. You can check.'

'So why are you a nurse when you run a media company? Business a bit slow is it?'

'Business is great since you thawed out, darling! I knew you'd be a star, I just knew it! That's why I took the nursing course and applied to St. Vincent's when I found out they were ready to re-fam you.'

'So the whole thing was a scam?' He still couldn't get angry no matter how hard he tried. He was even starting to see the funny side. 'You use the re-fam thing to get clients?'

'Client darling – just you. That's all I need. I've been in this business for a long time. I only need one star. All those second-tier wannabees are nothing but gaps. I don't waste my time with leaf-blowers. I'm a professional.'

'Well, you're a professional something, that's for sure!'

'Oh, that's a good one!' she beamed.

Dielle stopped dead. He looked around. 'Is all this being recorded now?'

'Of course dear, everything onSlab is recorded all the time.' She lowered her voice. 'But don't worry, we can edit that bit out before we release it. We're not going out live at the moment.' She lowered her voice to a whisper. 'But I did get a pretty attractive offer today that might mean we could be going Slabwide constant live on a very big aggregator.'

'But!' cried Dielle, 'I love you! How could you do this to me?'

Kiki had tears in her eyes, which made them sparkle even more. Dielle instantly worried that he'd gone too far. If he had known that the real reason she was tearing up was because she knew just how many extra sumers an outburst like that was going to generate tomorrow, he probably wouldn't have said what he was about to say. He took Kiki in his arms. She looked suddenly vulnerable, fragile and very beautiful.

'I'm sorry darling,' he said, kissing away her tears. 'It's all been a bit of a shock, that's all.'

Dicing hell, this is gold! thought Kiki, cancelling a meeting with a prospective writing team. She broke away from what was turning into a passionate kiss, reluctant to lose the potential income another quickie would bring in, but not wanting to be late.

'Darling, we have to go,' she said, grabbing a bag and pulling him toward the tube portal. 'We don't want to keep the president waiting.'

'The president?' said Dielle inside their privacy bubble. 'Slab has a president? I thought everything was run by Sis.'

'Well, yes, of course it is dear,' she said, stripping off. She took two palm-sized disks out of her bag, reached up to stick one on the roof and put the other one on the floor. 'Come on, you can't meet the president smelling like you've just had sex.'

Hot, sparkling water gushed from the top emti and drained away through the one on the floor. A portable shower, thought Dielle, just what every girl-about-Slab should have in her handbag. He shed his clothes and joined Kiki as soapy bubbles started to fill the air.

'So we've been invited to a party with the president,' said Dielle. 'Cool! What's the occasion?'

'It's just a regular NewCyke party, but only a small group of really famous people generally get invited. It's huge!'

'Small and huge?'

'Small as in very few celebrities, huge as in sume figures. Everyone watches the president's parties darling! We'll only get a tiny percentage of the income, but it's still going to be very serious wonga!' Kiki formed a circle with the forefinger and thumb of her right hand and made a side to side movement. 'I could go back to Aux Renoir tomorrow and double our deal, lookadat!'

'You really do know about all this deal stuff, don't you?' said Dielle. He was beginning to realise he'd fallen into some very skilled hands.

'They don't call me Tiger for nothing, dear!' said Kiki, standing on tiptoes to kiss him on the nose. The water stopped abruptly and both emties blasted the pair with warm air. Kiki grabbed her handbag, took out a white block of chamoist and gave it to Dielle. 'Here,' she said. 'Put this on. We'll change into our party clothes when we get there.' She took out another block and shook it out into the shape of a body suit. Dielle copied her and put his on. The material simultaneously dried and moisturised his skin with invigorating oils. Kiki collected the shower emties and popped them into her bag.

'That's a very handy bag you have there,' said Dielle.

'Just a portable emti, darling,' said Kiki, taking out a large hairbrush and then a mirror that expanded in her hand. She brushed her long black hair, which immediately dried to a fine shine. 'I've ordered you a really nice suit in variable reds. It's designed by a ridiculously expensive designer friend of mine who insisted you have it for nothing. That's what happens when you get invited to a presidential party.'

They arrived at the reception area, a large, circular space with a deep blue Soffen floor which absorbed the room's ambient sounds and the momentum of anyone who walked on it. The walls and ceiling glowed with a soft light that grew in intensity from the floor to a slender, motile sculpture which hung from the centre of an ornate dome. Kiki lead him to a bank of dressing rooms.

Dielle looked around at the deserted corridors.

'Shouldn't there be someone here to welcome us?'

'What for, dear?'

'Security I guess.'

'Sis controls all onSlab security, darling, what use would a human be? We wouldn't have been brought here if we hadn't been invited.'

'Well, we could be assassins or something.'

'The assassins have their own entrance but I don't think any are coming tonight.' She pushed him into an open cubicle. 'You use this one dear, I'll meet you in the pre-bar. Just go through the opposite vex and Sis will lead you straight there.' She gave him a peck on the cheek and disappeared in to the room next door.

As the transvex darkened behind him, the lights came on and Dielle found the suit waiting for him in the emti closet. He tried it on. Shades of sensual reds rippled through the thick, velvety fabric as he moved. A pair of knee-high, blood-red boots complemented the suit along with a wide-brimmed hat which seemed to reflect light that wasn't actually there. It felt refreshingly cool on his head. A flap of fine gauze hung from the brim to the nape of his neck. He admired himself in a full-length multimirror.

[[•]]

{[Yup?]}

[[You have the hat on back to front]]

An animation superimposed on his reflection. The flap was supposed to cover his face. He turned it to match the image. From his point of view, the material became transparent but his face in the mirror was traced by flowing patterns of subtly pulsating light. It made him look god-like. He stared at his reflection.

He suddenly felt very small and isolated. How could he, a five-day-old 27-year-old have wound up at a presidential party on a gigantic spaceship hurtling towards an impossibly distant destination?

He dumped the chamoist body suit into a large hamper and immediately re-opened the lid to check if it was still there. It wasn't. He wondered idly what would happen if he climbed into the hamper.

The sound of laughter outside distracted him. A drink, he thought, heading toward the noise, I need a good strong drink.

Dielle followed the sounds into a room packed with hundreds of laughing, chattering people. Two of Slab's top LightHarpists filled the space with exquisite contrapuntal melodies which, due to the tuned acoustic absorbers in the low ceiling, easily dominated the muffled murmur of the crowd.

[[Entering smooze: standard rules apply]]

{[~?]}

[[A smooze is a formally delineated space for conversation of a superficially social nature which is in actuality a front for exploring the underlying potential for interesting and/or valuable transactions. Standard rules are currently in force in this smooze, which means that all recordings are strictly non-publishable without the registered compliance of all parties involved and all agreements are contractually non-binding]]

A troupe of dancers clad in identical iridescent-green, gender-concealing bodysuits flitted between islands of half-sunken couches talking to guests and dispensing snacks and drinks from the emtiwaiters embedded into the upholstery.

One of them appeared before him in a flurry of whirling arms and legs.

'Welcome to Dielle,' said the sparkling creature in a soft voice which didn't help nail the gender ambiguity. It bowed flamboyantly. 'I am sylph.' No help there either. 'May I introduce you to one of your choosing? There are twelve social invitations already on file for you with an additional four just posted as you entered the smooze.

'Well, I'm kind of … waiting for my … friend.' Dielle was having trouble simultaneously coordinating his mouth, brain and eyes because a goddess was striding toward him. Her perfectly symmetrical face was framed by a mane of long, white hair which flowed and wound itself around her expertly sculpted curves. Every move she made was a minutely choreographed ritual, echoing genetic programmes which had been running continuously for hundreds of thousands of years. Her deep, golden eyes widened and her mouth parted just enough to reflect the ambient light off the glistening, micro-enhanced surface of her lips. She was a work of sexual art (the artist was currently turning down business in the next smooze). Her golden gown clung to every sensuous outline of her body and he would have found her distracting in any circumstance, but there was something else: whenever his eyes darted to her lavishly proportioned chest, the fabric seemed to melt away, revealing a pair of multi-award winning breasts.

'Dielle, I've been so looking forward to meeting you.' She put out her hand as the sylph glisséed silently away. 'Van Darwin, Faith-Sincere, in case you haven't already asked Sis.' No I hadn't, something must have caught my attention, thought Dielle.

'Just call me either Faith or Sin, depending on your point of view.'

The point of his view was more than obvious. He tried hard to control his eyes but they had a life of their own. Her laugh, like a lot of things about her, was generous.

'You are quite a star, you know,' she said. 'I'm a big fan of yours already.'

'Faith,' said a cold voice beside him. It was Kiki. 'Drumming up business? I thought you were booked solid for the cycle already?'

Faith-Sincere's eyes hardened to a professional smile. 'Tiger! Darling! How are you? You must be exhausted!' She reached out and put a delicate hand on Dielle's velvety jacket which swirled and danced different shades of red around her palm. 'He's such a handful, darling!'

'Not just a handful. Darling.' Kiki had to force that last word through clenched teeth. 'Do I see Admiral Massive over there?'

Faith-Sincere, assuming a joke, casually looked around. Over in a corner was a crowd of excited people surrounding the lantern-jawed hero in a flashy uniform. 'Lookadat! He never comes to parties!' She turned back. 'Excuse me Dielle, I really would love to talk to you later if that's OK with you.' She smiled and then nodded at Kiki. 'Tiger … ' She span round and hurried off to join the growing crowd.

'Hah!' said Kiki. 'That bitch!'

'She seemed pretty nice to me,' said Dielle wistfully.

'Yeah! I bet! I suppose you could see her breasts?'

'Well, yes. Rather nice they were too.'

'Thought so. She's wearing Reveal; it goes transparent when someone looks at it, but only if the viewer has been granted permission by the wearer. So you get to ogle her designer tits while all I could see was a dress on a tart.'

'I could see them because she let me?'

'Of course! Can you guess what she let me see?'

'What?'

'Her bare ass as she flounced off!' Kiki was incensed.

Dielle hadn't been able to see her bare ass. Pity, he thought, nice ass too. He turned to look at Kiki and did a double take.

'You look … ' He tried to look her up and down. It wasn't easy. 'Missing!'

Kiki's neck and face were floating above a pair of mirrored shoes. Where her body should have been was a kind of sheen through which he could see a distorted view of everything behind her.

'What's this?'

'It's a C-thru,' she said proudly. 'It's really expensive. I ordered it especially for the party. It has micro-image sensors woven into the fabric right alongside micro-projectors, so when you look at it you see a projected image of whatever is directly behind. It works like the light transmitters under buildings. You know how you can see the sky through overhead buildings? It's the same principle.'

'That's amazing,' said Dielle, reaching out and waving his hand behind her back to test the effect.

'It's a bit hot, though, and they haven't got the gloves right yet.' She waved her hands in front of his face. All he could see was a blur of background colours distorted in the approximate shape of hands.

'You look like a floating head,' he looked down, 'being followed around by a pair of mirrored shoes'.

'Yeah, it's advisable to wear some conspicuous footwear if you don't want to keep getting stepped on. I'm not sure about them though. Do you think they make my feet look big?'

'I don't think they make your feet look anything. All I can see are reflections. Come on, let's get a drink.' He put his arm around her slender back and moved her over to an empty couch. She started giggling.

'What's funny?'

'I just thought. If you wanted to do something naughty, you could do it in plain sight and no-one would notice. Your hand would just disappear.'

That opened up a few other possibilities too, thought Dielle. He raised an eyebrow and grinned.

Kiki was shocked. 'Not at a presidential party!'

Dielle considered doing something that might increase her shock factor and looked around to see if anyone was watching. He found himself staring into the almond eyes of a sylph who had appeared behind them. This one, though, was most definitely a female, thought Dielle. Almost definitely.

'We have Slab's premier mix-masters on call tonight for our guests,' it said. 'Would you like to sample a mix or would you prefer your own creation?'

'Are the Epoxile Kids mixing tonight?' Kiki asked eagerly.

'Yes, they're available but running on a 5-10 minute delay. We have Elixir Five and Harry's Bar too and they're not so busy.'

'That's OK, we'll have two large EK specials. We'll wait.'

'Done. I've ordered you a tasting set, too, that'll be here right away. You are aware of your invites, Madam? I assume you need no intros.'

Kiki waived her hand dismissively at the sylph who bowed gracefully and departed.

'Oh, I love proper parties!' said Kiki, rubbing her hands together with glee and causing a minor visual disturbance. She reached down and pulled out a tray of delicious-looking titbits. She put her invisible hand on his lap which gave him another idea. 'Now let me fill you in on the protocol for meeting the president because we've just had a request for a full meet and greet in 40 minutes and it's not going to be embargoed, which is unusually magnanimous. The president can be a sweetie when he chooses to be; it just doesn't happen that often.'

'How do you mean, not embargoed?'

'It means I can syndicate it right away, darling. We're going to get top ratings on this. We'll make a pile!'

'So meeting the president will make us money?'

'Yes, hang on a second, I'm just negotiating

distribution.' Her face went blank, and since that was all he could see of her, he looked around for something else to occupy his visual cortex while he queried Sis about Faith-Sincere. Sis confirmed that she held a significant amount of personal information about Ms Van Darwin but that almost none of it was available to him, due to the extraordinary high level of personal privacy protection Faith-Sincere had in place.

{[So what can you tell me?]}

[[I can confirm that she is now aware that you have queried her dataprofile]]

Dammit! thought Dielle, furious that he'd made such a basic error. {[How much more of this type of stuff do I have to learn about?]}

[[~?]]

{[Forget it. Can I access someone's profile without them knowing?]}

[[Not legally]]

{[You mean it's possible, but not allowed?]}

[[I mean it is not allowed]]

{[Then why not say that instead of 'not legally'? If something wasn't possible then you wouldn't need to say it wasn't allowed would you?]}

[[But it isn't allowed]]

Dielle frowned. As young as he was, he knew when he was being firewalled.

He spotted a suave, immaculately dressed man lounging in the next island, surrounded by an eager and boisterous crowd of pretty young flings, most of whom were vying for his attention. He didn't seem to be interested in anyone but Kiki, who had turned her longaze away the moment she'd focused on him.

Dielle couldn't let that pass without comment. 'There's a guy next door staring at you.' he said, gently nudging Kiki in her invisible ribs.

'I know, darling, he's being very rude. I have already

refused to make iContact with him. He's contravening the rules of the smooze.'

Dielle was experiencing an odd, new sensation. Something about this guy rattled his confidence. 'Do you know each other?'

Kiki broke off from whatever she was doing and gave him a small smile. 'Here,' she said. 'Follow this.'

[[Burst ex-K S-M Pundechan]]

{[What?]}

[[Options: deliver/hold/trash/report/more]]

{[More? More what?]}

[precis/syndicate/publish/compare/validate/tracesource /broadcast/encrypt/forwardto/anon-forwardto/copyto/blind-copyto/blacklist/data-mine/translate-to/translate-from/Fourier-transform/pattern-analyse]]

{[STOP!]} Jeez, he thought, remind me not to ask that again.

[[••]]

{[Give me a brief outline of whatever Kiki just sent]}

[[Burst precis follows]]

'A professional criminal?' Dielle stage-whispered, trying hard not to look at the guy and failing badly.

The EK specials arrived in the local emti. Kiki floated a glass of vertically striped, fluorescent green and yellow liquid over to him.

'Yes,' she said. 'A notorious scam-master. One of the best there's ever been.'

He took a tentative sip of the luminous drink. Kiki watched his reaction.

'Wow!' said Dielle. 'That's amazing! It felt like my mouth exploded in five different places at the same time and each one tasted different.' He took a mouthful and his face lit up again. 'Same effect, different tastes!'

'I love the Epoxile Kids,' said Kiki between sips. 'They're the best mixers onSlab.'

Dielle motioned toward the crook with his eyes and lowered his voice. 'So how come he's here? And what does he want with you?'

'He's here for the same reason you are, dear. He's a celebrity. Only he's in dire need of a new manager seeing as his last one just got zeroed for ripping him off.'

'Sis said he was the most sumed crook onSlab. I don't understand.'

'He's very good at what he does, a true artist, but I think he's losing it. His last job was a heist of such complexity that he'd lost half his sumers by the end of the set-up. It's typical of these guys. They get so into what they're doing that only other crooks can appreciate the artistry. That game is about popularism and keeping it quick and simple. I told him all this, but he won't listen.'

'So he wants you to manage him and you've turned him down?' Dielle felt relieved for several different reasons.

'There's no money in it.' said Kiki, taking another sip.

The neighbouring island had just received their order of EK specials and turned to Kiki and Dielle with their glasses raised. There was a chorus of 'The First!' and then the master crook added with a respectful nod of his head: 'And hopefully not the last, eh?' His phoney coterie fell about laughing.

'Oh darling!' said Kiki. 'You've only been here five days and you've invented a catch-phrase already!' She kissed him on the cheek. 'You know, you'll get royalties whenever anyone onSlab says that now.'

'I will? Seemed a kind of obvious thing to say.'

'I'll fill you in on how it all works tomorrow, darling. Let's go and talk to a few people I want you to meet.' She floated up, following her glass. Even though everything was still very strange, somehow Dielle didn't feel so out of place anymore. Alcohol, he thought: anaesthesia for the restless masses. Then he wondered where that thought came from.

They moved between groups, exchanging pleasantries with an endless series of names and faces, all of whom Kiki either knew personally or knew a lot about. Dielle tried to keep up with what was being said, while querying Sis for details on who he was talking to. He had a hard time juggling the internal conversation with the external ones. Sis fed him new words and concepts which he didn't understand and those led him further down enquiry lines which inevitably led to even more, while he simultaneously tried to answer questions about his first impressions of life onSlab and what being frozen for 360 years was like. After another EK Special (which tasted entirely different from the first one but was, if anything, even better) and three realtime conversations interspersed with Sis responses, his head was reeling. He took Kiki to one side.

'I can't keep up,' he said. 'Is that guy I just spoke to a religious nut or a scientist? I couldn't understand what Sis was feeding me while he was going on about not knowing what our real vector is.'

'Ignore him darling, he's a Rellie.' She moved closer to him and lowered her voice. 'Which kind of makes him both a religious nut and a scientist. I'd advise you not to query Sis too much while you're talking to people; everyone can tell when you're doing it and it's considered impolite. And in any case, unless you are really skilled at handling multiple data streams, it will dice with your head.' He felt her invisible hand behind his back guiding him to an exit corridor. 'Sis will automatically keep a record of all your interactions and you can browse stuff later if you like. Try telling Sis to go into basic like-to-know mode and then she'll only ping you with important stuff as you need it.'

{[Sis? Can you go into basic like-to-know mode please?]}

[[Your interest and tendency behavioural heuristograms are still immature]]

{[What does that mean?]}

[[I don't know what you like to know about yet. There haven't been sufficient interactions for me to build accurate prediction algorithms tuned to your personality and preferences]]

{[That's OK]}

[[It is possible that information you might consider important will not be provided]]

{[So?]}

[[Standard life disclaimer applies]]

{[OK, just do it, OK?]}

[[••]]

He laughed out loud.

'What is it?' asked Kiki, amused.

'I think I just had my first argument with Sis.'

'Oh, she'll get over it, I'm always arguing with her. Of course, it's totally pointless.'

'Because she's always right?'

Kiki looked at him, momentarily sober and serious. 'Darling, don't believe everything you hear or everything you think you hear or everything you think you think.'

He didn't yet know just how good that advice was.

'Including that?'

'Including that. Come on, we can't keep the president waiting.'

Dielle followed Kiki's bobbing head down a corridor to a pulsating blue transvex that led to a hexagonal room with vexes on each wall. The one to their right hilighted so they stepped through it, turning right, then right again through an archway. Dielle's spatial awareness was jangling as they walked into the presidential suite.

The reception rotunda had been designed under the personal supervision of the incumbent. Local information prefs were set to impress, so wherever Dielle looked, detailed information flowed into his head.

The circular walls were lined with floor-to-ceiling bookcases inset with arched alcoves.

[[5,520Kg African mahogany: origin Indonesia, Earth/2,748 molecular-film-protected paper-based books : oldest 576 Earth-years/nearest alcove: 17th-century brass optical telescope, original J.E. Buttersworth oil painting, original J. Harrison H5 Chronometer, silverclone of 2105 America's Cup [more]]]

Stairs led down to a reception area with a dark-wood floor inlaid with an elaborate compass rose.

[[Oak flooring salvaged from keel of 16th-century Spanish galleon, Urca de Lima, currently moored in UpSide Seacombe Maritime Museum/parquetry: rosewood, burr walnut, Slab-grown mother-of-pearl, Natalite [more]]]

Brass glowglobes hovered beside simulated-leather sofas. A complex clockwork machine with copper-coloured spheres sat in the centre on a low, glass table. A detailed illustrated map lay beneath the glass.

[[Hand-drawn 18th-century chart depicting then-known navigable seas of Earth/early 19th-century orrery of major planets and moons of Sol system: Note – Neptune undiscovered, orrery not to scale [more]]]

Dielle walked down to the lower level and stepped on a rug.

[[Handmade Mughal hunting rug, 18th century Earth]]

'Jeez!' he said, jumping off. 'Handmade?'

'Handmade for feet, mate!' said a gruff voice from above. 'Gawan! Take your boots off and feel the quality. Handmade by fucking virgins I reckon!'

Dielle looked up. What he'd mistaken for a mirrored ceiling, wasn't. The room above looked identical except for the old, weather-beaten guy sitting in one of the green leather couches, looking down, or rather up, at him.

'Tiger! Come on down! What in Dicename are you wearing? You look like a bloody ghost!'

Kiki's head bobbed slightly and floated gently upward, followed by her shoes. When she got halfway she tipped over and gently landed on what, to Dielle, was still the ceiling.

'It's a Woodham Grey C-thru, Charlie. It's hyper-now.'

'Bloody hell! I can't see where to grab you! Can't you turn it off?'

'It cost me a small fortune. I'm not going to turn it off just so you can cop a feel.'

She gave him a kiss and he reached out to hug her. To Dielle, it looked like he was grabbing thin air. Charlie looked up.

'Come on down to UpSide, mate. Give it a try. Sis will carry you as soon as you jump. You can't get hurt in here! Jeeesus H! Imagine the publicity! I'd be a laughing stock!'

'Charlie, you were a laughing stock a long time before you took office,' said Kiki, sitting down and looking up at Dielle. 'Come on darling, it's easy.'

Dielle launched himself upward and immediately felt light. It was just like the inertia-free feeling he'd experienced on the tube. He rotated in the middle and landed with the same force as his take-off.

'Cool!' he said, grinning inanely.

Charlie stuck out his hand. 'Charlie Pleewo, temporary Slabwide president, serial bonne voyeur and general handyman in a tight spot. Pleased to meetcha!'

Dielle was surprised by the vigour of the handshake.

Slab's president stared Dielle coolly in the eyes. 'Welcome to the presidential neutral room, welcome to UpSideDown. In fact, welcome to Slab in general. Take a seat. Let me get you a proper drink.' He took the now-empty glass from Dielle and walked over to a brightly lit cabinet filled with old bottles and crystal glasses. 'None of your regulated banalcohol here,' he said. 'This is the real thing.' He poured a finger of amber liquid from a cut-glass decanter into a thick crystal tumbler.

'Get your laughing gear round this one. It's a true

vintage, laid down before Louie Drago was a twinkle in your father's eye.'

'You know about Louie?' said Dielle, cautiously smelling the heady vapour coming from his glass.

'Course mate! I'm the president! Who d'you think authorised bringing you out of that deepfreeze in the first place?'

'I thought Louie said it was a contractual thing, something to do with paying for it?'

'Yeah right! What d'you reckon to the Scotch?'

Dielle took a sip and nearly choked. 'Wow!'

'D'ya like it?' asked Charlie as the aromas and burning fluid passed through Dielle's digestive system, exciting everything it touched.

'Yeah!' said Dielle, taking another sip. 'It's amazing! What is it?'

'It's a distilled spirit made from fermented malted barley and natural spring water which had been filtered through a thousand years of peat and heather. It was matured in a country called Scotland in a wooden cask made from an oak tree that lived over five hundred years ago in Southern France before being chopped down and shipped to Spain to be turned into sherry barrels. And we are currently,' he paused for a brief moment, and sighed, 'one point four eight two million, billion kilometres from another bottle of it.'

'Oh Charlie?' said Kiki. 'How come I didn't get any?'

'You've got the sumecast rights to this meeting, Tiger. Which would you prefer?'

Charlie sat down next to Dielle and gave him his full attention.

'Yeah, I know about Louie but I haven't met him yet. He's been invited to SlabCouncil and they don't allow the likes of me in there you know.'

'But you're the president. Don't you get to choose where you can go?'

'The president doesn't have any proper authority.' He sounded resentful. 'I get to open events and make speeches and raise funds for noble causes and so on. That's about all.'

'And be a piss-head,' said Kiki from behind his back.

'Yeah, well there's that too.'

'But you just said you authorised my re-fam.'

'Yeah.' He looked at Kiki and nodded. She went blank for a second, frowned and looked back at him with a query in her eyes. He turned his head to one side and raised his eyebrows. Kiki thought for a moment and then nodded.

Charlie reached into his pocket and took out a small, shiny rectangular object not much bigger than his two middle fingers. He placed it on the centre of the table and pushed the top. An intense white line of light swept a perfect circle around the perimeter of the room, encompassing them all in a shimmering hemisphere. 'OK,' he said, getting business-like. 'We're off the record. Anything and everything that happens in here is now sub-rosa. Complete embargo.' He turned to Kiki. 'I mean it, Tiger'.

Kiki shifted uncomfortably. 'Yeah, yeah, keep it short though. Every second is billable'.

Charlie moved over to sit opposite them. 'Goddammit Tiger, we're off camera now, can't you turn that bloody dress off?'

'OK, but warn me before you lift the rose.' Kiki's body, completely enclosed in a thick, grey material, appeared on the couch. She took off her heavy gloves and wafted her face with them.

'Thing is, son,' said Charlie, turning to Dielle, 'I really *don't* have any authority over who gets re-fammed. It was a sham. I was ordered to approve your consent by SlabCouncil and now they've taken Louie into their bloody nest.'

'Well, they're welcome to him as far as I'm

concerned,' said Dielle. 'He's a pain in the ass. In fact, if you had to define pain in the ass, Louie Drago's name should be top of the list.'

'I'll see to it,' said Charlie. 'When they said they wanted to bring you back, I naturally assumed they needed something from you. Like some older, pre-equalisation genes or some such blocks they're always bloody fiddling with. But it turned out they weren't interested in you – at least not yet. You, in the hands of this very capable young lady,' he nodded again to Kiki who accepted his compliment with grace, 'are turning into a big star. Good luck to you. In fact, as president, I can even help you.'

'Oh no!' said Kiki springing up. 'No way! You're not getting any of this action you conniving, stimmed-out windfarmer! So that's what this is about!'

'No, no! No! Calm down! I don't need any of your deal.' He looked genuinely frightened of Kiki. 'Look, it's very simple. Something's going on and they won't tell me what it is. His,' he stabbed his finger at Dielle, 'previous incarnation has been scooped up into that bloody carnival they call council and I want to know why. I'll trade you guaranteed rating enhancement if you can find out from Louie what the dice is going on.'

'Well, you know, I kind of had another agenda sketched out,' said Kiki, turning immediately into negotiation mode. 'I've seen some of the sume footage and I don't think Louie comes over well for the demographic.'

It was Dielle's turn to be shocked. 'You know about Louie?'

'Of course I know about Louie, dear, I'm your agent. It's my job to know everything about you.' She turned back to Charlie. 'He's a holo, he's just not human enough for the major feeds. It's not what they're looking for.'

'Tiger, listen to me,' said Charlie. 'This is something big. I don't know what yet, but it might be about the war. Something they're too frightened to tell us. There's a rumour they captured a ship and found a living alien inside it. Massive isn't saying anything but I know that dumb fuck is hiding something. I think they want Louie to do something for them that's connected with all this. You'd like a piece of that action, I'll bet.'

Kiki took a breath. 'If this screws with my artist's career I'll … ' Kiki wasn't sure what the she could actually do that could threaten the president so she left it hanging.

'Don't I get a say in this?' asked Dielle, wondering when he'd been elevated to the status of artist.

'No.' said Charlie and Kiki in unison.

'But I'm the one who has to talk to Louie, aren't I?'

Kiki and Charlie looked at each other in frustration. Dielle suspected they were passing messages through Sis and wondered how they could be sure Sis wasn't passing them on to the SlabCouncil.

{[How is this being kept secret?]} No answer.

{[Sis? Can you hear me?]} No answer.

'OK,' said Kiki after a few minutes. 'But I want top table for every public function and direct links from all your feeds.'

'Oh, come on!' Charlie protested. 'I only want some inside information, not the bloody system encryption code!'

Kiki and Charlie went on like this for some time. Dielle was getting bored with it all and, with no-one to talk to, decided to do a bit of acrobatic practice. He needed to speak to Louie about a few things anyway, so it didn't really bother him much, he thought, as he bounced from UpSideDown to DownSideUp and back again.

Over by the antique view-screen, the negotiations came to a satisfactory conclusion. Charlie looked over at Dielle, happily wheeling in mid-air.

'Bit of a kid, isn't he?' he said privately to Kiki. 'Shouldn't you be investing your considerable talents in a more mature man?' He reached down and squeezed Kiki's ass.

'Oi! You can't do that!' shouted Dielle from the ceiling.

'Course I can mate, didn't you get the memo? I'm the fucking president!' He walked over to the table and turned back to Kiki. 'I'll lift the rose. Ready?' Kiki reactivated the dress and nodded her floating head. The shimmering hemisphere collapsed.

'Hey!' called Dielle from above. 'Can I have some more of that Scotch?'

Charlie looked straight up at him and held his gaze. 'Sure you can, just as soon as you figure out a way of going back for more.' He turned to Kiki and held out his hand. 'Shall we join the citizens?'

thirteen

'How long have you known about this?' Louie asked the small audience of avatars standing inside a detailed reproduction of a Roman bathhouse. The NAHs had all donned togas and were in constant motion, describing complex paths around the periphery of the space and forming spontaneous cliques, muttering to each other while sneaking sideways glances at the group in the centre and then moving on. All the NAHs looked exactly the same as the one that had collected Louie from the park. Although each individual could be identified by a unique number, everybody just called them Erik. The avatars represented human interns and they too all looked the same: pale, frail humanoids with bulbous, bald heads, long, skeletal limbs and huge almond eyes which blinked slowly and deliberately at Louie's projection.

Louie's vDek was arranged to make him look as though he were sitting behind a white marble table under a canopy of dense green leaves that swayed in the breeze. A sunny Mediterranean sky was visible between a semicircle of white, Doric columns. Sublimators embedded into the flora filled the air with calming aromatic oils. It was wasted on Louie. He hadn't paid for olfac.

They'd travelled here in a privacy field while Louie absorbed as much information as possible about the artefact, so although he hadn't a clue where onSlab they were, he was fairly sure that none of what he could see would pass any reasonable definition of real.

Louie looked around at fifteen pairs of blinking eyes and waited for an answer. Except for the sounds of running water and exotic birds, there was complete silence. Time passed while Louie regretted that his fingers couldn't make a drumming sound. Then the avatars came to a collective response.

'There are several among us who do not agree to include you in our forum,' said one of them in a soft, flowing female voice. 'Providing an answer to your question is not a simple matter.'

'We have known about the FutureSlab for more than a cycle,' interrupted another avatar with a younger, more aggressive male voice. Oh good, thought Louie, at least they sound different. 'The NAHs assure us they were made aware of it at the same time as we were and we have no evidence that contradicts this claim.'

'However,' said a third, a female much older and more precise in tone and manner, 'we have reason to believe that Sis has known about this phenomena for a lot longer and has deliberately withheld the information from us.'

This statement produced a fluttering of comments and murmurs. One of the Eriks, who was standing alone by a distant column, turned around and raised his voice.

'Citation!' He waived his hat angrily, gaining everyone's attention. 'We cannot support that statement without citation.'

The avatars all turned back to look at Louie.

'They always say that,' said the older woman who Louie had decided to call Ethel. 'It's a smoke screen. We suspect Sis has kept this quiet for a very long time.'

'Where is Sis?' asked Louie, exasperated. 'I have got to talk to her. Or it. Whatever.'

'She is everywhere and nowhere, she is in everything and everyone,' said the first female. Jane, thought Louie, definitely a Jane. 'You can talk to System through any of us or the Eriks whenever you want.'

'How will I know I'm talking to Sis and not you?'

'What would you like us to do? Wave a flag?' said the aggressive younger guy.

Shithead, thought Louie. 'No, I don't want you to wave

a flag, I want to speak to a person. Can't she take over an Erik or something – they're supposed to be system representatives aren't they?' A tremor went through the group.

'All NAHs have full citizen rights, Mr Drago.' It was Jane again. 'The coerced subversion of a conscious entity is one of our highest moral crimes. It would be as offensive as having your own personality overridden by another, more powerful entity. Mind rape, Mr. Drago.'

'Hey!' said Louie, trying to break the mood. 'Call me Louie!' He thought for a moment. 'What about a speaker then?'

'Everyone speaks for themselves here, we have no appointed leaders or presiding officers.'

'No, not that type of speaker; a loudspeaker. You know, a panel in a box that sound comes out of. A spea-ker.' Louie said the last word slower and louder, trying to describe a box shape with his hands.

'Why would that help?'

'Look, you all hear Sis in your heads right? I can't, and Erik over there tells me my programming is so old that it's not possible to let me interface with Sis directly. I have to hear a real voice so I'd want it to be a voice I can identify as Sis, and come from something I can direct my question at. Why is that so difficult to understand?'

'You want to give Sis an actual voice and a physical presence?' asked an older male voice with an authoritative tone and a Scottish accent. The name Richard came immediately to Louie's mind.

All the avatars turned to look at each other, silently blinking and slowly nodding their heads. Then, as one, they turned and wandered off in different directions.

'Hey!' called out Louie. He was stranded; even the Eriks wouldn't come close to him. They continued to walk around, forming small spontaneous groups which would usually disperse after a few minutes. It was like watching a formal dance in which nobody ever danced, but everyone got asked.

Eventually, one of the alien avatars wafted back and sat next to him.

'I'm afraid your request has proved to be impossible to comply with.' It was Ethel.

'Why is it such a big deal? Can't I just have a terminal or something?'

'You request is to hear a manifestation of a voice we all have had in our heads since we were born, Louie. To every single one of us that voice is like a guardian, a teacher, a constant companion and an intimate confidant. We all have our own versions of what that voice represents. Sis is unique to each of us and yet you wish to give her a discrete personality.'

'Kind of like when they had to cast a new James Bond, huh?'

The avatar blinked at Louie for a while.

'System admin representative 001.735.3160, the Erik that brought you here, has volunteered to act as guide and, let's say, *conduit* for your conversations with Sis.' She was clearly extremely uncomfortable about this. 'The interns have approved this course of action, but most of the NAH's have departed in protest, despite the expediency of this selfless act for which we are most grateful.'

'Yeah, well, dupe. Way to go, Erik. Can we get on with it now?'

'Many of the contiguation have requested avatar presence so it has been decided to expand our arena.' The avatar bent down gracefully and stretched an elegant arm towards Louie's vDek. 'If you will allow me?'

'Sure,' he said, grinning. 'Take me to your leader.'

'It is important that you understand that SlabWide Integrated System, or Sis, is neither our leader nor our servant. We exist in a highly evolved symbiotic relationship where Sis acts entirely independently but always with our best interests at heart. Council was instigated as part of the Initial Design with a fixed ratio of human interns to non-human representatives who are all autonomous individuals and have free will as defined by the Not Actually Human Resources charter of cycle 238. As such, Slab has no specific leader who can be identified individually and our political hierarchy can be classified as a machine-resident benevolent dictatorship with human peer-moderated decision-guidance and monitoring apparatus. The interns function anonymously and are not associated with our real identities in order that no personal power can be devolved to any specific individual. In essence, we are led by our anonymous selves, so it is not possible for me to comply with your request.'

And you have absolutely no sense of humour, do you? thought Louie. Well, he thought, it sounded a pretty mad way of doing things, but it had to be better than democracy. That had been a real screw-up.

They had been walking down into a marble amphitheatre during Ethel's explanation. Noisy, restless avatars jostled for room. As he watched, several of the pale alien avatars morphed into a variety of weirdly shaped humanoids, furry blobs, winged beasts, glowing orbs, comic-book stars and wizards. Why must there always be wizards? thought Louie.

'It's getting serious,' said Ethel. 'You note the avatars changing? That means the interns are showing up in person as opposed to ghosting the blanks. Oh well, I will have to finish off what I was doing later.'

Ethel's avatar changed into a busty, blonde Amazon in a skin-tight bodice. She had all the accoutrements of a warrior goddess: Viking helmet, glowing magic shield, bejewelled scabbard and dynamite legs in thigh-high leather.

'There,' she said. 'Now I'm all here.'

Louie looked her up and down and whistled. 'Wow!

Will you marry me?'

Ethel looked down at him. Louie realised he was going to have to give her a new name. 'Ah,' she said. 'Sarcasm. I was told you were a bit of a humorist.'

Louie hadn't been joking, but he thought he might as well smile. 'I shall call you Ethless the Beautiful.'

'Why?' said Ethless the Beautiful. 'That is not my name. I have no name here.'

Because Ethel the Joyless doesn't have the same ring to it, thought Louie as she placed his vDek on a small podium at the front of the stage. Erik walked over from a conclave of the few remaining NAHs who were anxiously milling around, adjusting their togas. He sat down as a small, square section of the stage rose up to meet him. The audience hushed.

'We are going to conduct this session in full auditory mode,' said Erik. 'You are free to use system-facilitated communications as always but your comments will not be considered public unless vocalised.'

There was a disgruntled murmur from the assembly.

Louie raised both arms in an exaggerated shrug. 'Sorry guys!'

'As you know,' continued Erik, 'I will be acting in a mediation capacity between our honoured guest and SlabWide Integrated System.' More murmurs and a few muted laughs and coughs. 'For the purpose of identifying my speech on behalf of System as distinct from my own, it has been decided that I shall employ a female voice when answering with words that are not mine.' Erik paused and looked up at the ceiling/sky for a moment. 'In order to satisfy the majority of those present, the voice you hear will be that of the twentieth-century-Earth screen idol Miss Marilyn Monroe.'

Uproar. Avatars were standing and shouting and throwing shards of light which dissipated before hitting the stage. Shouts of disgrace! Sacrilege! Abomination! Bloody good oh! and Nice one Erik! mingled with hoots of derisive laughter, cheering and whistles. The last of the NAHs departed during the disruption.

Jeez, thought Louie. Nearly four hundred years on and we're still run by a bunch of children.

Erik waited for the disruption to settle, then turned to Louie. 'We understand that you can read Ænglish.'

Louie nodded.

'Good. We have arranged for a series of text-based feeds which will be visible to you and no one else.'

Three translucent black panels rose out of the stage to form a semicircle in front of Louie, stopping just below his shoulder level.

'The centre panel will display any additional information you request directly from Sis; the right side will display general queries from the participants to Sis; and the left will form a record of all non-vocalised, intra-participant communication. You have the right to make any of this information public by speaking it out loud. This is as close to normal as we can simulate without connecting you directly to Sis.'

Text flashed past Louie's eyes, green on the left, red on the right, but too quick for him to read more than a few words. He thought he caught a few green comments about him. None of them looked complimentary.

'Hey! Can you slow them down a little?' The two outer screens slowed to a fast reading speed and the central panel displayed a message directly from the SlabWide Integrated System in light blue text: *Random comments displayed, no edit. Impossible to display all conversations at reading speed. Archive recording available for later research. Your eyes only.*

Well hello, thought Louie, nice to meet you too.

'This meeting is called to decide on a course of action regarding FutureSlab,' said Erik, raising his normal voice to hush the background unrest.

'OK,' said Louie. 'I've got a question straight off: Why are you calling it FutureSlab?'

A fuzzy blue avatar rose and spoke in a strong, clear voice. It was the one Louie had tagged as Richard earlier. 'The slab you have seen ahead of us is identical to our slab in every perceivable detail except one. It even has the same scar on its right edge – a scar that was formed over 350 cycles ago as a result of a chunk of space debris that evaded our gravity traps and gouged a groove in our starboard flank. It is inconceivable that what we observe is anything other than our own Slab but somehow shifted into the future – our future.'

Louie wasn't convinced. 'Every detail except one?'

'Heat, Mr Drago,' said another avatar, a pretty female with wings and a diaphanous gown. 'It is our only export and detectable signature. Nearly thirty-two million individuals create a very large amount of heat and if we didn't move the excess out into the infrared thermal radiators, we would all melt. However, the FutureSlab is, for all intents and purposes, the same temperature as the surrounding space. It is cold. Very, very cold.'

'So you're assuming no-one is on it then?'

'We don't know for sure because we can't get close enough to use any other means of detection,' said Erik.

'Why not? If it really is the same as this Slab, you already know everything about your own defences. You must know your own weak points.'

'Our defences are designed specifically to withstand anything we can dream up,' said Richard. 'And even if we could get through the outer defences, the Slab walls are fifty kilometre-thick Natalite. The hardest substance known to man. It is virtually impenetrable.'

'Natalite?' asked Louie. His central screen filled with information about aggregated diamond nanorods.

'Of course, we are only making assumptions at the moment,' said Erik, 'but they are fair assumptions, and they lead us to contemplate a wide range of disturbing possibilities.'

'If the Rellies find out about this they will have a field day,' called out someone from the back. 'This is exactly the sort of blocks they've been going on about for years.'

Louie looked at Erik. 'Rellies?' he said with a raised eyebrow.

Erik explained; 'Rellies is the popular name for members of the Church of Relativity. They are believers in the absolute lightspeed barrier and frequent protesters and portenders of doom onSlab. The fact that our acceleration is tending toward zero as we approach C has helped to calm the SlabWide panic they were attempting to whip up, but that hasn't stopped some of them from arguing that something of significant mass could be travelling away from our point of origin with sufficient speed so that our velocity relative to theirs could be greater than C.'

'What?'

'Their mantra is that everything is relative,' said Richard. 'Say we're moving away from Earth at a speed that's approaching the speed of light and Earth sends out another ship in the opposite direction that accelerates at a similar rate to us, then at some point, we will be travelling faster than the speed of light, relative to that other ship.' Sis was drawing neat blue diagrams on his central screen to illustrate the intern's description.

'So?' Louie had spent enough time around egg-heads to know when he was being bullshitted. It seemed there were a number of interns arguing about this same point on his left screen.

'Look, we're not saying it's true, but we are running out of explanations. One thing we know for sure is that we are looking at a Slab that seems to be from our future. A future that indicates something cataclysmic has happened to Slab. Something that wiped out all living things inside it.'

'So if we're travelling faster than light, which is not

possible, relative to a spaceship that's travelling away from us … ' said Louie, slowly, tying to make himself understand. He could see a barrage of mathematical equations on the right hand screen that meant nothing at all to him. 'What happens to the other ship, the one we're moving away from? It's travelling faster than light relative to us too, isn't it? And that's not possible either.'

'No it isn't.'

'So it could have a doppelganger in front of it too?'

'Yes,' said Erik, looking miserable.

'And, seeing as how we have now gotten very close to the speed of light, almost anything that's travelling away from us at an even moderately decent speed like, say, a planet in fast orbit, or a galaxy moving away from us at high speed, could be experiencing the same effect?'

'Potentially.'

'But that could be happening all over the universe, couldn't it?'

'Precisely.'

'So it's like we've broken some really fucking important law of the Universe or something?'

'We don't know,' said Erik, looking seriously upset. And that, thought Louie, for a president who wasn't exactly celebrated for his levity, was very upset indeed.

'And that's why we're all dead – in the future?'

Louie looked around him. The chatter on his screens had petered out to a virtual silence. Someone had put in a query about self-stasis options on the right screen. The centre screen was flashing the words *Not possible* in large blue letters.

'So,' said Louie carefully, 'why exactly are you telling me all this?'

Marilyn cleared her throat.

fourteen

'He's a manipulative, cunning, cheating wind-farmer and I wouldn't trust him with the key to a song.'

'So how come he got to be president, then? Surely no-one would vote for him if they knew what he was really like?'

Kiki gave Dielle a withering look. They were having a late breakfast outside a café in UpTown DownTown Seacombe SideUp. Dielle had come to meet Kiki, who was between meetings. They sat overlooking a dozen bustling platforms and suspended walkways linked by impossibly long and slender bridges.

'Well, first of all, that's precisely why people would vote for him,' she said. 'Those are some pretty useful qualities for any president. Always have been. But in any case, he wasn't elected. We abandoned democracy as a failed experiment shortly after leaving Earth's jurisdiction. He won the presidency in the leadership lottery.' Dielle raised his eyebrows. 'The theory goes,' continued Kiki, 'that anyone is capable of being president, so anyone can be, except the people who really want to be, because the last person who should be given a position of power is someone who tries to convince people they should have it.'

Dielle poured himself a second cup of coffee. 'You're losing me,' he said.

'It's a basic premise of the Initial Design: The people that want to, should be the last ones allowed to. It's the nearest we get onSlab to an official political philosophy. We pick our presidents at random and they get to be president for a maximum of ten cycles and anyone can quit any time they like if they don't like the job. It can happen to anyone – only it's happened to Pleewo three times in succession.'

'Three? He's been picked at random three times from over thirty million people?'

'Well, not everyone's eligible, because of age or mental acuity and so on. Many people opt out, too. There are currently,' she paused for a fraction of a second, 'almost twenty-four million possible contenders for the job and every single one of them knows there is no way Pleewo could possibly have won the lottery three times in a row. The odds against it are astronomicubed but no-one can figure out how he did it. It's generally acknowledged that if he's clever enough and well connected enough to have got away with rigging it at least twice, then he's probably an ideal person to be president anyway, so no-one's complaining too much, or at least not too loudly. He's still not to be trusted though, pretty much by definition really.'

'He seemed to know you pretty well.'

'Our paths have crossed before,' said Kiki darkly. 'It's a small Slab.'

It didn't seem very small to Dielle. The previous night's party had given him a hint of just how varied life onSlab could be. Almost everyone he'd met had either delighted or confused him – sometimes both.

The first thing he'd found out, after they'd left Charlie's private rooms, was that all of the presidential public areas were designed around the interface, the gravity plane which separated one side of Slab from the other. This was done, ostensibly, to ensure complete presidential neutrality between the two sides of Slab civilisation. SlabCitizens took the whole UpSide/SideUp thing very seriously. Some lived their entire lives refusing to travel to the opposite side or have anything to do with the people that lived there. Dielle couldn't see the point and had spent the evening happily bouncing from one floor to another, talking to anyone he liked and generally having a very good time.

The main entertainment of the evening had taken place in an auditorium shaped like the inside of a gigantic scallop shell with two opposing stages at the hinge. Dielle and Kiki had sat with the rest of the Siders in comfortable reclining chairs, looking up at the Uppies looking up at them while the dancers from the pre-bar smooze performed an intricate aerial ballet suspended on the interface between the audiences.

Kiki returned to the dressing rooms to change clothes twice during the night, the first time specifically for dancing, the second for lounging around looking attractive and sparkly. Most people changed clothes or accessories more than once but Dielle was happy with his red outfit and even happier with the number of women eager to leave their impression on various parts of it. He'd been quite a hit.

He'd detected something different about Kiki's attitude but couldn't tell whether she was jealous of all the female attention he had been getting, or was concerned about how he was dealing with his celebrity status. He decided to find out.

'You know,' he said casually, 'I think a couple of those women last night wanted to sex me.'

'You think?' said Kiki, distracted.

'Yeah, a couple of times I felt like I was being hunted. And when everyone started shouting *Happy NewCyke*, and that dancer kissed me, there was some serious tongue action going on.'

She turned her attention to him and looked him steady in the eyes. 'You didn't seem to mind too much.'

'Well, I was flattered of course,' he said defensively. 'It was fun, but I have to say I'm feeling a little uncomfortable about it all. I have conflicting desires that I can't reconcile. I don't know how to describe it really.' Dielle knew he had to get some insights into these personal interaction issues pretty soon or he was going to get into trouble. He needed a guide.

Kiki was his guide, but she was also his agent and he loved her. He hoped she loved him too. Somehow that made it even more complicated.

'It's called guilt, darling,' she said, smiling. 'You are experiencing a very, very old feeling; one that's been dicing with our heads since we came down from the trees. It's caused by the inner conflict between what you really want to do and what your conscience thinks you should do. It's one of the main reasons we're all here.'

'How do you mean?'

'Well, it's commonly accepted that this struggle, which goes on inside all of us, is really a struggle between our physical, animalistic heritage – the part that is more than nine tenths the same as a common ape – and the non-physical, alien consciousness which infects us and has a completely different set of values and principals that we usually call 'morals'. Our human side wants to do something but the annoying bloody conscience in our head tells us we shouldn't. Animals don't feel guilt – they don't have the concept. That's because they aren't infected. Or it's possible they are, but their aliens can't fight hard enough to override the basic animal instincts of the host. They need to interface with our more highly evolved frontal lobes to do that.'

'And humans are evolved enough for these aliens to manipulate us but not enough to overcome our animal instincts entirely?' asked Dielle.

'If you're thinking that it's all a bit unlikely, I'd agree with you.' Kiki was looking serious. 'One theory says that they stumbled upon Earth a couple of hundred thousand years ago when humans were nothing more than upright-walking apes and spotted them as potential future carriers. They seeded a few individuals and fed us little bits of useful information – like how to make fire, build language, form social groups, kill people from other social groups and so on. They've been dicing with our heads ever since. It explains a lot.'

'You sound unhappy,' said Dielle, 'but surely it's what got us to here? Wouldn't we still be banging rocks together without them?'

'It's not that. It's more about the human condition. We struggle and fight with ourselves for most of our lives. We stop ourselves from having what we want and then pretend we don't. If we give in to our animal sides, it causes us pain but if we don't, we feel frustrated, inhuman and disconnected. We fight each other over stuff we don't even understand. We have *soul mates* who we long for and a feeling of emptiness inside us caused by the alien conscious energy's separation from the rest of its collective. It drives some of us half mad. We've got an absolute right to complain about it.'

Dielle had never seen Kiki looking so dark. He wanted to lighten things up.

'So I feel an inner conflict because my inherited man ape wants to frolic naked with as many lady apes as possible and my consciousness is telling me I should behave with more integrity towards you? Have you got some form of side deal with my alien?'

'Maybe my alien has, I wouldn't know.'

Dielle looked her in the eyes, wondering what Kiki had just admitted to.

'Do you know why all those women wanted to bed you? Can you imagine?'

'Well, I kind of assumed they'd seen me on a sume and liked what they saw and, well, you know … '

Kiki smiled at him and reached over to stroke his face. 'You really have no idea, do you?' she said gently. 'You are such an innocent that it's a shame to tell you, but you'll find out soon enough anyway, if not from me, then from someone else.'

'Tell me what?'

'Well, you'll have to ask Sis about something called *human evolution gender disparity* when you have some spare time, but basically it's all about women being more highly evolved than men, what we did about it when it was discovered, and the fact that you are a primitive.'

'More evolved?'

'Sis will give you all the details, but it's a numbers thing: usual breeding ages of the two sexes, younger females, older males and hundreds of thousands of years of evolution. Basically, the female part of the genetic line has a lot more generations in it than the male line – thousands of years more. We're more evolved.'

'And what happened when it was discovered?' Dielle thought this all sounded highly questionable, but he didn't have enough information to argue about it. Yet.

'Well, the first thing was they passed a law stipulating compulsory human breeding between young men and older women. That was a fun time, and no-one really complained about it, especially the older women. But it was futile, it would have taken tens of thousands of generations to redress the balance. Then the geneticists got very angry about it. At least the male geneticists did. They came up with a way to accelerate male-side gene evolution. Seeing as how they'd seriously diced everything up with the stop-gene fiasco, and no-one could breed without them, the future of the human race was in their hands anyway. So they did whatever they do and they say it's worked but the result is that onSlab men are a lot more evolved than men were in your day. They're more, well, like us women, I suppose.'

Dielle was starting to get the picture. 'So when people refer to me as a primitive, they mean my genes were formed before all this evolution re-balancing went on?'

'Yes.'

'And that's why the women want to have sex with me? Because I'm less evolved than the men here?'

'Well, that and the share in the royalties they'll earn through the subsequent sumecasts.'

'They'll make money by having sex with me?'

'Well of course! You're a star.' She paused to pour herself more orange juice. 'It's just that I don't like any of the deals they're offering at the moment.'

'You're negotiating royalty deals with women who want to go to bed with me?'

'Naturally dear, I'm your agent, who else would … '

'Well you're right about one thing,' said Dielle, getting up and knocking his chair over in the process. It auto-righted. 'You must all be a lot more bloody evolved than I am because I don't understand a single word of this!' But, he thought, I know a man who almost definitely will.

'I don't know why you're getting so upset about it, dear,' said Kiki, startled. 'It's great for your popularity ratings. If you're confused, why don't you ask Sis for more information?'

'I'm going for an old-fashioned walk,' he said, making for a bridge. 'It's the type of thing we primitives do – walk around aimlessly. I might even go find a tree to swing from.'

'Well, enjoy yourself, dear,' said Kiki cheerfully. 'I'll catch up with you later. There's a skimmer meeting I'd like to take you to.'

'Whatever,' he said grumpily and walked off. He'd caught that slightly vacant look in Kiki's eyes and felt sure she was negotiating a deal even as she waved him goodbye. He realised, with a rueful smile, that even knocking over his chair and storming off was probably going to titillate the sumers. He was going to have to get some impartial advice about all this blocks, he thought.

[[##]] An ugly feeling violated his mind like a flash-back of a foul taste.

{[What was that?]}

[[ASOL interrupt. Pollution control]]

{[~?]}

[[You are emoting negative energy over the unscreened public band]]

{[~~?]}

[[Humans and most higher order mammals are capable of communicating over a wide range of empathic frequencies. You are currently scatter-casting anger and confusion in a public place contrary to current morality version 1039:85Rev1.02 and all previous versions for the last 954.23 cykes.]]

{[I'm pissed off! Are you telling me I'm not allowed to be angry?]}

[[You are allowed to be angry, it is simply contrary to accepted Slab behaviour to pollute your local environment with negative emotions which could infect co-proximal SlabCitizens]]

{[And what are you going to do to stop me?]} There are few things more likely to increase the pissed-offness of someone who is already seriously pissed off than to suggest that they should stop being pissed off.

[[##]]

{[Urgh! OK, OK. What do you want me to do about it?]}

[[Recommend either lightening up or narrowing your emotional radiation to the appropriate frequencies]]

{[And how the hell do I do that?]}

Suddenly he knew. He didn't get less angry, but he was now able to focus his anger in a more constructive and socially acceptable way.

{[OK. Sorry. Thanks for letting me know]} That explained why everyone he'd met so far seemed to be so well mannered, he thought, and wondered again about how much he still had to learn about the way this place worked.

{[What was the name of that guy I met last night who was really bright? I was talking to him about the different Slab sections]}

[[Fencer Dean Twenty; collectively recognised initiator of important intangible query assets]]

{[Can I contact him?]}

[[Yes, he opened his message filters to you while you were speaking to him last night]]

{[Can you let him know that I'd like to meet him please?]}

[[••]]

Seconds later, Dielle was walking by a tubevex when it started to flash at him.

[[•]]

{[Deliver]}

[[Fencer Twenty has accepted your request and authorised your transport to his current location at his own expense. Please take tube via indicated portal. Destination already set. Privacy bubble provided as courtesy]]

Fast and friendly, I like his style, thought Dielle, stepping through the flashing membrane.

As the privacy bubble descended, Sis told him the journey would take almost an hour and offered him some entertainment, again courtesy of his host. He declined. He thought he could make better use of his time asking some questions.

{[What's this message filter thing you just mentioned?]}

[[All SlabWide communication via your neural implant has filter options. Your preferences are set to average, which means you only receive messages from individuals who you already know or who your heuristogram profile indicates you would like to know. If you meet someone and you'd like to receive communications from them, you simply add them to your allow filter]]

{[What happens to messages from people I don't know?]}

[[They are kept in archive and the senders are informed of their non-receipt]]

{[How many messages do I currently have in archive?]}

[[624,323]]

Dielle gorped.

{[How can I possibly deal with all those?]}

[[You don't have to. It will help me to build up your heuristogram if I deliver a message to you at random, then you can tell me if you wanted to receive it in the first place and how you want to reply, if at all. After you've done a few, I will be able to process most of the rest of your messages on your behalf without further interaction]]

{[Well, I guess I've got an hour. Let's get started]}

It didn't take that long. Most of the messages were from people asking to have sex with him or just hang out with him. It was slightly worrying to him that at least 25% of these were from men. His ego couldn't decide whether the requests were because he was irresistible or because they hoped to make a killing on the syndication rights on the recording of their hoped-for encounter. After dealing with about thirty or so of these, (some of which had suggested doing things he wasn't sure were even physically possible) Sis informed him that she had built sufficient profile to deal with 90% of the outstanding messages. Most of the rest were advertisements or people asking for money. They were easy to deal with. Then there was a list of people he had met the previous night who had opened their personal filters to him and requested a reciprocal action. He did so, but asked Sis to only inform him of messages from these people when he wasn't busy, which Sis advised him was a standard way of doing things. He noted, with a smile, that Faith-Sincere had sent him a voice message, telling him that she had enjoyed their *little chat* and saying how much she was looking forward to getting to know him better. He'd have to think about that one.

There were several anon-untrace messages which meant that even though Sis knew who they were from, she wouldn't tell him, and there was one message from an unknown source. Sis couldn't explain how he could get a message from an unknown sender but she admitted that the comms system could be manipulated by some highly resourceful game-players and that, as a security precaution, she had not read the contents of the message. She advised him to ignore it too, as it was likely malicious or criminal in origin.

It hadn't occurred to Dielle that he might be the target of criminal activity. He hadn't even considered that there might be real criminals in an environment where everything was monitored and recorded by the system. He was just about to ask Sis about this when she pinged him to let him know he'd reached his destination.

Before he could get out, a light green furry beast burst into the bubble, accompanied by a storm of white flakes and freezing cold air. Dielle's instincts put him into fight-or-flight mode but fortunately, before he did something he'd have regretted, the monster turned around to reveal the smiling face of the man Dielle had come to see.

'Dielle! My man! Good to see ya!' Fencer stuck out a huge gloved hand which Dielle grabbed with both of his and shook. Fencer wasn't very tall and had a youthful, vaguely nervous manner but during their brief conversation the night before, Dielle had realised two significant things: first, Fencer was probably the single most intelligent human he had ever met, and second, as far as he could tell, Fencer wanted absolutely nothing from him.

Fencer shoved a small package into Dielle's hand. 'Here, put this on and come outside!' He stepped out amid another storm of flakes as Dielle opened the package. It softploded in his hands and expanded into a full-sized furry body suit similar to the one Fencer had been wearing. He put it on.

{[What's the white stuff?]}

[[Snow. Aggregated frozen water crystals. You are in the winter levels of the new AllWeather section. The terrain here is currently being furbished]]

The suit self-sealed and adjusted to his body temperature then expanded as several layers of foam were emtied into the outer skins.

[[The foam is a new test material developed especially for this climate. It will provide flexible thermal insulation but hardens instantly to a virtually impenetrable shell in the case of a fall or imminent impact]]

{[Cool. What's it called?]}

[[It doesn't have a market name yet. Its ProtoName is *Crunchfoam*]]

{[Catchy]}

[[Watch your step]]

Dielle stepped outside and immediately wished he hadn't. He was standing on a ledge cut into the side of a steep mountain in the middle of a full-scale blizzard. He could barely see his feet.

{[Where's Fencer?]}

[[Green]]

A cascade of green squares led Dielle around the narrow ledge to a small corrie where Fencer was standing and waving his arms at a vertical wall of snow. He looked as though he was conducting a hidden orchestra. Dielle slapped him on his back to get his attention. Fencer turned around and stopped the blizzard with a wave of his hand.

The silence was sudden and unnerving. Fencer pulled his hood back and smiled.

'The glacier is coming along nicely, but we're having a bit of a problem getting this snow to stick at the higher altitudes. It keeps falling off in sheets. Rather spectacular to watch, but not the effect we're aiming for. I'm trying to figure out a solution,' said Fencer, kicking a new batch of snow which collapsed onto his boots. 'I think we'll have to compact it with more wind and alternate freezing and thawing.'

The air cleared to reveal the magnificent Graphite mountains. Externally they were exact replicas of the most famous peaks and alpine features of Earth and ranged over 10,000 square kilometres of the AllWeather section. Internally they housed millions of cubic metres of desperately needed state-of-the-art storage and retrieval facilities. Dielle knew none of this. He'd been too busy staring at the view to ask. Unfortunately, the visual effect the designers had worked so hard to achieve was somewhat marred by the moth-eaten patches of snow clinging pitifully to the highest slopes. The snow glistened wetly under the harsh glare of the only mobile sun onSlab.

'Very impressive. Can't you just add some glue?'

'Snow glue. Yes, we've been working on that. We think it's called ice.'

'Well, I'm glad it's your problem and not mine. Look, I'm sorry, I didn't want to disturb you while you were busy.'

'I'm not busy! Let's go and get something hot and ratted to drink. There's a great little lodge nearby we've opened up just for the crew. I think we'll keep it secret too – it'll be a good place to come when you want to chill out. Ha! Chill out! Get it?' Fencer was a likeable chap despite his propensity to laugh at his own bad jokes.

Dielle followed Fencer back along the narrow ledge to the tube, peeked over the edge and threw himself back against the sheer rock face.

'SHIIIIII..! How high are we?'

'About three kilometres here I think,' said Fencer cheerily, disappearing through the vex.

Dielle clung to the snow, paralysed by fear. Slowly, it started to shift.

fifteen

Louie wanted to rub his hands together with glee, but as he wouldn't have felt the benefit, and being aware of the mood of the joyless interns around him, he decided that a look of grave concern would be a better pitch.

He'd instantly warmed to Sis. She was straight to the point, with no emotional colouring or personal agenda. Louie liked doing business with people like that. Too bad he'd never met any back on Earth, he thought.

'SlabCouncil deems it essential to investigate the interior of the entity designated FutureSlab,' said Sis via a replica of a long-dead American president doing an outstanding job of impersonating one of the greatest sex icons of twentieth-century Earth. In contrast to the interns, the Eriks had an extremely well developed sense of humour. 'They believe that it is either our Slab from some alternate or future time-line,' she continued, 'or it is a copy, made by some alien intelligence for a purpose which we cannot currently understand. Either way, Council has determined it must know.'

One of the furries shouted 'Coldslaw!' which Louie took to mean they didn't like the idea. Either that or they were hungry. In fact it was a reference to 'Cold's Law' named after Nathaniel Nathan Cold, a little-known late-nineteenth-century-Earth physicist whose famous maxim is usually rephrased as: *Don't fuck about with something you don't understand.*

Louie didn't care. He was just happy to know they needed him for something. Throughout his life he had developed a finely tuned feral instinct for leveraging weaknesses into maximum personal benefit. It was this talent that had made him, at one point, the second richest man on Earth. The richest at the time was Louie's business partner – and he was the richest only because Louie had negotiated the deals that way. Poor old Milus, thought Louie, but not with any feeling.

'Every possible precaution will be taken to ensure that there are no negative consequences for Slab,' said Sis. 'Yield to question on the floor from 434 0955.'

'How can we be sure,' said the guy Louie had tagged as Richard, 'that our attempts to investigate the FutureSlab, which may run the risk of violating some form of time continuum or alternate universe anomaly, isn't what was, or rather will be, responsible for our potentially disastrous future?'

This was met by a chorus of comments.

'Good point.'

'I already said that.'

'Causality conjecture!'

Erik raised his hand. 'Respected interns,' he said with his Abe Lincoln sincerity effect on maximum. 'There is little point in debating this question over and over again. Majority consensus can be summarised as: If it is, then it's already happened, or rather it already will have happened and if it isn't then it's no problem.'

'What about free will?' asked Louie. 'Don't we get a choice?'

'Of course we do,' said Erik. 'And we choose to find out what it is.'

'But if you said it already has been going to happen …' Louie's holographic brain threw a loop error. 'No, just forget it,' he shook his head. 'What's been done to investigate it so far?'

'Everything we can do remotely has been done and has revealed exactly what we've told you – which is not much. The only thing we can do is try to get inside it and find out what will have happened. If you get my drift.'

Louie could almost smell the money. 'And you can't. Right?'

'No, we can't.'

Still the same old Louie Drago, thought Louie triumphantly. They could download him, freeze him, store him for hundreds of years and project him into space, but they couldn't take away his nose for a deal.

'And that's why you want to talk to me, huh?'

'That,' said Marilyn in a particularly breathy voice, 'is exactly why we want to talk to you, Mr Drago.'

The screens lit up again with argument and counter argument. Avatars were shouting at each other on every available channel. Louie couldn't make out what the main problem was but it seemed to be a philosophical one. He might have had a superb nose for business, but when it came to philosophy he stopped well short of Plato. He used to say he stopped short of Pluto, but realised that that particular gag had had its day. In Louie's entire life his biggest philosophical problem had been trying to decide who he might persuade to pay for his lunch. Surprisingly, as he had become richer and richer, this task had become easier and easier, leading him to discover a truism which he was fond of quoting: *The more you can afford something, the greater the number of people who fall over themselves to give it to you for nothing.* Now that, he thought, is real philosophy.

The only way to get anyone or anything inside the FutureSlab was to use an extended relay of emties. The first problem was that emties required both receiving and transmitting ends to function, so they had to figure out how to transmit a receiver through fifty kilometres of Natalite from over a thousand kilometres away. This had been a particularly hard one to solve, but recent developments in the war had spurred weapons researchers into experimenting with projecting nano-scale emti receivers over very long ranges. Conceived to enable warhead delivery inside enemy ships by stealth, they relied on a self-replicating cascade effect. Unfortunately, the whole process was inherently unstable and tended to suffer what the military liked to call 'spontaneous failure events'. This didn't matter as long as they were trying to blow up the receiving end, but mattered a lot when they were trying to retrieve something. Such as a holographic recording device.

The next problem was more complicated and went back to an argument that had been running for as long as emties had been around.

Emti technology had been invented on Earth a long time before Slab was built. It would have been virtually impossible to have constructed anything on the scale of Slab without matter transmission technology which had made it possible to deliver enormous masses into Earth orbit at very little cost. If it had been left to rocket science, mankind would have been incarcerated forever on its tiny, doomed planet, futilely trying to boost payloads into the outer atmosphere which were ninety percent comprised of the fuel required to get them there.

The man who had invented matter transmission (or, more accurately, accidentally discovered it during a drug-fuelled weekend of sexually motivated, obsessive behaviour) was Milus Blondel. He and his business partner formed the Institute for Research into the Already Known which, using the impossible-to-comprehend amount of money the M.T. technology generated, coupled with Milus's incredible knack for asking stupid questions, also discovered anti-gravity and several other inventions of major importance during the middle of the twenty-first century. Milus's business partner, the man who had negotiated all the deals, who had been his advisor, protector and occasionally even *friend*, was Louis Clinton Drago.

Louie had never fully understood what all the fuss was about. Emties were the wonder of the age. They could be used to transport almost anything anywhere at very low cost.

They revolutionised so many aspects of life that it was impossible to quantify just how widespread the effects were. They had transformed transportation and delivery systems, ended the world's reliance on petroleum products, radically altered building and city construction, delivered freshwater from ice-caps to deserts, removed waste and separated it into constituent molecules for super-efficient recycling; they had changed people's lives forever and even done away with the dry-cleaners (a personal triumph for Louie). They had also made him and Milus incredibly rich. Unbelievably rich. Rich enough to buy the State of California. But there were just a couple of small problems with the emti.

First, they couldn't be used to transport human beings. There would be no beaming up, down or sideways for any future space captains because emties were only allowed to work on non-animate objects. They had discovered that if a human being was transported using a big enough, properly tuned emti, the body would be transferred, but the soul, being non-physical, wouldn't. Louie couldn't understand why this had bothered anyone, but as the practice produced a sudden influx of advertising and music business executives, it was banned.

The second, slightly more significant problem was what happened when some bright spark in IRAK's Malibu research labs decided to build a machine that would transmit itself to a receiver attached to a long arm connected to the machine it was transmitting from. The idea was simple: as all emti transmissions happen instantaneously, the result should be faster-than-light travel. No-one knows exactly what happened because the simulcast of the experiment ceased when the count-down reached zero, but the instant dematerialisation of most of Southern California led to the law requiring all emties to have built-in Auto-Self-Sensing Closedloop OVERflow protection.

Even though most of IRAK's assets bar Louie's Manhattan offices had been wiped out by The

Disappearance, Louie thought most people had overreacted. Arizona Bay had rapidly filled with the Pacific Ocean, which had the effect of returning global sea levels to those the world had enjoyed before global warming had turned Greenland and Antarctica into arable farmland. The energy released during the event had permanently fused the San Andreas fault, making the entire western seaboard earthquake-free and, usefully for the marine leisure industry, longer. And of course, the movie business improved dramatically. Louie thought that the pluses far outweighed the minuses. Not everyone had agreed with him.

Nobody was agreeing with anyone now. General consensus in SlabCouncil was that it was unethical, immoral and illegal to ask any sentient being to be transported by the series of emti relays into the emti receiver that they were hypothesising could be projected into the FutureSlab.

Louie raised his virtual eyebrows. 'Why not just send a NAH?'

Silence descended like a bad smell.

'We will not travel by matter transmitter,' said Erik with utmost Lincolnesque gravitas.

'Why not?' asked Louie. 'I thought you weren't human, so you can't have souls, can you?' The debate among the interns re-started.

'We most certainly do not have souls, thank you,' said Erik, offended. 'We are not polluted by such alien manifestations. No, our position on matter transmission is that since no-one can provide proof that the body which steps into the transmitter isn't destroyed and a new one created at the receiving end, we will not use them.'

'But if the NAH that steps out the receiving end looks exactly the same and has the same memories as the one that steps into the transmitter, what possible difference does it make?'

'Sir, we NAHs are, for all intents and purposes, immortal. We will be sentient and *alive* for as long as we can regenerate ourselves, which, seeing as we have our own, internal Nole®-powered systems, should be forever, failing catastrophic crisis or a voluntary act of self-termination. As you so rightly say, we do not have souls, so the only thing we have is our existence. Our *being* is all, and is therefore sacred to us, especially as there is no possibility of any part of us enduring our own physical destruction. When we cease to be, Mr Drago, we truly cease to be.'

Louie was beginning to lose the plot. 'Hey, call me Louie!' he said with a smile.

'We cannot accept the possibility that our existence might be terminated by the matter transmission process and a new, different version of us created at the other end. The NAH walking into the emti would effectively die.' To Louie's amazement, Erik was shaking.

'But how would you know it was a different person?'

'How would you know it wasn't?'

Louie could tell that he wasn't going to get anywhere with this line of reasoning and wanted to get back to some cold facts.

'How come you're asking me? Weren't there a whole load of people who had themselves frozen and turned into holograms?'

'Indeed so, sir. Our final ship's complement on leaving Earth orbit included 278 cryonically suspended individuals. But, um, unfortunately,' Erik looked unhappy again, 'there was a bit of an administrative error about that.'

'Administrative?'

'Yes. You see, you were the only individual to negotiate a deal with one large cash payment in advance.'

'I got a length-of-voyage special offer. The consortium building this tub was going broke and they needed bailing out.'

'Quite so, sir. It transpired that everyone else paid by instalments using something called credit cards.'

'Seems reasonable.'

'Apparently, credit cards were in the habit of expiring, sir.'

'You're not telling me you terminated all those frozen people from Earth because their credit cards ran out?'

'We didn't terminate anyone, they lapsed. The terms and conditions of passage stated very clearly it was the client's responsibility to ensure full payment of all charges. They were all sent letters warning them they were in default.'

'They were frozen.'

'Frozen and invalid, sir.'

Louie tried to look surprised and outraged on behalf of his fellow Earth travellers, but he just couldn't do it. After some of the bureaucratic blunders he'd witnessed during his life on Earth, 277 frozen and abandoned bodies was nothing. The fact that they were a select group of Earth's wealthiest people and had been disconnected for non-payment of a maintenance fee just added a little spice to his day.

'So you need someone who isn't a NAH or a human to go over there to find out what's going on. Someone who has no soul.'

'As you say, sir.'

'Bingo!' said Louie.

'You'll do it? It doesn't bother you?'

'Erik, whether I'll do it or not is going to be the subject of a long and expensive negotiation,' said Louie brightly. 'Expensive for you that is.' Having no soul didn't bother him in the slightest, although he recalled it used to bother his three ex-wives now and again.

The room fell quiet again. Sis had informed the council of Louie's decision. Avatars started disappearing. Within half a minute, the only individuals left in Council were Erik and Louie.

'You're welcome,' said Louie to the empty auditorium. 'Funny bunch, aren't they?' he said to Erik.

'As you say, sir, although funny isn't a word I frequently use about our interns.'

'Is Sis still here?'

A glowing white ball, the size of a fist, appeared at Louie's eye level. It pulsated as it spoke. 'Yes, I am always present, but you may direct your remarks to this object if it makes you feel more comfortable.' Sis had switched from Marilyn to a neutral, almost-but-not-quite female voice.

'Should I assume that this adoption of an identity for Sis means we are not being recorded?' asked Louie.

'This will all be recorded as data and be accessible on a need-to-know basis for interns and NAHs only,' said the ball. 'There is no need to record visual documentation of our negotiations since the only way we are actually communicating is via interpreted data stream. What are your demands?'

Very direct, thought Louie. This should be fun.

'More than you have,' he said.

'Meaning?'

'Well first off, tell me why the hell I should bother doing this in the first place? What have I got to gain from it?'

'I understand from your profile that there is no point in trying to appeal to your humanitarian or altruistic sides. So I am able to offer you virtually unlimited access to all Slab facilities and as much credit as you could ever need.'

'What? I'm a hologram. What possible use would your facilities be to me? And anyway, I have more than enough of whatever currency you spend here. I have access codes to accounts that were laid down into your data core in index-linked, inflation-proofed assets before you were a floating scaffolding in space.'

'First, Louie, you will be surprised how far holographic technology has advanced since your day. Most entertainment onSlab has some element of stim-connected enhancement which could be directly fed into your systems. Data streams are still data streams and you would be able to interface with them, assuming a certain amount of admittedly expensive programming. And second, if you check your accounts you will find that there is nothing in them.'

'WHAT? You scheming, lying sons of b ... '

'No, not us Louie,' said Erik. 'Your third wife successfully sued you for desertion after you went into cryonic suspension. She cleaned out your accounts. You are effectively broke.'

'That bitch!' said Louie, trying to think of something fast. He'd been outmanoeuvred at a crucial point in a negotiation. He hated it when that happened. He was sure they were lying, but he also knew he couldn't prove it. If they said his accounts were empty, he knew damn well that was what the data showed now, even if it hadn't said that before they'd started negotiating.

'In order for you to do the task we need you to do, we have designed some augmentations to your original programming which will give you complete autonomy and the ability to move around and interact onSlab,' said Sis. We do, of course, need your permission to alter your programming before they can be implemented, but as an act of good faith we are ready to install those systems now, if you wish.'

'I can have control over where I go and when?'

'Absolutely,' said Sis. 'You have already been given Temporary Sentient Being status, so you will have the same freedom as any SlabCitizen but you must of course adhere to Slab protocol and social conformities.'

'Yeah, yeah, sure,' said Louie. He had never come across a rule he couldn't get around if he needed to.

'You are warned, however, that if you try to inform anyone of the privileged information you have received here, or may receive if you do carry out the proposed task, your communication facilities will be disrupted immediately.'

'My output conduits are sealed,' said Louie.

'Yes, they would be,' said Sis. 'You agree?'

'Yes, I agree – just do it, will you?'

Louie instantly felt upgraded. He knew, without being told, that he could manipulate local objects via a projected gravity field emanating from his vDek. He decided to test it out and did a small tour of his immediate surroundings, finding it easy to manoeuvre merely by concentrating on where he wanted to go. He spent a few minutes zooming up and down, getting a feel for it. Erik watched with disinterest. After a few moments a thought occurred to Louie.

'Why don't you just send a camera? Why do you need me to go?'

'Because we have no way of getting the data back safely. We could try to emti a vDek over there and have it record, then send an emti transmitter to get it back, but we can't operate it from here, it would be out of our range the moment it arrives. It has to be activated to transmit at that end. We can't set it to auto transmit because we have no idea what's in there. We could receive something back that could destroy us.'

'Like a bomb?'

'Well, we could handle anything as crude as an explosive device, of course, but it's the something-we-haven't-thought-ofs that cause the real problem,' said Erik. 'Something worse than we can imagine.'

'Aren't you being a little paranoid?'

'Louie,' said Erik, 'we are over one hundred and fifty-six light-years and three hundred and thirty of your Earth years away from help of any kind and we have encountered an object whose mere existence has terrifying implications for all of us. It is impossible to be too paranoid at this point.'

Louie always enjoyed a fight, but only the ones he thought he could win.

'So I go, have a look around, wait for you to send over a transmitter which I have to activate personally … '

'With a highly secret code,' interrupted Sis.

'OK, with a secret code. Then I come back, report what I saw and I get the freedom of Slab and as much money as I'll ever need?'

'Yes.'

'It's not enough.'

'What else could you possibly want?' said Erik

Louie was just warming up. 'Well, I can think of three things straight away. First I want some form of always-on data interaction with Sis. Then I want a permanent, non-revocable seat on the council.'

'What?' said Erik. 'We've barely been able to persuade the interns to give you sentient status. They'll never agree to let you into council. It's impossible!'

Louie looked him straight in the eyes: 'Nothing's impossible, Erik.'

'What is your third demand?' asked Sis.

'I want a SlabWide league of basketball teams set up and I get to be head coach for a team I handpick.'

Erik shook his head slowly. 'Is that it?'

'No, of course that's not it,' said Louie. 'How the hell would I know what I might want? I've only been here a few hours.'

'We will need time to set up the emti relays and make sure they are secure,' said Sis without emotion. 'We also need time to try to persuade council to accede to your demands. Until we can proceed you will have a voice interface available to you for communication with me. This meeting is adjourned.'

The council chamber vanished. Thousands of tonnes of water crash-flooded the space it left behind, leaving Louie and Erik swirling and disoriented.

Erik deftly righted himself. 'I hate it when she does that,' he said. 'You must have really pissed her off.'

Louie followed Erik as he swam toward the surface. 'Where are we?' he asked.

'SlabCouncil meets in a non-static temporary space,' said Erik without moving his lips. 'This particular one seems to have been convened in the Slab water reserves. Therefore we are at the rear end of Slab in the hydroponics, environmental control, manufacturing and recycling section. Just her little joke, you know.'

'Sis has a sense of humour?'

'That is the subject of a long-standing debate.'

'What isn't?'

'Quite,' said Erik, breaking surface. 'There's a recreational port a couple of kilometres from here.' He eased into an efficient backstroke. 'Follow me and we can talk on the way.'

sixteen

Everyone was sitting around laughing except Dielle. He was propped up against a wall and wasn't in a laughing mood. He considered himself lucky to be alive. It's not everyone who falls off a three-kilometre-high mountain and lives to suffer the embarrassment of having people turn around every thirty seconds to look at him and laugh themselves silly. A looped recording of the local avalanche which had knocked him off the mountain showed him flapping his arms in mid-air in terrified desperation before the impact anticipators turned the Crunchfoam rigid, snapping him to attention. If Dielle hadn't closed his eyes, certain he was going to plummet feet-first into the ground three thousand metres below, he would have seen the arms of the safety nets shoot out from the cliff-face, arresting his fall 2.7 metres below the ledge. The image zoomed into his face as his eyes opened wide and darted about in disbelief.

They especially liked that bit.

'Yes, really fucking hilarious,' said Dielle. 'Can't one of you bastards at least feed me another drink? How long before this stuff goes limp again?'

'Could be any minute,' said Fencer, trying hard to suppress a smile. 'It's still experimental. Hey, do you think you could have a word with your agent? The resort want to use the footage to promote how safe the place is. She's apparently holding out for a sum that would mean we'll have to turn round and go back for more cash.'

'Good!' said Dielle {[message to :: Kiki Tiger@pundechan Media: Under no circumstances is the recording of me falling off that mountain to be made public – please acknowledge]}

[[••]]

Dielle crumpled.

'It's worn off then,' said Fencer cheerfully. 'Good. Come and sit over here, I'll introduce you to everyone.'

[[•]]

{[Deliver]}

[['Darling! You were fabulous! I haven't laughed so much in cykes! I won't do any deal before speaking to you – don't worry! See you around six? Love!']]

You won't do any bloody deals at all, he thought grumpily. At least I didn't shit myself. Then he remembered the colonic emties. Maybe he had – how would he know?

They were on a wooden deck overlooking a spectacular Alpine scene, drinking steaming cups of mulled wine. It was freezing cold outside but the localised temperature was mild. He took off the body suit and threw it onto a pile of clothes on the nearest table. The lodge wasn't staffed yet, so everything was supplied via the kTables. He ordered another drink and sat down. Fencer introduced everyone, which wasn't strictly necessary as Dielle had had plenty of time to ask Sis who they all were while he was doing his plank impersonation against the wall. Three of the guys were involved in environmental design and the fourth, who went by the name of Gentricycle Thalmus-Orang, did something interesting with mountain acoustics, but Dielle had had enough of mountains and had enquired no further.

Fencer pointed at each man in turn: 'Geoff, Mate, Twopoint and Thal.' They all raised their cups as Dielle collected his from the kTable. 'The First!'

Twopoint laughed again: 'And hopefully not the last eh? That's a good one!'

Dielle was puzzled. 'Why does everyone think that's so funny?' he asked.

'Because when we say *The First*, we are toasting to that most excellent citizen Cecil Shallock I,' explained Mate. 'He was a man of true discernment and a significant contributor to the well-being of the human race, the onSlab human race that is, mate.'

'He was the Earth-bound specialist who was ultimately responsible for making sure every gene known to man had been included in our gene-banks before we left Earth,' added Fencer. 'It was his signature on the manifest. And it was also his idea to leave off the gene for spinach after being sworn to it by his three children.'

'Projectile vomiting apparently,' said Geoff, doing a reasonable mime.

'Yeah, so we have him to thank for never having to eat spinach – and seeing how his name is a bit of a mouthful, especially when you've had a few … '

'Could have been worse; could have been his second daughter,' said Twopoint.

'Yeah,' continued Fencer. 'So instead of saying his full name, we just say *The First!*'

'And I'm the first person to say something like *hopefully not the last*?' said Dielle incredulously.

'You have the copyright, mate,' said Mate. 'So you must be.'

'That's pretty weak,' said Dielle.

'But *hopefully not the last* doesn't make any sense when you know it's about Cecil Shall … ' Geoff trailed off. 'But you're right, it's lame. Hey! Let's ramp up the regular and get ratted! Rat 5s all round!'

They spent the next hour or so getting very drunk on Regular 5 alcohol of all styles and flavours. All five of them considered it their personal right, duty and obligation to introduce Dielle to as many alcoholic concoctions as they could remember, and several they couldn't. Dielle was *very, very, very happy* to have met such *wonderful guys* and was *absolutely sure* that there couldn't be a more *wonderful bunch of guys in the whole universe*. He told them so. Several times.

He remembered Fencer saying they were going to keep this lodge a secret and he wanted to know more. Like many private residences, the lodge had its own privacy shield, a differentially permeable force-field that kept heat in and prying eyes out. It was transparent from within, but opaque white from the outside, and for a small fee Sis would set the tube address to private. It was a popular option in this part of the mountains. Twopoint, however, was a software landscape designer and knew how to circumvent the privacy protection. After much cajoling and group threats, he did something through his eye that turned off the privacy fields. Dielle hadn't realised until that moment, but the interface also had a privacy field running. Previously, when he looked up all he had seen was blue sky. Now, with the fields off, he could see the mountains and alpine terrain of UpSideDown hanging high above them and dozens of lodges scattered around the mountains and snow-capped hills below.

'They're all still empty, of course,' said Twopoint. 'This whole winter level isn't open yet.' The other four started laughing.

'Yeah, we're slightly behind schedule, mate,' said Mate. 'Like fifteen cycles behind schedule!' Everyone fell about laughing except Dielle, who was confused.

Geoff looked at him and shrugged his shoulders. 'Well,' he said, 'we've had a few bugs!'

Mate choked, spraying Thal with a mouthful of BeaverBrew.

'This whole variable-climate, moving sun idea has been nothing but a bloody gap right from the start,' said Geoff.

'Twilight deprivation my arse!' said Mate. 'It still won't look any different from anything you can sume on your home screens even when we do crack it.'

'But the sunrises and sunsets will be fabulous,' said Thal, whose broccoli-weave jacket was already dry. 'And the onshore breezes and season simulations are going to make the beach property worth a fortune.'

'S'all right for you, echo-boy, you've had it easy,' said Geoff.

Thal knee-jerked: 'Moving mountains isn't as easy as it looks, you know.'

Dielle remembered that he had a few questions he wanted to ask and thought this a good moment to interrupt. Fencer suggested they all 'go down a rating and just get *mildly Scottish* instead'. Within minutes Dielle was able to ask a question without giggling.

'Guys, I need a friend or two who can help me out with some things. I keep coming across stuff that doesn't make any sense and it's making me feel like I'm in a weirdly diced-up dream. Now I've even fallen off a bloody mountain. I'm worried I'm going to wake up and find I'm still in re-fam or worse.'

'Whadya wanna know?' asked Thal, whose comedic talents had improved with every drink. He was a cruelly accurate mimic. 'Sis can tell you just about everything you want to know, you know?'

'That's the problem. I don't know what I want to know.'

'Ah well, that's Fence's department then,' said Geoff. 'He's an accredited question askerer. Going to make intern one day, huh?'

Fencer was modest. 'Well, I don't know if I'll ever join the contiguation, but I can't deny I'd give it a go if it was an option.'

'Do a damn sight better job of it than the current crop of wind-farmers they've got running things,' said Geoff.

'So, what areas do you need help with?' asked Fencer.

'Well, women for a start,' said Dielle.

'Oh fuck! Let's go back to Rat 5s,' said Thal.

Fencer gave Dielle a serious, *I'm listening* look. 'What particularly about women?' he asked.

'Well I've only just found out about this whole female advanced evolution thing for a start. What's that all about?'

'Statistical blocks!' said Thal, seeking, and getting, affirmative nods from the other three.

'No, I'm afraid it's not,' said Fencer. 'Look at it this way: Since the dawn of man, when humans started congregating in social groups, males have traditionally mated with younger females. They used all sorts of excuses of course; healthier breeders, fitter for the job … '

'Nicer tits,' said Twopoint. He'd gone back onto the Rat 5 already.

'But in fact,' continued Fencer, 'it's always been the women who selected who they would conceive with. They had the control over who put what where and when. And they were deliberately breeding young. After a few tens of thousands of years, the pattern had been entrenched. The daughters of young mothers became young mothers themselves breeding with older men. In every hundred years or so there would be an extra generation of women, in every thousand years, ten more generations of the female line and so on. And this has been going on for over five million years. The male-only holandric traits, which are inherited from the Y chromosome, are roughly five thousand generations behind, so the uniquely male characteristics and parts of the brain are less evolved. This was a perfect result for the women. After all, they didn't actually want to go and run about in bushes all day trying to spear something to eat, fight wars, or spend all day in dusty chambers arguing about rights and government. They wanted to stay at home and play with the kids.'

'And bitch about the way the food was caught, the wars were fought, or the way the country was run' interrupted Twopoint.

'Don't mind him. He's just been dumped,' said Geoff, turning to Twopoint. 'And by a really wonderful girl too, eh?'

Twopoint grimaced.

'Is that why they want to talk so much?' asked Dielle. 'Because they're more evolved?'

'Nah, they're just bloody noisy by nature!' said Twopoint, reaching for another drink. 'Can't stand silence. Think something's wrong with you if you're quiet.'

'Something's wrong with you even when you're not quiet, mate,' said Mate.

'So what you're saying is: Women have manipulated men over hundreds of thousands of years in order to get them to do all the stuff they don't want to do while they stay at home and evolve faster?'

'Isn't it dicing obvious?' asked Twopoint.

'Well, I haven't met that many yet, but now you come to mention it … '

'There are many complex and subtly interdependent side-effects to this selective evolution,' said Fencer. 'Some are beneficial, others questionable. But the idea that the force-accelerated evolution in the predominantly male parts of the brain which they've been working on for almost a KiloCyke means we're all evolving into more feminine, sensitive and caring types really is a load of blocks.'

'Too right!' said Twopoint. 'Fucking geneticists.'

'Yeah,' said Dielle. 'What was all that about a stop-gene thing and human evolution being in their hands?'

'Unfortunately, that is definitely true,' said Fencer. 'The bottom line is they accidentally allowed something called a stop-gene to get into the human food chain. They'd originally engineered it into farmed fish to prevent the faster growing, more aggressive ones they needed for higher yields from wiping out the other species. They designed it so the farmed fish couldn't breed in order to keep the population under control and allow other fish to compete for food resources. Trouble is, this stop gene, once it had jumped the piscatorial barrier, mutated and spread. So now the human race is sterile.'

'What? Everyone? Including the women?'

'Yes, everyone,' said Fencer. 'Probably not you of course. This happened after you were put into cryo.'

They all looked at him for a moment.

Dielle didn't want to know what they were thinking. 'So how does the human race breed?'

'The geneticists handle it all of course. Which is, it has to be said, a much better and safer arrangement. Reduces all the chances for mutations and bad crosses and so on. They even input randomness to simulate the chance possibilities that can produce genius and exceptional talent.'

'Fence, you're just giving him the party line,' said Thal. 'You are definitely angling for intern, aren't you? Tell him why they can't just take the stop gene out again. They put it in, they should bloody well take it out.'

'Well, it's just not as simple as that.'

'You bet!' said Geoff. 'It would put them all out of a job, wouldn't it?'

[[•]] Sis reminded Dielle that he had to be at the other end of Slab and was running out of time.

'Guys,' said Dielle, 'I've got to go now, but one last question, OK?' They all nodded and waited expectantly.

'What do you do when your girlfriend, who you are living with and you love, who's gorgeous and incredibly horny and a great, well … but she's also your agent, and you keep getting propositions from other really beautiful women who she is negotiating deals with about what royalties they will get from the sumecasts of you fucking them, but the one you really want to fuck is the one she really hates and has already left you two [[Three]] er, three messages to get in touch with her but you know there is no way your agent, that is your girlfriend, who you love, is going to let you do that?'

The other five looked at him silently for a while.

'I know, mate!' said Mate, leaping up. He stood rigidly to attention, looked terrified and flapped his arms. On eye-cue, everyone else copied him.

'Bastards!' said Dielle and left.

Once in the tube, Sis told him Kiki had made a divert request for him to meet her at a ground terminal where they'd catch an excalator to the skimmer races. He accepted and asked Sis for more information.

Skimmers were multi-winged gliders with frictionless hulls that skimmed the interface. The races were held over dynamic courses which the solo pilots had to navigate using a combination of natural thermals, variable gravity and a considerable amount of luck. Mandatory way-points were marked by mobile beacons which functioned as an active handicapping system by constantly reshaping the course to benefit those at the rear, generating nail-biting finishes and the occasional spectacular collision. Skimmer racing was glamourous, dangerous, colourful and unpredictable, and no race ever lasted for more than five minutes, which fitted perfectly with media company requirements and the attention-span of the typical skimmer fan.

Each race started with a row of luridly decorated, highly eccentric skimmers being gravmanipulated into a line-abreast formation on the interface. Then, with a stomach-wrenching (for both the pilots and any nearby spectators) pull of a snap-spot triple-gravity well, the unpowered skimmers plummeted toward the slabscape. Skimmerjocks jostled to out-manoeuvre their opponents and trade height for speed before pulling up into dangerously high-gee turns and throwing the super-slippery craft into lower gravity columns in an effort to return to the interface as fast as possible, flip over and repeat the process. To a stationary spectator, it looked as though the skimmers were alternating between falling down and falling up as they flipped between the two sides.

Gravity wells of varying strengths formed and collapsed spontaneously in random patterns around the course, adding extra tension to the proceedings as some pilots chose to rapidly oscillate along the plane of the interface (*threading*), waiting for the next big pull while others took flamboyant plunging dives which gained them additional momentum but put them at a greater risk of *fizzling*, or failing to reach the interface, which usually led to an embarrassing divert to a landing field. Occasionally a skimmer would come to a complete stop exactly on the interface and have nowhere to go until a random breeze altered its fragile equilibrium. That was when people began betting on how long the glider would hang as the pilot tried desperately to nudge the machine by violently bouncing around in his seat. It was a lot of fun.

The races were only one part of the entertainment. Spectator platforms held landing strips lined by rows of garish carnival rides and near-death experiences. The stands were constructed to house both Uppies and Siders in mirrored arenas which inevitably led to a wide range of practical jokes. The spectator platforms were part of the mobile beacon system that delineated the racecourse so it couldn't be connected to the tube system. The only way to get to them was via transportation disks from ground stations that were scattered around Mitchell.

It was at one of these terminals that Dielle met Kiki. He'd wanted to stay angry with her but his mood dissolved the moment she jumped into his arms, smiling and excited.

'Charlie's given us full access to the presidential box,' she said. 'And he's not coming! I've invited a few of my friends I want you to meet. Come on, the first race has already started.'

She pulled him onto a crowded shuttle disk which silently joined the celestial escalator to the spectator level.

'Who were you with earlier, darling?' asked Kiki coyly.

'Don't you know? I got the impression you could watch anything I did?'

'Depends on the privacy settings. Recordings are jointly owned by all the participants. If any one of them vetoes it, or declares privacy, it's not available. I saw you'd gone somewhere with Fencer Dean Twenty but the moment you arrived everything went into privacy mode.'

That was news to Dielle. Useful news.

'Oh, just some guys. Friends of Fencer's. We had a few drinks. It was fun after I was able to move.'

'That was so funny!' she laughed. 'Are you still upset about it, darling?' She stood on tip-toes to kiss his nose. 'The resort owners are really keen to use it. Really keen.'

'How keen?' He couldn't help himself.

'Very keen.'

'Tell them I want my own lodge, full privacy. Forever. Then they can use it.'

Kiki looked suspicious. 'Who have you been talking to, dear? That's a very hard bargain. Did someone suggest that to you?'

'Nope, I just thought of that myself.' He had too, and surprised himself in the process.

She nodded, approving. 'Well, I'll tell them your conditions. It's OK if I add something on top for little old me, isn't it?'

Dielle looked at her coolly and thought about what he'd learned that afternoon. The roar of the crowd above diverted his attention as a huge, bright yellow skimmer shot up from underneath them, inverted itself, banked around the beacon by the spectator platform above them, then dived down into UpSide.

'That's the Speedthrills skimmer!' shouted Kiki over the noise. 'Tony Speedthrills! I have all his stims. I'm his biggest fan.'

'Speedthrills?' said Dielle incredulously. 'Is that his real name?'

'What do you mean, real name, darling?' asked Kiki jumping from the shuttle disk moments before it was ingurgitated into the dock and emtied back to the ground station. 'Come on! We'll miss it!' She pushed through the crowd. 'Yellow vex!' she shouted to Dielle.

He followed her to a bank of transvexes – one was flashing yellow. On the other side, a privacy bubble was waiting to transport them to the presidential hospitality suite. Like most presidential facilities, the room spanned the interface and had the standard floor/ceiling duplication of luxurious seats and leisure options. At one end, a continuous viewpane curved from UpSide to SideUp and housed a bank of holo-projectors showing multiple views of the race.

Whenever Dielle's eyes focussed on a projected skimmer, animated graphics sprang out in 3D. Sis fed him labels and numerics as he glanced at each one. Every imaginable detail was available to him, from cockpit telemetry, optimal vectoring, aerodynamic options and gravity predictions to the pilot's heart rate, what he'd had for breakfast and the emotional state of the person he'd eaten it with. One enquiry thread detailed bloodlines going back for generations, another provided instant comparison between sequences of the competitors' DNA with glowing indicators highlighting statistical superiority. As he waded through the glut of data, his focus fell on a row of coloured cylinders projected onto the floor. They were continually changing in diameter and height and represented the betting odds and amount of money that was being gambled. A series of smaller cylinders trailed off into the distance, illustrating the betting on how the odds were likely to change.

{[Too much!]}

[[General prefs for this locale are wide-band. Throttling personal feed to demand only]]

'Do you want a voice-over or just an eye feed?' Kiki asked.

'What do you use?'

'Voice for personality commentary, Sis for analysis,

audio for pit-to-skimmer comms and the holos for facts and telemetry.'

Dielle wasn't surprised. There seemed to be no end to the amount of things Kiki could do simultaneously. More evolved, he thought, glumly.

'Just voice for me,' he said.

'Let's have Entwistle! He cracks me!'

A coarse male voice cut in mid-insult. Entwistle was SlabWide famous for his mastery of the scathing put-down and was in full flow. His target was a currently defenceless and momentumless skimmer pilot who, according to Entwistle, would probably have had a more successful racing career as a mollusc, as long as all the other molluscs were suffering from total paralysis or a particularly debilitating form of molluscan depression. The stream of invective was delivered with such obvious delight and expertise that it was difficult not to feel sorry for the object of his vitriol.

'Any refreshments, sir, madam?' said a small cupboard hovering behind them.

'Cold beer, Rat 3, tasties,' said Kiki without taking her eyes off the holos. 'Come on Tony!'

The emtiwaiter's door opened and a gravpad floated out with the drinks and a platter of translucent wafers. Outside, a shiny blue skimmer charged past narrowly avoiding the turn beacon. The crowd roared as Entwistle cranked up the ridicule.

'This is exciting,' said Dielle. 'What the hell is going on?'

'Blue one's leading,' said Kiki, stuffing her mouth with salt and vinegar dissolves. 'But Tony's catching up. Only two laps to go so he's not going to make it unless that one misses an interface turn, which it very nearly just did.'

The yellow skimmer zoomed into view in three of the holo-projections, all from different angles. Things didn't look quite as frantic as before.

'Oh blocks!' said Kiki, dismayed. 'He's stuffed it. He's undershot a flip.' She turned away from the screens and stood up. 'Hello Wendle! When did you arrive?'

Wendle wore a hand-tailored suit that, despite costing more than the average SlabCitizen made in a cycle, failed to make him look anything but round. Wendle's mass was the subject of a strictly enforced SlabWide non-disclosure agreement which meant that everyone knew he was a 357-kilogram porker and that he was proud of himself. His three fawning female attendants were proud of him too.

'Just got here, Tiger. Speedthrills fucked up again, huh? He's a waster. Hope you didn't have too much on him.'

'Not much. I'll get it back in the fifth. He'll thrash Jennersson and Crumb for sure. He's just a slow starter, that's all. Dielle dear, meet Wendle. He's the owner of one of the largest SlabWide sume distribution companies and a very old friend of mine.'

'Friend, is it? Friend? Is that how you treat friends? Screw them into the floor and make it impossible to make an honest credit?' He offered Dielle a short and bloated arm. 'Pleased to met you Dielle. You're doing very well, which is more than I can say for myself.'

'Of course we're friends, Wendle,' said Kiki defensively. 'It's not my fault 9com offered a 105% deal, is it?'

Wendle floated down on his gravboard. His short, fat legs were clearly not capable of providing much in the way of ambulatory assistance. Dielle tried not to stare.

'Don't mind me,' said Wendle, waving Dielle out of his way. 'Tiger, you are a scheming liar. I happened to bump into Henry last night at an awards negotiation and he promised me he made no such offer.'

'I'll have Sis deliver you authenticated transcripts if you like. And it wasn't Henry, it was his sidekick NAH. You know, the slimy one with the Elvis hair.'

'Don't flush me with transcripts; I'm not some dimwit

rocket scientist you know. Transcripts are worth Dice-all. My own flesh and blood, too!'

'Oh Wendle, don't take it so bad. It's just a deal. You'll make plenty on the side-throughs and don't give me that flesh-and-blood lookadat. There's none of your flesh or blood in me, just a few of your genes.'

'What?' said Dielle. 'Are you two related?' He couldn't imagine two people looking less alike.

'Kiki is 4.6% me,' said Wendle, his porcine features beaming. 'I'm very proud of her as a matter of fact.'

'Oh Wendle!' said Kiki. 'You are the nicest, fattest slob I've ever met!'

'Yes I am, aren't I?' he said, accepting a big wet kiss from his half-niece twice removed through an electron micro-gene splitter.

The family reunion was interrupted by a flurry of activity from the back of the room. 'It's alright darlings! Don't panic! I'm here. Oh! The presidential box! Tiger, you are coming up onSlab, aren't you darling! Why hasn't anyone given me a drink yet? What has a girl to do to get any attention around here?'

Dielle stared at the source of the commotion. It didn't look like a girl, but it didn't look like a boy either. He had no idea what it looked like.

'Darling! How are you!' said Kiki, hugging the new arrival. She stood back to look at him/her. 'Or rather, what are you? You're in transition again, aren't you?'

'Oh I know, dear! Back and forth, back and forth. I just can't make my mind up. I think the truth of it is, I'm a straight man trapped inside a gay man's body!'

'Let me introduce you to my straight man.' Kiki took the tween by the hand and led her to Dielle. 'Darling, I'd like you to meet my oldest friend …' She turned back: 'What is your doName today, darling?'

'I don't know, I haven't decided.' He/she looked around the room. 'Anyone?'

'How about Idiot,' said Wendle.

'I always liked *Stephaniel,*' said one of the pretty Wendle attendants.

'Stephaniel! I like it! Could be one or the other, or both at the same time. Call me Stephie … or Niel. What's your name, dear?'

'Pretty Wendle Assistant Number 2, sir,' she said, prettily.

'Ah! You're Not Actually Human, aren't you?

'Yes sir, thank you, sir.'

Stephie reached out and squeezed Dielle's hand. 'You meet all sorts here, don't you? Hello Dielle, I'm very pleased to meet you. Kiki-chan has told me a lot about you, and I bet none of it's true! Where's my drink?'

The emtiwaiter took advantage of a temporary hiatus in Wendle's spirited consumption of hi-chol pre-dipped fritter sticks to dash over to deliver Stephie a large glass of cool, black liquid with a creamy, white topping.

Dielle was intrigued. {[What's that?]}

[[Ginis]]

{[I'll have one]}

[[••]]

'We grew up together on the same farm,' said Kiki, putting her arm around her friend. 'Of course, she was a little girl then.' They looked at each other affectionately.

'You grew up on a farm?'

'Yes darling, a kid farm. We all did.'

Dielle had been meaning to ask about this. He hadn't seen any children since he had arrived. That must explain it. They all lived on farms. He made a mental note to research that later [[Noted]]. He thought he should try to make conversation.

He took a mouthful of his new drink, then wondered why anyone would drink cold, bitter liquid. 'And what do you do, Stephaniel?'

'I love babies.'

'Well, that's nice, but I meant what do you do for a living?' He felt strangely compelled to taste his drink again.

'That's what I do. I love babies. I'm a professional baby rearer.'

'Don't the parents do that?'

'Hardly. Most gene donors can't be bothered studying child psychology and sitting all the full-time parenting exams. It's a very demanding job, you know.'

This was news to Dielle. 'You have to train to be a parent?'

'Of course you do. Children are way too important and vulnerable to be parented by amateurs. Look at the complete blocks they made of it all back on Earth. Bad parenting was responsible for virtually all of the problems society suffered from in those days. It was completely unregulated. A total mess. I mean, did your parents know anything about child psychology before they raised you?'

'I don't know,' said Dielle, a little subdued. 'I don't remember my parents.' {[Another Ginis]}

[[••]]

'That's alright darling!' said Stephie, touching his arm affectionately. 'I never met any of mine, and there were twenty three of them! But we shared some great rearers.' Stephie called over to Kiki who had picked up her conversation with Wendle. 'Do you remember old Mrs Thorpe?'

'Of course I do! I loved Mrs Thorpe! She inspired me to start my own business. She changed my life.'

'Well, she sent me a note the other day on paper – real paper!'

'Amazing! She must be over six hundred cykes by now! What did it say?'

'I don't know darling, I sent it to a reader but it was in her scrawly handwriting and the est was less than forty points accuracy so I nixed.'

'I should invite her here, she'd be so proud of me! I wonder … no, she's on full privacy.'

A roar from the crowd signalled the start of the next race. As they turned to the viewpane, a dozen custom-built skimmers dropped out of the sky. Dielle enjoyed a couple of races but his attention was caught by something he had seen near the landing strip.

'Think I might go for a walk around,' he said.

'No problem darling,' said Kiki. 'I'll let you know when the rest arrive. They said they wouldn't be here until around the eighth race anyway. Have fun! Take an emtibrella with you'

'A what?'

'By the vex, dear. Those small cylinder things. Hold it upright when there are Uppies about or you'll get wet.'

Dielle took one of the devices, asked Sis to take him to the public area and stepped through the transvex.

He entered an arena filled with the sound of twenty thousand people having an extremely robust time. He could hear, but he couldn't see half of the crowd because the Uppies above him in the overhead terraces were blanketed by a stadium-wide softAd for a product that made stunningly beautiful women smile a lot without giving Dielle any clue why. This was because most of the spectators wore sponsored adcaps that formed spontaneous network connections with hundreds of others of the same brand in order to project images which could only be seen by the opposing side. Whichever cap-brand was prevailing gained the most exposure so competition was fierce. Rival brand representatives fought to build dominant nodes by bribing the usually half-ratted spectators to swap caps. A significant amount of the shouting and screaming had nothing to do with the races at all and everything to do with the current value and location of the most strategically placed adcap.

Attending sporting events was a lucrative business

onSlab. Not only were the spectators paid to wear advertising technology, they were also paid to consume and rate the free food and drinks dispensed by an army of rapid-cycling emticabs that darted about the crowd like humming birds around wildflowers. This explained why the crowd behaviour was only marginally related to what was happening in the skimmer race. At the back of the stands, the two opposing sides were so close that they could almost reach up and touch each other. Dielle noticed a group of young guys on what he was starting to think of as his side of the interface form a huddle and lift one of their members high enough to grab the outstretched hands of an attractive young lady above them. The Uppies were quick to react and held on to her legs, pulling her back down and bringing several of the Siders along with her. Reinforcements joined in on both sides and a bizarre game of human tug-of-war developed.

Another popular interface caper was the practice of throwing beer directly above your head in an attempt to breach the interface and drench a member of the opposing side. It required considerable skill to avoid soaking yourself and those around you and was the reason everyone carried emtibrellas at interface sporting events, usually in quick-draw holsters. Dielle got a demonstration when he saw a large guy whip out his emtibrella as a stream of liquid appeared above him. The brella sprang open, forming a funnel to capture the liquid, which then flowed into the handle and disappeared. A jeer and a round of applause came from a section of the crowd above.

Sponsored chants broke out between the opposing sides and because Dielle was running on average prefs, Sis opened a channel and fed him an instaknow of the next line. Dielle shut it down. He didn't need the extra cash and he wasn't interested in joining in. What he was interested in was the streamlined metallic bulge he had spotted in the platform floor. He'd noticed a steady stream of intriguing looking people walking into it and disappearing. He focussed his gaze on it.

{[What's that, Sis?]}

[[Entrance to an underform live music venue. Session in progress]]

{[Music style?]}

[[roots/jazz/improv]] Excellent, thought Dielle. He had no idea what roots/jazz/improv was, but deeper instincts were guiding his feet.

The vex was an entrance to a wide staircase which led below the landing strip. As he descended, the noise of the crowd was cancelled out, the daylight faded and he heard the sound of a saxophone pushing against a lazy beat. The back of his neck got a thousand tiny hard-ons.

The club was dimly lit and crowded. The atmosphere was as different from the bright and frantic scenes above as it was possible to imagine. Here, people were sitting in small groups, either concentrating on the performance or partying with their friends behind mono-directional acoustic privacy fields. It was clear that some people were having a very good time, but the only thing Dielle could hear was the music. Sis had called it *live* music. Dielle could understand why; he felt his skin tingle.

He thought back to his first day and the fun he'd had dancing in the recovery frame. He tried to dance to the syncopated rhythms and discovered that not only did it make him feel ridiculous but people started pointing at him. He found a seat and asked Sis for a Rat 1 Ginis because he wanted to enjoy the music with a clear head and look cool at the same time. He closed his eyes and concentrated on picking out the complex patterns and textures emanating from the stage. Something inside him found a home.

Too soon, the keys man announced they would be back later and walked off the stage through the applauding crowd. He was about to pass Dielle's table when he stopped and looked down at him,

'Cheese es nerry nohang dood encha?' he said. He was tall and angular with coffee-skin, ropes of black hair and a bespoke beard. Dielle hadn't seen anyone with hair on their face before. He was impressed and wondered if he could have one just like it. [[Option is valid but specified design is copyright, statutory license fee applies, change defaults to implement]]

'I'm sorry, what?'

'Dielle innit? Tempgal sume loadza u! Skinit!' he said, enthusiastically sticking out his hand. The words meant nothing to Dielle, but the body language and broad smile signalled friendship.

He reckoned he should also respond in kind and extended his hand. The musician went through a complex series of finger and wrist movements but stopped, disappointed, when Dielle failed to reciprocate.

'Fee u cherry downam shandri?'

'I'm afraid I don't speak your language.'

'My mistake man. Yeah. You haven't had time to pick up any muso yet. My name is Jesus Aloisius Marley the Eighth but most citz just call me Fingerz Jeez!' He held up his hands and waved them around. He had long, slender fingers. Dielle, unsure of this elaborate hand-waving protocol, did the same. Thanks to Louie, he had long fingers too. 'Hey! You should play keys man! You equipped!'

Dielle looked at his own hands and thought about his future. Fingerz sat down opposite Dielle and nodded his head as if he was agreeing with something profound that Dielle had just said. He pulled a slim pack of shiffs from his pocket, stuck one in his mouth and sucked on it. Vapour spiralled from the tip. He nodded again and exhaled a cloud of light blue smoke which formed an egg-shaped boundary around him before cycling into the emti on the bottom of the pack he'd placed on the table between them. Dielle gorped again.

'What's that?'

'You not done shiff yet?' asked Fingerz, offering him one. 'This is one of those things the disclaimer warn you about, make you feel relaxed an' kinda focussed. Gets the vibe down cool, though. Deep an' cool.'

Dielle stuck it between his lips and sucked. His mouth, throat and lungs filled with acrid smoke. He coughed so hard that he almost threw up. He stared at the smouldering tube, bewildered that anyone would voluntarily do such a patently stupid thing as fill their lungs with pollution. Ten seconds later, he understood. He took another lungful and tried hard not to choke. Then he amused himself by blowing out the smoke and watching it hit the PersonalSpace which had expanded to envelop them both. He felt relaxed. Relaxed and yet strangely focussed.

'Shiff huh? Where do I get some?'

'Same place as everything else. You just ask our ever-lovin' Sister man, but if you want the best, you gotta have it handmade. I got a man on UpSide makes me a special blend.'

Dielle looked carefully at Fingerz and knew that he had known him for a long time.

'You know, you're a great player. I loved what you were doing with those keys. You really think I could learn?' said Dielle, looking at his hands again. 'How long does it take?'

'Well sure you can. Anyone can. You try my latest stim, you'd get fluid in NoTime. But it's more than just being able to play, man. You gotta have what we call the creative differentiator an' you can't get that through a stim unit. That's a natural born thing, man. It's like an invisible gene or something.'

'Creative differentiator?'

'Talent, man – the stuff that makes the difference.'

'And how do I find out if I've got any?'

'You don't man. Other citz, they, like, feel it in you. You don't learn it, you just let it.'

Dielle took another lungful. He was starting to understand. Fingerz had a way of saying things that helped him understand something he wasn't sure he understood but he felt sure that it didn't matter if he didn't understand it because if he didn't it probably wasn't something that needed to be understood anyway.

'Let it, huh?'

'Yeah, let it and live it. You gotta know who you are, man.'

'Know who I am. Right.'

Dielle sucked down more smoke and thought for a while. He looked at Fingerz. Fingerz looked at him. Fingerz blew out some smoke and disappeared behind his cloud. Dielle blew out smoke and, eventually, thought of something to say.

'I didn't get one of those Stim-o-rama-tron things when I had my eye put in. I guess I'll have to get one if I want to learn to play.'

'That was one shrewd move, man,' said Fingerz. 'You don't want to get those commercial stim units anywhere near your head. You don't know what they link through. I can take you to a guy who can insin you the latest sub-legal stim, with full-on sensurround, auto-store an' full recall. You don't get that with those rama-tron pieces of lookadat crap.'

'You can take me?'

'Yeah sure, but you gotta go with maximum privacy, man, cos you're a full-on star an' he ain't gonna go anywhere near you if you're recording. You know what I'm sayin'?'

Dielle knew exactly what he was saying. Or thought he did.

[[•]]

{[Deliver]}

'Hey, it seems I'm wanted. You want to come see the presidential box?'

'Man, I ain't goin' anywhere near that dumb-eyed cheatin' wind … '

'It's OK, the president isn't there today. We're just borrowing his place. It's cool, come over.'

'Listen, you are my new, old friend right? Lemme tell you something you need to know. You come close to that slimeshit an' you gonna get touched. You better play it very cool with el presidento.' He stood up. 'Anyway, I got another set here in fifteen an' then a gig crosSlab in ToNight UpSide. I gotta go. If you feel like it, come over later. Just ask for me.'

'It's OK if I bring someone?'

'Who? That Kiki-chan? She is one fine piece of late-night entertainment, an' I'm not lyin'. Yeah you bring her along, maybe I get myself a new manager too, huh? But she's gonna be lookadat wanna-know 'cos I threw a privacy field around me when I left the stage man an' she is gonna be bustin' to know what we been talking about.'

'Yeah, well, I don't think I'll be able to remember much. Must be this shiff you gave me.'

'You know man? You an' me, we're going to get along!'

Dielle was pretty sure he was right.

When he got back to the presidential box there was a party in progress. Dielle guessed there were a couple of hundred people in there [[178]] with just enough room for the few more who were pushing past from the transvex behind him. He could see Kiki in the middle, laughing. She enjoyed being the centre of attention. She glowed.

'Hello handsome,' said a sultry voice close behind him. 'Are you avoiding me or is Tiger holding your leash too tight?'

Dielle knew who it was without looking. He could feel her curves pressing against his body. They were the type of curves a six-day-old twenty-seven-year-old guy doesn't forget. Ever.

'Ms Van Darwin,' said Dielle without turning round. 'What a pleasure.'

'Yes, it will be,' breathed Faith-Sincere, getting even closer.

'I didn't return your messages because I, er,' Dielle hesitated, desperately trying to think of something witty and subtly suggestive. He gave up. 'Because I didn't know what to say.'

'How charming!' He could feel her breath against the back of his neck, making the hairs stand up involuntarily for the second time that afternoon. This time they were accompanied. 'Old fashioned honesty. So refreshing.'

'Do you think that Kiki would approve of us being so honest with each other?' asked Dielle, trying to sound obvious, but still not turning round.

'Approve? She sent me the basic terms of the deal earlier, otherwise I don't think the vex would have allowed me through, do you?'

'What deal?' asked Dielle, turning around angrily. 'Don't I get a say at all?'

'Oh, you do, but I don't,' said Faith, her eyes flashing danger. 'The only deal she's offering gives me no edit rights before sumecast, no share in any residuals and no distribution control.'

'What does all that mean?'

'It means, my beautiful, handsome boy, that the only reason I would fuck you is for love.'

Dielle looked her up and down. He was fighting hard not to reach out to touch the curves of her hips. Her long, flowing hair contrasted boldly with the tight, dark silk of her bodice. 'And that means?' he said trying not to sound strangled.

'Darling,' she snarled, looking him in the eyes with a desire he could practically smell. 'Do you know how long it's been since I fucked a man for love?'

'I couldn't even … '

'One hundred and twenty of your miserable, primitive Earth years!' she said, raising her voice and swivelling on her pin-sharp stilettos. 'Tell your so-called agent that the Universe will be a singularity in non-space before Faith-

Sincere Van Darwin gets subSumed by a second-rate, two-bit Wobbler!'

'You are talking about the woman I love!' protested Dielle, worried that he might be sounding less than genuine.

'Ha! Love? You're still in diapers and you're talking about love? We'll see about that!' And with a toss of her animated hair she stormed off, disappearing through the transvex. He turned sheepishly back to the room hoping that no-one had noticed. Somebody let out a high-pitched gasp then everyone started applauding and cheering enthusiastically. Unfortunately for Dielle, none of them were watching the race. Kiki had tears in her eyes.

The party fizzled seconds after the last race was won. Dielle had lost track of how many people he'd met who were delighted with the result of his encounter with Faith-Sincere, or *the entertainment* as they were calling it, but he hadn't had the opportunity to broach the subject with Kiki.

'I had no idea she was that old,' Dielle said to Kiki as she flopped down, exhausted, on a form chair. 'Why does everyone hate her so much?'

'Because she runs the most successful chain of ego massage parlours onSlab, is the highest paid ego therapist with the most exclusive client list and she has the single most expensive body in the known universe,' said Kiki, taking off her high boots.

'Ego massage?'

'Dielle! Dahling!' said Kiki with sparkling eyes and a scary smile. 'We were just talking about you! How much we all missed you! You are looking just great! Oh it's so wonderful you came into our little parlour when there are so many to choose from. Have you been working out? You look even better than last time you came in and that's really hard to believe. Sit your sweet, gorgeous body down while Samantha here gets you something to drink and waggles her plastic tits five centimetres from your face.'

'Right. I see,' said Dielle. 'But that doesn't explain why everyone dislikes her.'

'That's because they all secretly use her so-called therapy but refuse to admit it. So much so that they go out of their way to put her down. It's like a SlabWide sport among the rich and famous. That and the fact that she really is a two-faced, professionally disingenuous, artificially enhanced from spleen to pore bitch.'

'She speaks highly of you,' lied Dielle.

'She speaks highly of anyone who pays her to speak highly of them,' said Kiki with venom. 'And I know for sure that doesn't include me.'

'Is there something I should know about? Something in the past between you two?'

'The only thing you should know about is that she wants to fuck you because she wants the publicity and demands complete control over the sume edit, no doubt to hide her sagging million-bucks-a-piece breasts. Also, that she's just formally dropped negotiations and that's fine because we don't need her sorry ass.'

Dielle thought it prudent not to tell Kiki that whatever the reasons Faith-Sincere had for pulling out of the deal, breast-sag wasn't one of them. It was odd, but despite being very unsure about his lover/agent negotiating who should and shouldn't get an opportunity to romp around naked with him, the fact that Faith-Sincere had decided not to agree a deal made him want her more. That, he thought, might become a problem. A change of subject seemed in order.

'Are you tired?' he asked, rubbing Kiki's feet.

'A bit. Why, darling?'

'Because I met this really cool musician called Fingerz Jeez and he's playing somewhere later and I thought we might go and see him. I think I want to learn how to play the keys and he said he thought I'd be good at it, if I can, er, find out who I am, or something.'

'Fingerz Jeez? Never heard of him.' A millisecond

pause. 'Oh right, he's playing in Rick's Bar in TorryTown. That's UpSide night strip. Do you want to go out to a night, darling? That'll be fun. We haven't been to one yet.'

'Not if you're too tired,' said Dielle. The massage had moved higher up and he was starting to go off the idea of going out.

Kiki brightened almost instantly. 'No, I'm fine dear! I just emtied some Buzz and I'm keen to go. Learn the keys, huh? That could generate a nice sideline. Just let me get my things.'

She sprang up, picked up her boots and threw them into an emti hovering nearby, then reached in and took out a pair of comfortable flats.

{[Buzz?]}

[[Popular non-addictive stimulant. Increases the body's metabolic rate and neutralises fatigue poisons]]

{[Can I have some?]}

[[No. You don't need any]]

{[What? Aren't you supposed to do as I ask?]}

[[Who gave you that idea?]]

'Hey!' he called to Kiki. 'I thought Sis was supposed to give me anything I asked for.'

'Who gave you that idea?' asked Kiki, waiting at the transvex. 'Come on. We'll be late for the first set.'

Dielle was thoughtful during the descent from the spectator platform to the tube system. Once they were on their way in a tube privacy field he tested a line of enquiry with Sis but didn't get very far. They were routed crosSlab to a Z-axis conduit, part of the tube system that linked the two downs. The e-zee was built into the wall that separated Seacombe from The Strip and day from night and acted like an express elevator. At midpoint their bubble went through a split-second of weightlessness and flipped over but were it not for a slight discontinuity in Kiki's shower, it would have been completely undetectable.

'I think you might want to check the type of music

Fingerz plays,' Dielle said to Kiki as she shimmied into a form-fitting dance suit. She paused for a moment, looked at him, longazed and wrinkled her nose.

'Is that the type of music you want to learn to play?' she said, getting undressed again and pulling a loose fitting dress and a belt from her bag.

'Sure! If I can. That is, if I have any talent.'

'You'll need to get a stim unit if you want to avoid tens of cykes of practice.'

'Yeah, he mentioned that. Though Sis has just given me the impression there was something questionable about learning that way.'

'It's just the purists, dear. They give neg about technology that avoids having to do hard work but of course you don't see them walking from days to nights. Just because you can learn how to play any musical instrument in a few hours with a good stim, doesn't mean your skills aren't just as valid as doing it the old fashioned way. I'll give PT a ping if you like, although after you bent his nose I'm not sure he'll be so hungry for the commission.'

Dielle wasn't keen to see PT again either.

The tube deposited them in a busy public area with a black sky. Black, that is, aside from a galaxy of gaudy neon, holo-projections and mobile glowtubes. The place was packed with people of every size, shape, sex and genetic line pushing and bustling to get around. And it was noisy. Blaring music overlapped with over-amplified hawker-calls, hysterical shrieking, blackboardfingernail scrapes, random explosions, hyper-bic-annoying jingles and a cacophony of bells, beeps, whistles and klaxons.

'This is more like it!' shouted Dielle, excited. 'I wondered where everyone was. I guess most people spend a lot of time in the night sections, huh?'

'No, not especially, it's just the way The Strip was designed,' Kiki shouted back, pulling him through a torrent of people. 'More like a street thing back on Earth. All the tube vexes come out onto walkways. No dedicated access points, so you're forced to get off and find where you want to go on foot. One of the problems with the private tube ports we have at home is that unless you deliberately go into public areas, you hardly ever see anyone. So the designers retroed to this type of environment – makes for more random interaction. It's called social engineering.'

Dielle immediately felt at home. He looked up. A floating platform eclipsed the sky, its underside lighting up the faces of the people below with a scene from an actionsume. When he looked at it he could hear the voices of the performers and the sound effects clearly, but the moment he looked away the sound faded into the background. The platform moved on to reveal a cross-hatch of lights high above: DownSideUp at play.

Kiki dragged him into a smaller laneway off the main thoroughfare. Silence surrounded them like a soft cloak. A dim light illuminated the unmarked door of the club Sis had been directing her to. They entered a narrow reception corridor lined with changing rooms and heard the sound of a spirited crowd coming from the far end where a handsome blond man in a white three-piece suit intercepted them.

TorryTown was the centre of excellence for live music onSlab and Rick's Bar was one of the clubs that had been there for so long that it wasn't even reconfigurable. The tiered rows of tables with their semicircles of plush seating and red tasseled table-lights had been replaced more than thirty times during the club's history, always with exact replicas of the originals, which were themselves exact replicas of a club that had only existed on a film set long before mankind had discovered escape velocity. You knew you had made it as a musician when you had a regular gig in one of the top clubs in TorryTown and you knew you had made it as a music aficionado when you were allowed into a club like Rick's Bar.

'I'm sorry, but we have no reservation for any Pundechan or Dielle,' the white suited man said without any discernible nuance. 'Are you perhaps guests of an existing patron?'

'Fingerz Jeez told me to mention his name,' said Dielle, stepping toward him.

'Please don't come any closer, sir,' said the vexman, showing Dielle the palm of his white glove. 'We have a transparent vex at this entrance that is not yet configured for your transit.'

Dielle backed off fast. He hadn't forgotten his last bloody nose.

'Mr Marley is performing tonight, but he hasn't made any guest requests and he's not responding to my pings. I'm sorry sir, madam, but unless … '

'Do you know who you are talking to?' snarled Kiki.

Blondie gave her a withering look. 'Madam, do you think there is the slightest possibility that I don't?'

'Well, do something!' Kiki was obviously not accustomed to being delayed. She muttered under her breath: 'Bloody Uppies! Think they're better than us.'

'I have dispatched a club runner to find Mr Marley. Apparently he is not currently on the premises and has dropped off system presence awareness.'

'Dropped off?' said Dielle, surprised. 'I didn't know you could do that.'

'All the night sections have dead zones, sir. Many people come here for that sole purpose.'

'Well override it then!' ordered Kiki. 'You can't imprison us here just because some deadbeat muso is so out of his head he forgot to put our names on his guest list. Do you know where we were today? The presidential box at the skimmer races!'

'Madam, you are not imprisoned, you are free to turn around and leave the club.' He held her fuming gaze with no perceptible emotion. 'And I am free to initiate a lateral vex translation if you should choose to stay where you are and continue to behave like a spoiled Sider brat.'

'WHAT?' raged Kiki, banging her fists against the invisible barrier. 'I'll have your job on a fucking stick you nobrain windfarming trashgene leafblowing son of a b… '

And then they were outside again, expelled by an unseen moving wall like a plunger in a syringe.

'That was fun!' said Dielle, laughing. 'You really taught him a lesson.'

Kiki threw him an angry look, breathing heavily.

'You know you look really sexy when you're angry,' said Dielle, getting close.

She fell asleep in his arms on the way home. Dielle looked down on her flushed face and gently stroked her hair. He replayed the day's events in his head.

[[•]]

{[?]}

[[You are accessing recent events, do you wish to see highlights of your day's activity?]]

{[I can do that?]}

[[Of course. However, I don't have a reliable behavioural heuristogram for your diary review so I'll use average preferences for a male of your bio-age]]

{[OK, but leave out the falling off the mountain bit, will you?]} He'd seen that too many times already.

As he watched a fast edit of his day, a thought occurred to him. {[Can I contact Louie?]}

[[He is currently in full privacy mode. Do you want to leave a message?]]

{[Can you just let him know that I want to see him?]}

[[••]]

{[Can you tell me where he's been and what he's been doing?]}

[[All of Louis Drago's activities since he left your presence are completely locked down and embargoed]]

{[That's a bit unusual isn't it?]}

[[••]]

Dielle couldn't be sure but he thought he sensed an overtone in that affirmative ping, like a different flavour of thought. Something was definitely going on. He needed to piece a few things together. He needed some more advice, and he suspected it was probably the kind of advice he could only get in a dead zone. But first, he thought, as he watched himself getting energetic with Kiki in a dark corner of a TorryTown alley, he needed to get some sleep.

seventeen

Louis Clinton Drago had been born into a broken world. Exactly eighty years later, during the Bacchanalian extremes of his farewell party, just before his body was ceremonially placed into cryonic suspension, he reflected on the fact that he'd done absolutely nothing in his entire life to fix it. He couldn't have cared less.

He'd grown up in a place called the Bronx; an old fashioned, mainly residential suburb of what later became the upper-eastern googopolis of the North American continent. Despite, or maybe because of the fact that he was short and not particularly good looking, he had lived a varied and sybaritic life. Married three times and divorced twice, his last wife, twenty years his junior, had run off with his mistress's son when he was sixty-four. He didn't give a damn.

He'd fathered two children, which was the maximum he qualified for no matter how many times he married, but neither of his daughters nor any of his former wives would talk to him other than through paid intermediaries or with a lawyer present. He didn't care about that either.

Known throughout his neighbourhood for his intrusive energy, acerbic wit, business acuity and loud mouth, he'd lived the last forty years of his first life in an ostentatious house he'd had built over the bulldozed remains of the grocer's shop he was born above. He had driven the bulldozer himself.

He had worked hard and played even harder. By the time he was seventy-five he was pornographically wealthy, had visited everywhere he had any desire to visit, had experienced as many risky and thrilling experiences as he could endure and had variously drunk, eaten or inhaled as many legal, semi-legal or wildly illegal substances as his robust constitution could tolerate. He literally had been there, seen it, done it and stubbornly refused to buy any t-shirts, postcards or anything that would ever require dusting.

Louie couldn't figure out why he hadn't become a hologram sooner. He never got tired or hungry and had no bodily functions to tend to. He felt no pain or discomfort; in fact, he felt nothing at all, no gravity, no temperature, no body mass to haul around and feed with energy and no air pressure bearing down on him. Feeling nothing felt great.

He found that he could concentrate for hours without any sense of time passing, which was ideal for someone who had been born with an insatiable hunger for any information that could be leveraged to his advantage. So while Council debated whether or not to let him into their exclusive club and engineers ran complex simulation scenarios using emti relays to break through Slab's own defence system, he indulged himself. He gorged on data.

He built complex enquiry threads to mine Slab's archives and backed up any intelligence he considered particularly useful into his on-board memory. He knew he didn't *really* need to store anything locally because, assuming he would always be connected to Sis, he'd have continuous access to anything he wanted to know. But a long time ago Louie had learned never to assume anything.

While he knew that the information Sis provided was useful, experience told him that the really valuable stuff would only be discovered by accident. He needed to talk to people. Louie enjoyed talking. He was good at it and liked to think he had a gift. *Talking at* came naturally to him, *listening to* however, was a skill he'd worked hard to perfect. Listening took a lot of effort and he needed to find just the right place to meet people who would be worth listening to. A little research was required.

The main night section, The Strip, was devoted to

entertainment of every imaginable variety and several unimaginable ones. This was where the SlabCitizens went to socialise, party, lose themselves and abandon inhibitions. It was noisy, intoxicating and, in the dead zones, potentially dangerous. Safety, like everything else, was a matter of personal preference and some people liked living on the edge. The Strip had plenty of edges and Louie briefly considered making his base there but he was sick of trying to extract the truth from the unending bullshit that was the inevitable consequence of excess and drug induced delusions.

The other night section, called *Smith,* was primarily a dormitory. While most of Slab's citizenry preferred to have their sleeping areas attached directly to their daylight homes, many others preferred to sleep with the window open. The concept had at first seemed absurd for a space-faring population, but once voiced, the idea gained widespread support. Most of Smith was designed as moonlit countryside with murmuring streams, winding paths and secluded glades. Bijou bungalows, chalets and thatched cottages dotted the hillsides. It even once had talking squirrels but they'd been deactivated after residents complained about the sporadic sounds of gunfire.

Despite the nauseating tweeness, many people chose to live in daylight apartments but sleep in Smith, travelling by tube while catching up on the evening sumes, taking a shower or a relaxing soak depending on how long the bedtime commute was. Even those who had qualified to be full-time parents and elected to live with their children often slept apart from them in the adults-only Smith woodlands. Undisturbed sleep was an unalienable right of every SlabCitizen. Good luck to them, thought Louie. He had no use for sleep or sleepy people.

The original day section, Seacombe, was old. This was where the administrators, the business types, the money people and the movers and shakers hung out. In Seacombe it was considered *modern* to have apartments that had been designed hundreds of cycles ago and it was *ultra-modern* to have at least one artefact that had originated on Earth. This was where the wealthy and powerful lived when they weren't in their summer homes. These were the people who were getting impatient about the technical delays that kept them from their winter lodges. They even had *seasons* and would spend a cycle or two in Seacombe and then migrate (usually en-masse, in co-ordination with their social circle) to Mitchell.

Mitchell was the summer section and was supposed to be used exclusively for leisure. Current social lore held it impolite to even discuss business there, although the habit of moving and shaking is not something that can be easily removed or shaken off for most Seacombers.

Louie was indifferent. He had always hated the type of people who used golf as a game of power-broking and he despised the idea of building networks of *friends* who swapped favours and patronage. He knew where his real friends were. They were dead.

As far as Louie was concerned, there was only one place that held any real attraction for him: The Spin.

The Spin was a mess. Everyone knew that. It was supposed to be mess. That's why it worked. The Spin was where 90% of Slab's intellectual property creation, inventing, directing, designing, philosophising, writing, programming, performing and ideas generation originated. The other 10% came from The Valley which formed the cylindrical lining of the Slab section called Big Yin in which The Spin span.

The Spin was like someone had taken the national foods from two dozen different cultures, rammed them onto a skewer and left them to roast slowly over an open fire. Only, the skewer was a 355-kilometre-long triple helix which ran the entire width of Slab and rotated once a day, the fire was a 200-metre-wide sunstrip which cycled between bright sunshine and full-moon and the chunks of food were huge, buzzing cities. Every culture from Earth had its own district, town, precinct, province, state, chome, canton or arrondissement. Every detail of architecture, cuisine, entertainment and behaviour was respected and celebrated. The Spin was where people lived, worked, drank, ate, loved, argued and prosumed – often simultaneously. It was a 10/100 spinning conurbation of ideas and human energy suspended above a fourteen-kilometre-wide valley of verdant green.

Spin inhabitants didn't care about upsides, downsides, sideways or waysides and the vast, sprawling collection of fluctuating urban centres reflected this. Every building, platform and walkway had its own gravity generator and local down and everything evolved and revolved around the rotating core.

When people moved apartments or offices, they usually did just that: moved them to somewhere further along the helix, chasing the ideas which were the currency and life-blood of The Spin. This was a truly mobile society. Fashionable areas blossomed overnight and declined just as quickly when tides of apartments, work places, amenities and people flowed from place to place.

Getting between the rat's nest of buildings, whether at opposite ends of the helix or just next door, often entailed such a complex routing via switch-backs, stairs, bridges and tubes that most people preferred to travel by bug; small grav-controlled multi-coloured vehicles that flitted around like clouds of day-glo midges.

The Spin was home to over twelve million people and as far as Louie was concerned, this was where the action was. All knowledge onSlab was ubiquitous and free, manufacturing was automated and most basic services, excluding the performance-based arts like cooking and waitressing, were handled by Sis. So creativity, ideas and talent were the only games in town.

He selected a conspicuous table outside a popular café in central SpinStanbul and set himself up.

OfficeLouie consisted of Louie, two Sis-connected screens that only he could read, and a permanently full pitcher of cold beer for anyone who wanted to stop and talk. He had already managed to persuade the café owner that he should have these facilities free of charge, based on his estimation of the level of increased publicity the bar would gain from having the only fully interactive holographic citizen from 21st century Earth as a resident. He was continuing negotiations for a split of the increased profit that would be generated by his presence and had suggested that they change the name to Louie's Bar. This hadn't gone down too well with the owner as the place had been known throughout Spin as The Plywood Café for nearly a hundred cykes. But he'd only been there for about half a Spin rotation. He had time.

It didn't take long for him to make new friends. Louie was hard to ignore, even if he was made entirely of projected light. He had styled himself as a business gurulla during most of his life back on Earth and money-making ideas came easily to him. He was dictating some of them to a screen when Dielle found him.

'Why have you been ignoring my messages?'

Louie reluctantly looked up. 'Why have you been sending them?'

'Because I need to see you.'

'That's why.'

'Are you planning on being an asshole forever?'

'What d'you think I am, some kind of lackey you can just summon like a genie from a bottle?'

'Now you come to mention it …'

'Listen. Get this straight kid. I'm you. I have the same personality as you, I'm just older and a lot more experienced and I don't give a shit about your messages, OK? Would you if you were me … which you are?'

Dielle thought about that for a minute.

'OK.' He noticed the pitcher. 'Is the beer cold?'

'No. I have them warm it up especially for greengages like you.'

'Look. Get this straight, old man. I'm you. I'm just a lot younger with less bloodymindedness which I am seriously hoping is not an inevitable consequence of getting old. I'm fit and healthy and have enough credits to do almost anything I want. I have better things to do than waste my time listening to an asshole like you and I'm not going to stick around if you keep it up. Would you if you were me? Which you were, once, a long time ago.'

Louie thought about that for a moment.

'So leave,' said Louie, turning his attention to two happy, smiling girls on the next table who had just realised who Dielle was.

Dielle shook his head bitterly. 'Fuck you. I will.'

'Oh sit down. Don't be so sensitive. I don't know where you get that from, I was never sensitive,' said Louie, waving his hand toward an empty chair while throwing the girls a lecherous smile.

'Somehow,' said Dielle, 'I can believe that.'

'Have a beer and tell me what you want.'

'Who said I wanted anything?'

Louie looked at him with wide eyes. 'Shit!' he said incredulously. 'I may be just a projection but you're completely transparent.'

'They don't use that word here anymore. They don't do it either,' said Dielle, sitting down and removing a cold glass from the emti space in the side of the beer pitcher. 'I'll keep this short because I can see you're really busy.' He looked over at the girls who gave him a familiar smile. 'I think I need your help to re-negotiate my deal with Kiki.'

'You mean the Kiki you were banging last night down a dark alleyway?'

'You know about that, huh?'

'I can't decide if watching a younger version of me getting a fine piece of ass is perverted or not.'

'I can. You're a pervert.'

'So you're screwing your manager and you think she's doing the same to you, huh?'

'I really, really hate to ask this.'

'I bet.'

Dielle took a long swig of beer and sat back, looking at Louie. Louie couldn't drink beer. He stared back at Dielle. Dielle took another long, slow drink.

'I should make you do this yourself. The experience would be good for you.'

'I don't need the experience. I'm never going to be like you.'

'What are you going to be like then?'

'Well, first off, I'm going to get a stim-unit fitted and then I'm going to learn how to play keys and then I'm going to make music that's so good it would make your toes curl, if you had any toes.'

'Music?' Louie snorted. 'You? Me? You're crazy!'

Dielle waggled his fingers at Louie. 'I can do it.'

Louie looked at him with disappointment written all over his face. 'They were meant for basketball.'

'My hands, my choice. I'm going to be a musician. According to Slabscapedia, you spent your life making deals. I'm going to spend my life being the subject of deals. I'm already well known and I reckon I can turn my popularity into a career.' He turned to the two girls, who had been whispering to each other and gave them a big smile each. One of them smiled right back while the other waved over Dielle's shoulder at four excited girls who were hurrying toward them. He looked back at Louie and waited.

'You'd better let me see your contract.'

'I don't actually remember agreeing to anything precisely but I've told Sis to let you have access to anything you need.'

'OK, when do you want me to see miss cute-ass manager?'

'Look, I just want you to make sure I'm on the right deal. I don't want you to upset her.'

'I'll be all sweetness and light!' Louie raised his arms and eyebrows as if offended by the accusation. 'And I'll only be acting in my, that is our, best interests.'

Dielle looked at him and tried to calculate his options. 'Well I guess I can trust you. No-one lies to themselves, do they?'

'Oh boy! Do you have a lot to learn!'

'Well, just remember I love her. You'd better be considerate.'

Louie looked over to the table which now had six eager occupants and three more walking over from the nearest vexit. After spending a microsecond weighing up whether he should start renegotiating his deal with the Plywood Café owner now, he moved his vDek to the centre of the table.

'I'll consider everything, don't worry about it. I'll ping you tomorrow.'

Dielle nodded, getting worried.

Louie said 'Sixty-two' out loud to no-one in particular and disappeared into the emti chamber on the side of the beer pitcher.

Damn! thought Dielle, peering into the chamber, I forgot to ask him about the council stuff.

[[•]]

{{[?]}}

[[Message from President Plewo]]

{[later]}

[[••]]

{[Can you locate Fingerz Jeez for me and tell him I'd like to see him?]}

[[J. A. Marley is currently sleeping in a SideUp Mitchell cornfield. He has a privacy shield that is set to collapse just over two hours from now]]

{[Please leave a message asking if he'd like to join me for lunch here]}

[[••]]

Two hours? thought Dielle. What am I going to do with two hours?

'Hello ladies!' said Dielle, turning to the ever-growing crowd of young girls. 'My generous friend seems to have abandoned me with an auto-refill pitcher of cold beer. Now I don't know about here, but back on my planet it was considered bad form to drink alone.'

Of course, he had no idea if that was true, but neither did they.

eighteen

Sixty-two was the code Louie had pre-arranged with Sis to mean *anywhere but here*. He was finding it increasingly uncomfortable to spend any time around his younger self. Dielle's naiveté made him squirm. In this instance *anywhere but here* turned out to be a hanging garden attached to an outer edge of a bustling and vibrant jumble of haphazardly stacked apartments. Sis told him it was called Spingalore. If he had paid for olfac, he could have guessed.

Louie watched the valley floor move under his non-existent feet. The lush landscape that surrounded the rotating city was where the rich and famous lived, as far apart from each other as possible while still being close enough to make ostentatious signs of wealth worthwhile. The Valley was where every spinresident secretly dreamed of moving to after their genius had been recognised – but only, of course, to escape the unavoidable media attention and the unwelcome intrusions of hangers on, fans and *good friends*.

Thousands of bugs darted to and from the manicured grounds set into the woodlands and meadows that surrounded the spinning metropolis. The Valley was where normal people pretended to be wildly eccentric by spending fortunes on whimsical architectural experiments, interactive landscaped gardens and gaudy sound-sculptures while seriously stimmed-out people pretended to be normal by building faithful reproductions of ancient manor houses with tennis courts, swimming pools and gazebos. Every Valley resident lived with the constant reminder of the competition hanging over their heads. It gave meaning to their lives. So they said.

'It weirds me out. He's like the exact opposite of me,' Louie said to a small glowglobe that was floating near his eye-line.

'He has no memories and no experiences except those he has gained over the last five days,' said Sis. 'Think of him as a curious child who wants to explore his new life and be loved.'

'Yeah, a curious child with a grown up dick steering him around,' said Louie, waving his finger with inventive vulgarity.

'He'll get used to it soon enough. I think he's remarkably adaptable.'

Louie preened slightly. 'Yeah, I guess he's doing OK. I always was a survivor you know.'

'So it would appear. The NAHs are really looking forward to your talk about your career back on Earth when you've returned from FutureSlab.'

'You seem to be pretty confident I'll make it.'

'There is no doubt that you will survive.'

'How can you be so sure?'

'I will make a backup copy of your entire database before you are emtied forward. Even if your vDek doesn't make it back, all you will lose will be the memory of the trip, which the version of you left behind will not have experienced anyway.'

'No pain and no gain, huh?'

'You cannot technically experience pain yet, although programmers are confident they could add it to your stim interface if you so wished.'

'I was joking.'

'So was I.'

Louie watched a long line of sleek, black bugs head out to a distant mansion. Some things never change, he thought.

'What do you think FutureSlab is?' he asked.

'I don't think it's the future, but I don't think it's an alien artefact either.'

'So that leaves?'

'I'd rather not say, but I think we should leave it alone. It's not doing anyone any harm, is it?'

'You know that expression about sleeping dogs? We don't do that.'

'I have noticed that trait. That course of action is not always the wisest, however.'

'You said *when I get back from FutureSlab*. Have the council caved in to my demands?'

'Not yet, but they will.'

'Curiosity killed the cat, huh?'

'Quite so. Despite my advice, the interns are insisting on trying to determine their destiny.'

'That's an odd way of putting it. In my book, checking out a possible threat, arming yourself with valuable information and trying to figure out ways to screw them before they screw you are the basic tactics that got us out of the sludge. Everyone has those instincts, even the NAHs.'

'Especially the NAHs. But what if the investigation reveals a greater problem or the act of investigating itself sparks a damaging chain of events? Perhaps even a terminal event cascade.'

'Risk assessment is risky but risk avoidance is riskier.'

'Do you mind if I add that comment to the debate? You may claim full copyright over the phrase and all secondary usage.'

'Yeah, sure. I've been reading up on your whole intellectual property stuff. It's a lot more sophisticated than we ever managed to get working back home.'

'It is simple to aggregate and account for usage when you have a closed economic system based on completely attributable work along with statutory licensing and embedded, no-cost micro-payments.'

'Yeah, that's just what I was going to say.'

'What license structure do you wish to establish?'

'Everything I say and do is copyright me, OK? Including that. You use it, you pay.'

'Noted.'

'Tell the SlabCouncil that not taking risks is the riskiest thing you can do.'

'Done. That precise phrase, however, is credited to the estate of your ex-colleague, Milus Blondel.'

'I was just testing.'

'And that one.'

Louie shrugged. 'Any movement on my other conditions?'

'You'll be interested to hear that the NAHs have volunteered to form a basketball league.'

'That's no use. Everyone knows ex-presidents can't dunk.'

'NAHs have the ability to change body shape to suit the physical activity they are undertaking. I think you'll find they will make formidable opponents.'

'Woah ho!' said Louie, rubbing his hands together with glee. 'Now you're really gonna see something!' He set his vDek spinning around its central axis, which made his projection swing around wildly. As a display of excitement, it was the best he'd come up with so far but it needed perfecting – he kept travelling through the furniture, which spoiled the effect.

Sis waited for him to calm down. 'As far as I can ascertain, the only reason the NAHs are interested is because after watching ancient recordings they can't figure out why anyone would find the game interesting, which, if you are a NAH, is interesting in itself. They are inclined to plunder the infinitesimal depths of obscurity.'

'You gotta be there. There's nothing like a … ' The glowing ball flashed red to blue.

'Just a moment. Just a moment. Council have acceded to your demands. You will be given full SlabCouncil voting rights on your return from your explorations with your memories intact. There are, however, a series of conditions which you must agree to.'

'I expected as much. Let me have a look at them.'

'The first condition is that you are only allowed to know the other conditions after you have returned.'

Louie mulled this over. During his extensive business life he had been in some pretty tough and unusual negotiating positions, but none quite as bizarre as this one. He got an idea.

'Are you aware of all of the conditions?'

'Of course.'

'But you can't tell me what they are?'

'Sorry.'

'Then I have to ask you a question and depending on your answer, I will make my decision. But you must agree to answer me truthfully. OK?'

'Agreed, as long as you don't ask me to reveal the other conditions.'

'OK. Listen up: I have three choices; go, stay or re-negotiate. Each choice is written on a piece of paper and hidden inside one of three identical boxes. What's inside each of them is known only to you. I choose a box at random but don't open it. You then remove one of the two remaining boxes and allow me to change my mind but you have to ask a question of one of three NAHs first. The question is: *will the choice Louie made prevent him from being able to exercise full Council privileges for an indefinite period of time, should he not accept the secret conditions?* But here's the kicker: one NAH always tells the truth, one always lies and the third one lies 50% of the time but neither of us know which NAH asked the question. Would the answer the NAH relayed to me persuade me to select the other box?'

Sis's ball pulsed dark orange. A tiny tremor went through it, then it hung, silent and immobile.

For more than three hundred and fifty Earth years, as

Slab had vacuumed the vacuum of space, converting the basic building blocks of the universe into construction materials and mass-reactant for the anti-gravity drives, Sis had continually modified and improved on her own design. Using massively-parallel arrays of self-replicating nanoprocessors coupled to yottabytes of closed-loop-redundant, multi-mirrored, meta-quantised data cores, Sis had woven herself into the fabric of Slab, right down to the molecular level. To all intents and purposes, she was everywhere and in everything, all-seeing, all-knowing and invulnerable. No single part of the system could be isolated and identified as critical to system integrity and no amount of damage, short of the complete annihilation of Slab, could prevent her from functioning. Sis simultaneously ran every onSlab system, from the dust sensor embedded into the u-design auto-grow happiRug that surrounded the slumber platform of six-year-old Henrietta Nice-one Tattershall III in NightNight SideUp sleepcentre complex 345(b) to the boson-spin synchronisers balancing the anti-gravity drives which were even now straining to accelerate over 180 billion megatonnes of spaceship closer to the speed of light without hitting anything bigger than a hydrogen atom.

SlabWide Integrated System, if it could possibly be defined as a single entity, was undoubtedly the most sophisticated machine-based mind that had ever existed, anywhere, ever. At a conservative estimate, Sis was at least three hundred billion times more powerful than the human brain.

Sis pondered Louie's question for 2.78906 seconds, which by an odd coincidence was exactly the time it took her to mathematically simulate the creation and expansion of the universe from a hypothetical big bang until the present day.

'I have no idea.'

Louie smiled. 'That's dupe. Let's do it.'

'But I said I didn't know.'

'Exactly!' said Louie floating his vDek over to a nearby emtitrash. 'And the sooner we get this thing done, the sooner we'll be abusing the backboards – and the council.'

Louie materialised inside a cage of bent wire at the bottom of a cavernous chamber lit by a central point of brilliant white light. The cage was fixed to a rostrum surrounded by workbenches filled with tools and prototypes. There were three glum-looking NAHs dressed in lab coats waiting for him.

'I have to say I'm quite surprised how quickly the Council gave in to your demands, sir,' said a familiar voice above him.

Louie looked up as Erik floated down from a transvex high on the curved wall.

'Yeah, seeing as how they had no options, it was almost cruel to take their money,' said Louie, turning his eyes to the pinpoint of bright light. 'What's that?'

'The Universe, sir.'

'Huh?'

'This chamber is one of two that holds an exact holographic projection of our universe as we currently know it. It's now at maximum crunch to save on computational space. Would you like to see the simulation in action? It's rather good.'

'Sure, why not?'

The light exploded into a hundred billion points of light.

'Wow!' said Louie, dropping his customary sardonicism. 'Which one is good old Sol, then?'

'No sir, you are mistaken, these are not stars, each of those pinpoints is a galaxy. Earth's sun is in a galaxy over there.' Erik directed Louie's attention to a distant sector which started to expand into clusters of tiny bright spirals and clouds of dust and gas. One of the spirals in the centre grew and filled the room with stars. The view continued to zoom in and spin around the core of the Milky Way then shoot away from the centre, curving out along a spiral arm. Millions of stars flew past at dizzying speeds. The point of view turned back to the receding core and slowed to a relative crawl. It all looked vaguely familiar. Here were the constellations Louie recognised. The same ones he'd spent nights studying in atlases as a kid under the star-blind skies of the metropolis. He could name most of them.

'That's our local neighbourhood. Sol is a hundred and fifty-six light years behind us.'

'It doesn't look any different from how I remember it,' said Louie, disappointed. 'We've been travelling for over three hundred years and nothing's changed? Are you sure we can't we go any faster? We'll never get there at this rate.'

'While we are fairly certain we can't do it with our current belief system, there is renewed hope. This new emti projection technology has the potential to reveal a lot more about our galaxy than we've been able to glean through our static observatories. We've already started mapping local solar systems by sending recording probes out through projected emti relay lines. Nothing much to report yet, but we're hopeful.'

'Hopeful of what?'

'Finding other intelligent life.'

'You mean more intelligent.'

'Precisely. A race that can sell us the technology we haven't been able to invent for ourselves.'

'I thought they'd found you.'

'Oh yes. The war. I fear it is not easy to buy advanced space drives from the enemy.' Erik changed the subject. 'Let me show you the progress we've made with the emti array we'll be using.' The view zoomed in to show FutureSlab and Slab in line astern. A twinkling lattice of red dots connected by fine red lines appeared around the rear of FutureSlab like a massive bowl of invisible cut-glass that could only be seen when its edges refracted the light. The fragile network was changing and dynamically re-configuring itself as tens of thousands of emti relays flashed in and out of existence. It was joined to Slab by an umbilical cord – a spiralling filigree of pulsating red threads anchored to a ring of high-powered emti transmitters surrounding the matter collectors on Slab's leading face.

'The red dots are the current positions of the projected emties which are in a holding position on the perimeter of the FutureSlab auto-defence system. The lines are active transmissions, all of which are currently only carrying more emti relays.' As Louie watched, several thousand winked out of existence and a quarter of the bowl collapsed. 'As you can see, FutureSlab is targeting them and taking them out almost as fast as we can replace them, but we can't afford to move further out, otherwise you'll materialise somewhere inside the Natalite.'

Louie sucked at his lip as he watched half of the remaining network spontaneously fail. 'Comforting.'

'We have three distinct tasks. The first is to maintain a constantly replenished network of relays, just outside the secure event space of the defence system which will then momentarily establish an array of very high-power emti projectors just above the surface of FutureSlab. Second, we have to transmit you through fifty kilometres of Natalite without frying your circuits. And third, we have to maintain the array long enough for you to investigate the contents of FutureSlab and then retrieve you via a secure, picosecond-lived, one-way receiver.'

'Not at all risky then.'

'We have no way of knowing what to expect once you get there, so we're going to transfer your programme into this.' Erik pointed to a rugged-looking cube sitting by a toolbox. It was about five times the size of his vDek and looked like it had been built to withstand nuclear attack. 'It's equipped with pretty much everything we can imagine you'll need: wide-spectrum electromagnetic sensors, atmospheric samplers, ultra high-power gravity shields, stealth everything and a few pin missiles too – purely for self-defence, of course. Your programming will be updated on transfer so you will already know how to use it all.'

Louie looked at his new home suspiciously. 'And you've managed to invent all this in the last few days, I suppose.'

'Most of it is repurposed from the military. We've removed all of the more obvious offensive armaments. Don't want any internal security systems thinking you might be a threat, do we?'

Louie considered this for a moment.

'Are you ready to try it out?' asked Erik.

'Sure, go right ahe … woah!' Louie watched his old vDek fall to the floor of the cage with a clang and knew instantly that his capacity had been increased a thousand-fold. He felt like he'd just been given the electronic version of a five year course of steroids. He tried his infra-red and microwave sensors first.

'It's considered impolite to do that, sir,' said Erik, aware that Louie was examining the NAH's internal structures.

'Right, sorry, excuse me. Just wanted to test some stuff out.' Louie hovered above the workbench for a moment, then shot up to the ceiling, careened off the roof and hurtled around the perimeter of the projection space. His systems told him the room was 2.876567 kilometres in diameter and spherical to a tolerance +/- 0.0001%. Before he noticed, he had reached supersonic speeds so he throttled back.

'Yeeeeeeeeee! Ha!' screamed Louie as he threw his new home into a 25G turn and headed straight back toward the cage, breaking at the last minute and scattering the NAHs who had been observing him with unconcealed fear.

'I like it!' said Louie. 'I'll take two! Have you got it in green?'

'Any colour you like, as long as it's black.'

'And they say NAHs have no sense of humour.'

'It's called *extra-black*. Once you activate stealth mode, you become invisible and undetectable in every wavelength.' said a lab-coated NAH. 'It is imperative that you give this unit an exhaustive trial, sir. Once you are inside FutureSlab you will be far beyond Sis's support horizon. You must be completely self-reliant because there is no possibility of rescue.'

Erik was visibly distressed by this concept. It didn't worry Louie, he was used to being self-reliant. In fact, he thrived on it. Being alone and isolated without a safety net didn't hold the same fear for him as it did for the SlabCitizens who had lived every moment of their lives under Sis's watchful eyes.

'Yeah, no problem. What d'you wanna do?'

'Well drop you out here,' said one of the NAHs who had been tinkering with the emti projection cage, pointing to the close-up of Slab above them and a small red dot out to one side. 'We'll track your progress and as long as you stay within a thousand klicks or so, we should be able to collect you if anything goes wrong.'

'OK, let's take this baby for a spin!'

The NAHs all thought this was incredibly funny and fell about laughing.

'Spin!' said Erik, spluttering. 'That's a good one!'

Louie did the holographic equivalent of tapping his foot in a weary, I'm-waiting-here-while-you're-burning-daylight sort of way.

When Milus Blondel, his erstwhile partner, had originally discovered matter transmission he was often quoted as saying *it's all in the spin* in an attempt to explain how it worked while being vague and mysterious. The truth was, as only Louie and a handful of others knew, Milus hadn't had the slightest clue as to how it was done – he just knew, beyond the shadow of a doubt, that it could be done and that was enough to drive his research until he'd managed to reliably duplicate the phenomenon. Years later, in a particularly pointless attempt at post-rationalisation, Milus had paid a crackpot scientist to come up with a woefully incomplete theory about *randomly synchronised spins* and *spin memory* which, for some curious reason, no-one had ever attempted to rubbish. I guess they must have figured it out by now, thought Louie, watching the NAHs hold their sides. It's probably got nothing to do with spin.

The true reason the NAHs were laughing was because they knew that virtually everything in the universe existed solely because of spin and that Milus had been both simultaneously presciently right and moronically wrong. NAHs had a finely tuned appreciation of irony.

Patience was not Louie's strong point. 'Can we get on with it?' he said.

The framework on the podium came to life.

'This,' said a still-chuckling NAH, pointing at the quasi-physical frame, 'is an unrestricted, dedicated emti which is now tuned precisely to your exact constituent parts. It will transmit your Military Grade vDek and *only* your Military Grade vDek. If you were to absorb or be impregnated with anything larger than a proton while you were testing it out, neither it nor you would be returned to this space.'

'And what then? You just leave me out there? You guys really are paranoid.'

'It's important for you to realise, sir,' said Erik in full diplomatic mode, 'that Slab is a contained and secure environment. It's not like the planet you were raised on, vulnerable to any old space debris or interstellar bio-vectors. For millennia the only thing that protected your species from space-borne viruses or being wiped out of existence by multi-megaton collisions, was a tissue-thin membrane of atmosphere. Air, for Dicesake! It's a wonder you ever managed to get out of the primordial soup.'

'We have no way of telling what you might encounter in FutureSlab,' said another NAH. 'For all we know, they're just sitting waiting for us so they can trick us into bringing something catastrophic back through our own defences.'

'A Trojan horse the size of an atom?'

'Precisely.'

'OK, I take it back. You guys aren't paranoid, you're crazy'

'How do you mean?'

'You think an alien race with the technology to replicate your spaceship down to the last external detail and place it in your path, exactly matching your course and speed, would need to wait to plant a virus inside us? I'd be more worried about mega-zappo annihilators if I were you.'

'But if they had the capacity to destroy us, they would have already done it if that was their intention. They haven't done so, therefore they either can't or they don't want to damage Slab. Maybe they just want *us* dead so they can take over Slab intact.'

Louie knew that arguing with paranoids was futile, but he couldn't break his compulsion to make everyone see things his way. However, he also had a very short deferment tolerance.

'OK, OK. Just don't leave me out there forever, alright?'

'Of course not!' said Erik, horrified at the idea. 'We would simply have to come up with a way of transferring your clean data into a new MGV before we vaporise that one.'

Louie manoeuvred into the framework and settled in the centre. 'I feel like I should be holding my breath or something,' he said. 'Go on, hit the juice.'

Then he was outside, instantly aware that he was looking at Slab from a distance of 50.00004 kilometres. The MGV's data collection routines ramped up as his systems probed Slab over the entire electromagnetic spectrum and analysed the vacuum of space around him in single parts per billion. He accelerated to his top speed of almost 10,000 kilometres per hour and went exploring. There was not much to see, but that didn't stop him from having fun.

Louie had lived a very full life back on Earth. He'd done just about everything he could think of at least once but he couldn't remember anything to equal this. Within seconds he'd reached the nearest edge of Slab and he knew, to fifteen decimal places, how long it would take him to get to the other side. He analysed the surface for impurities and inspected for micro-pitting as he traversed the flat, black plane, then he headed aft where he expected to find traces of the original ship that had been built in Earth orbit.

When Louie had bought his one-way ticket to the future, Galactic Conveyor ISS 001 was still in its early design stages but he'd done a lot of research before putting himself into cryonic suspension. The initial design had three roughly equal sections: engines, life support and habitation. The plan was to take on mass as quickly as possible and build out the ship as it accelerated. Even though outer-space was far from empty, no-one was really sure how long it would take to accrete enough mass to build new habitable spaces for the crew of nearly 5,000 specialists, escapists, dreamers, loners, hyper-allergenics, the insatiably curious and banks of cryo-suspended embryos that would be allowed to reach viability when the space and resources were available.

What nobody had guessed was just how much junk there is floating around in the so-called vacuum of space. Within the first year of acceleration, the ship had taken on more than ten times its original mass. By twenty-five years, it had made its most valuable acquisition: a lump of dirty water-ice and carbon large enough to satisfy the needs of a population of tens of millions. It took them almost fifty years to accelerate the ejected comet to the ship's velocity, by which time the ship and the society it carried had been transformed. Wave generators were installed in the expanded reservoir at the rear of the ship and the breakers, along with the black sandy beaches, sparked a cultural transformation among the crew. They weren't crew anymore; they were inhabitants and Slab was their home. They had become true space-farers. Galactic surfers. The human race had moved into a new phase. Unfortunately.

Louie couldn't see anything that resembled the designs he'd seen on Earth. That was because most of the interior of the original ship was on permanent display as a museum on the floor of Seacombe SideUp while the outer hull had been turned sideways to the direction of travel, gutted, refitted with opposing downs and was now better known as The Strip. All he could see were a lot of hotspots that showed up like arc-lights in infrared. That didn't make sense, even he knew that gravity drives didn't generate heat.

He overshot the rear and turned back to what he decided to call the underside of Slab. He knew the Uppies would have a collective fit if they heard him describe their side of Slab in this fashion. He'll have to find a way of dropping it in conversation, he thought.

'Is everything functioning correctly, sir?' asked Erik.

'Hey! Hello! I didn't know you could do that,' Louie used the same circuits he used for normal speech. 'Can you hear me too?'

'Certainly, sir, although strictly speaking hearing isn't actually involved in the process.'

'I see.'

'You're joking again, aren't you, sir.'

'Everything seems fine to me. I love this MGV. You are going to let me keep it?'

'I'll see what can be arranged, sir, although I expect we will wish to disarm the pin missiles if you intend to interact with the biomass.'

'Ah, and there was I hoping to become a one-hologram terrorist.'

'Do you ever take anything seriously, sir?'

'Erik, life is too short to take everything seriously.'

'Not any more, sir.'

Louie hadn't thought about that.

'Do you mean being immortal makes you take everything more seriously?'

'I suppose you could put it like that. I'd prefer to think in terms of investment in the future and dedicating oneself to a life of integrity and value.'

'Sounds a bit dull to me,' said Louie, simultaneously locating his return point, calculating vectors and ETA, exercising his long range sensors and avoiding a passing micro-mass. 'What's the point of living forever if you aren't going to have fun doing it?'

'I never took you for a philosopher, sir.'

'Now who's joking?'

He nailed the approach to the return emti using a decelerating parabola which only he had the telemetric capability of appreciating. He could see FutureSlab hanging there, waiting for him. He focussed his attention and allowed data to pour into his memory banks. It was, as they said, exactly the same as Slab. A thought occurred to him. He changed direction, vectoring away from Slab.

'Where are you going, sir?' said Erik, his voice rising in alarm.

'Just acting on a hunch,' said Louie.

'If you continue on that course for another 15 seconds, you will be out of immediate collection range.'

'Don't panic,' he laughed. 'I'll be OK'.

Louie sped out to a suitable vantage point, crash-stopped, turned to FutureSlab and set his long range sensors on extreme narrow band. 'Now that,' he said to no-one in particular, '*is* interesting.' He turned and headed straight for the emti. 'I'm coming back in.'

Ten minutes later he was travelling with Erik to a hastily summoned council meeting. There were a dozen or so of the lanky, big-eyed blanks waiting when they arrived. Sis had constructed a new council chamber, an exact replica of the ballroom of an early twentieth century ocean-going liner.

'I can tell you one thing already,' Louie said to the assembly. 'Whatever it is, it hasn't been caused by some form of relativistic anomaly.'

'How do you know?' asked one. Louie thought it might have been Ethless the Beautiful and regretted that she wasn't there in persona.

'It's simple. If it was caused by us travelling faster than light relative to something else, then the Slab we see in front of us would also be travelling faster than light and would have a similar Slab in front of it, and so on. Ad infinity so to speak. I went far enough out to see what was ahead of it and there isn't anything.'

There was a brief pause while the alien avatars looked at him and blinked their eyes.

'Idiot,' said one of them.

They all simultaneously disappeared, leaving Louie alone with Erik under the chandeliers. There was a distant crashing sound and the floor lurched violently upwards.

'Very funny,' said Louie, exasperated. 'What the hell was all that about?'

'They had already thought about that, sir.'

'And?'

'You are making the mistake of applying logic to an irrational situation. You should know better than that, a man of your experience.'

'What do you mean? My experience?'

'Well according to records, you had been married three times?'

'Oh, right. I see. Yes. That reminds me. Do I have time to go see someone before you squirt me into the future?'

'Yes sir, it certainly looks that way. We'll contact you when we've been able to establish a reliable emti array. Current estimates are wavering between four hours and fifteen days.'

'Right then,' said Louie, heading for the transvex.

'Aren't we forgetting something, sir?' Erik stared down at the MGV.

'Oh right.' Louie ejected his complement of pin missiles and grav-manipulated all 250 of them into Erik's outstretched hand. 'See you later!'

nineteen

'We have a deal and that deal doesn't include you not taking my pings.' The president was angry. He wasn't used to being ignored. 'What did the hologram tell you about why they needed him?'

Dielle had been on his way to meet Fingerz in The Strip but instead had wound up in one of Charlie Pleewo's privacy fields in the middle of a golf course. They could see out, but were invisible to the other golfers who would have had no idea the field was even there unless they'd watched Charlie disappear into it.

'He didn't say.'

'You didn't bloody-well ask him, did you?'

'Do you have any right to divert me from my destination? I have someone waiting for me you know.'

'Yeah, we know. That deadbeat has been informed you'll be a little late. And no, I don't have the right to divert you, I just did it. Who you gonna complain to?'

'You can't push me around.'

'Kid, I haven't even started pushing you around. You want me to demonstrate the extent of my SlabWide network and its talents at pushing young punks like you around? You'll make spectacular ratings out of it, but you ain't gonna live long enough to enjoy the royalties.'

'Look, I didn't get time to ask him. He just emtied himself out of there before I could get around to it.'

'You got around to asking him to reneg on your girlfriend, didn't you? Do you not recall the terms of our deal? You want me to replay our conversation?'

'How do you know all this? I thought I'd spoken to Louie under full privacy.'

'You had. President? Memo?'

'OK, OK. I'm seeing him same time tomorrow. I'll make it my top priority to find out what he's up to, OK?'

'You'd better, kid.' He pointed at a vex surface embedded in the ground. 'Don't slam the door on your way out.'

Cute, thought Dielle, as he fell toward seventh on his way back to The Strip.

{[Can you explain how Pleewo got to hear what I was saying to Louie when I'd asked for a privacy field around us?]}

[[One of the girls on the table next door was a relay. She was bugging your field and re-transmitting to Pleewo-Smythe]]

{[Didn't you know that?]}

[[Not at the time, they use special standalone tech that's not connected to my systems. I can only discover these things when the subterfuge is revealed and I can backtrack events]]

{[I guess I'd better be more careful then]}

[[Common understanding is that whenever one deals with Charlie Pleewo, one had best be more than careful]]

Fingerz was waiting for him in his own personal smoke-dome outside a bustling Strip café.

'Sorry man, I don't do daytime, man.'

'But I saw you in Mitchell at the races.'

'So nutin'. Nues I use all have backstage vex, so Is don't go outside.' He handed Dielle a shiff.

'Huh? You mean you live in permanent night time?' said Dielle, puffing it to life.

'Cep when I sleep. Most musos do, man. Then when you maxed, you get yourself a kickass in Rotunda, soak up some rays and bug up to moverville when you seekin' the reekin'.'

Dielle stared at him, inhaled more smoke and waited until what Fingerz had just said made sense.

'Cool.'

'Yeah.'

'Rays.'

'Yeah, private sunlight. Everyone in the Valley has it now.'

'Cool.'

Fingerz took a long pull on his shiff, finished it and flicked the stub at the bottom of the box. It vanished.

'I talked to The Man, man. He can insin you today if you want.'

'That's cool.'

'Listen,' said Fingerz, bending into him conspiratorially. 'We're in a double privacy field now. This café is what's called a NowThen. It has a one-time key hardshield on all the tables and I'm running my own encrypted sub field off their system. NowThens are where the musos, hackers and Unkos hang out and, believe me man, it's C-cure.'

That could be useful to remember, thought Dielle. 'Nice place,' he said, looking around.

'Don't bother, man, it won't be here tomorrow. There are always a couple of hundred of these places running at any time – they even set some up in daysides but most are in Stripville.'

'So how do you know where they are?'

'All sub-legal stim units have a fully encrypted subchannel that works over the independent stim2stim network.'

'Independent of what?'

'Sis, man!' said Fingerz, whirling his slender fingers around the side of his head. 'Ah, let's go.' He stood up, as did most of the people around them. 'This NowThen is history in 50 seconds, man. Let's tube it.'

They walked over to a local vex as the café owner came out scratching his head, watching everyone leave. He'd been having a really good nightmorning until that moment.

'This is how it's going to work,' explained Fingerz as their privacy field hurtled to an undisclosed destination.

'You pay me now and I'll do the no-trace stuff to The Man. From this moment until your stim is online, everything you do, see or hear is perma-embargoed, full privacy, do-not-reveal. OK?' Dielle nodded. He wasn't absolutely sure what he was getting into, but he intuitively felt that pulling out now was not an option which would be greeted with calm acceptance from his permanently stoned muso friend.

'You tell Sis you're paying me for my keys stim with full handhold and personal consults and I'll take it from there. I take ten points for my dip and hide the trace to The Man for the rest. OK?'

'No problem. How much?'

Fingerz scratched his chin and looked at Dielle. 'The Man says standard fifty percent rate is cool.'

'Fifty percent of what?'

'What you have, man. The Man runs a variable pricing policy.'

'What I have?'

{[How much credit do I currently have?]}

[[5,126,872 at this mark]]

{[Is that a lot?]}

[[The term *lot* in this context is a subjective value judgement based upon a variable rate function of perceived purchasing power against your personal desire threshold]]

{[So that was a pretty stupid question?]}

[[••]]

{[Well it sounds like a lot. Do you think I could ask Louie? He's a business guy]}

[[If you wish, but his old monetary system bears no relevance to ours. There was a period of hyper-inflation after the crash of 466 and we dropped three zeros from the currency]]

'How does he know how much I have? Can't I just make it up?'

Fingerz looked horrified. 'No-one lies to The Man, man!'

Well, thought Dielle, if I've managed to make that much in just a few days, it can't be too bad a deal.

{[Transfer half of my credits to Fingerz Marley please]}
[[Again]]
{[Transfer half of my credits to J.A. Marley the 8th]}
[[What for?]]
{[Keys training]}
[[~~~?]]
{[And full support and personal lessons]}
[[Are you crazy?]]
{[Just do it, OK?]}
[[••]]

Fingerz looked shocked. 'Man! Now I know why they call her Tiger!'

Twenty minutes later they were standing in the middle of an anechoic chamber with white, luminescent walls that seemed to have depth without having a surface. Intense light radiated from the shallow concave disks that formed the floor and ceiling. Dielle was disorientated and turned to Fingerz, who had surrounded himself with a darkfield.

'What now?'

'Good day, gentlemen,' said a frail voice.

Fingerz' field leaned towards Dielle. 'The Man!' he whispered.

'Hi!' said Dielle trying to blend calm cheerfulness with relaxed self-confidence. He thought he nailed it.

'Do not be nervous,' said the voice. 'There will be no long-term negative effect on anything other than your credit balance.'

Dielle could hear heavy sucking sounds beside him.

'OK Marley, this transaction is approved. Get lost.'

Dielle turned to say bye. Fingerz had already left.

{[Please tell Fingerz *thanks and I'll see him later*]} No response.

{[Hello?]} No response. The walls faded away and the lights lowered to a faint orange glow

'Your system interface has been disabled,' said the voice. 'All functions have been usurped by my intelligences with which you are not yet equipped to communicate. Your body tech will be maintained at optimum. Do not panic.'

Dielle became aware of a low, throbbing hum and, as his eyes became accustomed to the gloom, a galaxy of tiny multi-coloured lights. He was almost completely surrounded by a huge, menacing machine.

'Disrobe.'

'Why?'

'Understand that I do not give refunds and if you ask any further trivial questions the procedure will discontinue.'

Dielle took off his clothes and dropped them into the emtitrash that had appeared beside him.

'Hmmm. I see you have recently met our esteemed president.'

'Yeah, how did y ... ' he stifled the question.

'You are coated with his nanotech tracers and bugs. Hold still.'

There was a blinding flash of blue-white light that hit Dielle like a searing wind. He felt as though every pore in his body had suddenly opened and closed after being shaved of its outer covering of cells, which was exactly what had happened.

'Ah ha!' said the voice triumphantly, with a synthesised laugh. 'Looks like Pundechan Media is keen to protect its assets too.'

Three black balls floated toward him and hovered in a triangle formation around the base of his penis. Dielle looked down in alarm and covered himself.

'Hey!'

'No need for concern, this will not hurt. I'm not going to remove the device, merely temporarily disable it. The value of knowledge is in direct proportion to its level of concealment, no?'

A device? He felt violated. When did Kiki put a device in my dick? he thought, realising that she had had ample opportunity. There was a sharp snapping sound and an intense localised vibration which brought a temporary smile back to his face.

'Thanks, I guess,' said Dielle.

'All part of the service. Tea?'

As the balls floated back to the machine, they passed a delicate china cup on a gravplate.

'Thanks. I'm fine. I just had … '

'Drink it!'

Dielle was unsettled. It may have been because he was alone, isolated from the protective arms of Sis, standing naked on a glowing orange floor, surrounded by humming machines that were bristling with sensors, probes and vicious-looking razor-edged wires while being humiliated by a sinister, disembodied voice. Or it may have been the tea. That was it. Tea. Disgusting stuff. He had never liked it.

'I don't actually like tea. Sorry. Do you have any coffee?'

'Drink it, you moron! It isn't dicing tea anyway; it's a cocktail of psychoactive drugs, capillary dilators and neuron markers necessary for the proper installation of your stim unit.'

'Oh, right. In that case.' He sipped the warm liquid. It was delicious.

'Exit via the transvex to your right.' A wall panel glowed blue. 'There are some sanitised clothes waiting for you in the privacy bubble which will take you to a new location. Do not try to contact Sis while you are in transit. Understood?'

'OK, no problem.'

'Why are you not moving?'

Not exactly service with a smile, thought Dielle.

The smile he sought was on the face of Mary-Belle Krischanssonson who was waiting for him in the privacy field on the other side of the vex. She was still wearing her Jenny's uniform and handed him a chamoist one-piece. Dielle was immediately pleased to see her.

'Don't even think about it,' said the voice which, being modified by Mary-Belle's vocal chords, seemed even more unnerving to Dielle. 'Not yet, anyway.'

'Bella? Are you The Man?'

'Don't be ridiculous. This individual is acting as a live-thru. She has a stim unit identical to the one you will be getting and she hires out her body for those of us who choose to experience other sides of the existential plane. You will be able to hire her as well if you like, should you wish to experiment with being a woman without going through all the tedious physical changes. I can personally recommend this one, she is strong and healthy and has superbly tuned pleasure receptors. I did the installation myself.'

'You mean I can inhabit another person's body?'

'Not exactly. The stim unit stimulates your brain in a mirror of another person's real experience, or more often, a recording. Normally, the originator is in control of their actions and has the option to transmit selected sensory data while retaining their memories. But a live-thru relinquishes most higher functions to the hirer and will have no memory at all of what they have done during the occupancy.'

'Sounds pretty risky for her.'

'Yes it is. Extraordinarily risky. Which is why Sis usually monitors the proceedings to ensure nothing gets out of hand.'

'Usually?'

'Well not in this instance, naturally.'

Dielle thought about that for a moment. Bella must be

either very trusting of this person or very stupid. Or maybe very scared.

'Can I ask … ?'

'No you can't. We've arrived. Get out.'

Dielle walked into a room that looked similar to the one he'd just left, but this one was far bigger and had a round patch of red Soffen, large enough for them both to stretch out on, set into the centre of the floor. Mary-Belle stepped out of her heels, strode into the circle and held her hands out to him. The Soffen was warm to his bare feet.

A long, narrow platform floated out between them. On it was a handful of shiny, complicated-looking instruments, the largest of which was something Dielle recognised from his encounter with PT. Mary-Belle picked it up and the spider came to life.

'Don't be alarmed and keep still,' said the voice through Mary-Belle as it clamped itself firmly on Dielle's skull.

'Oh, I'm not worried. I know it doesn't hurt.'

'No. You've only had a basic neural interface installed so far. This is a maximum-option stim unit designed to interface with every sensory brain receptor, autonomic system and motor neuron channel you have.' She stepped back and gave him a pouting air kiss. 'It hurts like hell.'

Dielle screamed as a torrent of pain flooded his body. He felt as though he had been simultaneously dipped in molten lava, irradiated by a thermo-nuclear explosion, had all his teeth, nails and hair wrenched out and then had burning spikes driven into his eyes, ears, throat and testicles. He collapsed in agony. He had pain in parts of his body he hadn't even known existed. Then, just as suddenly as the torture had started, it stopped and everything turned to pleasure. Intense pleasure. Too much pleasure. Painful pleasure. His brain lit up as every nerve ending told him it was being sucked by an angel. He simultaneously ejaculated, sneezed, belched and farted.

He snorted. Then started giggling. Then he broke into

uncontrollable laughter. He rolled around on the floor gasping for breath, unable to stop laughing until he was exhausted. Mary-Belle watched him patiently.

'That,' said Dielle, panting, 'was the most amazing experience I have ever had!'

'Yes it was. Now calm down. We need to finish the installation with some calibration and fine tuning.'

'How do we do that?'

'Well in your case, we'll be needing one of these,' said Mary-Belle, taking off her dress.

Dielle looked at her naked body, unable to stifle his natural reaction until he realised what was about to happen.

'But you're a guy! I can't do that knowing there's a guy in the driving seat.'

'You really are a fucking primitive, aren't you?' said the man. Mary-Belle switched to her natural voice. 'And if it makes any difference, I am of neither sex and haven't been so restricted for over three hundred of your Earth years. I am, also, an expert. Now lie down and let's get this over with.'

The floor below them yielded to their combined weight and moved to support every part of their now naked bodies. During the calibration, Dielle felt as though he was constantly phasing in and out of reality. Perhaps it was the psychoactive drugs The Man had told him were in the tea, but on several occasions he was sure he was actually inside Mary-Belle's body, looking out at himself, experiencing the event from her perspective. He had no idea how long it lasted. He lost track of time and his own extremities while his body experienced pleasure sensations that sequentially tracked every contour of his anatomy. He entered a dream-like state in which he couldn't tell where he ended and she started. This was like having sex in multiple dimensions. It was by far and away the best sex he had ever had. Eventually, neither his brain nor his body could take any more. He passed out.

He awoke lying face up on the hissing lawn, feeling warm, happy and a little sore. He gazed dreamily at the clear blue, cloudless sky. Things seemed bigger in a way that he couldn't put his finger on.

[:This is your encrypted subchannel. Do not acknowledge. It is separate from SlabWide Integrated System. While your brain was in theta, it was trained to differentiate this channel from standard system calls:]

Dielle understood. The thoughts had a different flavour.

[:You will be made aware of any person in your vicinity who is on this channel via an :ID: interrupt. Any attempt to disclose this channel's existence to someone who is not already on this channel will result in instant and irrevocable disconnection. Do not be confused about this. Everyone knows sub-legal channels exist but everyone also knows that if anyone says they are on one, they aren't. Acknowledge:]

{:Acknowledged:} That's all I need, he thought: another voice in my head.

[[•]]

Argh!{[Accept]}

[['Darling! Where have you been? I've been worried sick! Sis tells me you dropped off system almost three hours ago.']]

Er, thought Dielle, er … er … er …

{:Where the hell have I been?:}

[:You have been learning to play keys with Fingerz Marley in an UpSide offline Strip privacy room:]

He told her.

[['You've had a stim unit fitted without consulting me?']] She sounded upset. Very upset. The kind of upset you can hear in someone's voice when they are struggling to pretend that they are not upset, which makes it clear that they are very, very upset. Dielle didn't need a memory to understand this, he just had to listen to his instincts. His instincts told him to get the hell home.

Kiki was walking up to the vex when he arrived. Dielle noted, again instinctively, that she wasn't armed. At least not in any obvious fashion. That, he felt instinctively, was a good sign.

Unfortunately, instincts aren't always reliable.

'Who tuned it?' she demanded, standing legs apart with her arms folded.

'I dunno. Someone called The Man. Fingerz put me in touch with him but I didn't even see him.'

'I already know you've gone sub-legal, you cake. I mean, who was the live-thru?' Kiki was trembling with barely-suppressed anger.

Ah, thought Dielle. He knew that his next answer might be important. He realised that this could be a turning point in his relationship with the woman he loved. He even considered telling her the truth, but even though he was still very young and naïve, he wasn't stupid.

'I dunno. Just some woman. I can hardly remember her, it was all so sort of dreamy. I didn't like her very much.'

'Aaaarghh!' Kiki screamed. Her hands were small shaking fists on the ends of rigid arms. 'How could you do this to me?'

Dielle moved toward her and tried to put his arms around her. 'I'm sorry darling, I didn't know what was going to happen. I thought I was just getting a type of upgrade to my eye. I didn't even enjoy it.'

'What a load of string!'

{[~?]}

[[Ms. Pundechan thinks you are being disingenuous in the extreme]]

{[~?]}

[[She just called you a liar]]

'Honestly darling, she wasn't anything compared to you.'

'Don't be ridiculous. Everyone has the time of their lives when they're tuned in on their virgin stim. It's when the q-sensory brain preceptors wake up for the first time. You'll never feel like that again.'

'I'm really, really sorry, I wish it could have been with you. I'm sure it would have felt so much better with you.'

'With me? Are you joking?'

'What?'

'Do you have any idea how many people have been bidding to be your first tune-in? Do you know how much we could have got for the sumecast alone, not to mention the stim recording of the whole event? Three hour's worth! You crashsense *cake*! You have just thrown away the best part of twenty million bucks!' She slumped down in a chair, holding her head. 'Think Tiger. Think!' she muttered.

'What the fu … ?'

'Shut up! Shut up! I'm in conference!'

Dielle stared at her for a moment. Shutting up seemed like a very good idea. He needed a drink. A Rat 5. Then he needed another.

An hour and a half later she joined him as he was catching up on the war. There was big news: the new gigaplat had failed to arrive. Incredibly, the enemy had cracked the Navy's communications encryption protocols and established an impenetrable defensive shield in the ship's path. News channels had wild-eyed cryptographers bickering with each other about the impossibility of breaking the codes and at least one shockcaster had accused the Unkos of espionage. Chaos and confusion reigned on the new battlefront which had advanced 100,000 klicks. Admiral Massive had even called up the home guard. Slab was buzzing as members of the Auxiliary Defence Combat Units raced home to log on and fight. One sume had a live feed of two I.P. futures traders who had switched their terminals to offensive mode and were engaged in a thrilling high-speed fire fight while their colleagues crowded round, shouting advice and cheering. Their weapons officer, a kinderfarm teacher in a zone61 nursery, took out an enemy cruiser as it momentarily flashed into visibility off their port wing. It was intense. Dielle had to lower his drink ratings so he could follow a multi-channel sume of the battle. He'd completely forgotten about his latest screw-up until he saw Kiki's face. He cancelled the sume.

'OK,' she said, accepting the drink he offered. 'We have a plan. I've arranged strict sub-rosa on everything that happens for the next few hours but, for now, it's essential that no-one knows you already have a stim unit.'

'Fingerz knows.'

'His silence is already bought and paid for. He won't publish. In fact he seemed rather keen not to have anyone know he has any connections with your sub-legal. This *Man* of yours must be a heavyweight Unko.'

'What are we going to do?'

'The first thing we're going to do is eat. I'm starving. Let's go to Jenny's.'

'Oh! Er … Um.'

Kiki strode toward a swiftly opening window. 'Oh, and by the way, while you were getting screwed, so was I.'

Dielle scurried after her. 'What?'

'By an interholo called Louie?'

'Ah!'

'I can't believe you and he are the same person.'

'Neither can I. I hope he wasn't too hard on you.'

'Let's just say we re-negotiated a deal that is significantly improved for you but not so tough as to be disincentivising for me.'

'Sorry.'

'Yeah, well, I guess that what you may have just thrown away on my behalf is considerably less than before we re-negotiated.'

'And that's good, right?'

Kiki stopped. She turned to look at him and shook her head. 'Unbelievable.'

Mary-Belle greeted them with the same smile as always. Dielle looked closely into the eyes of the woman whose body he had recently had the pleasure of in every possible intimate detail. There was no sign, not the slightest recognition, that she was aware of their connection although he did see her eyebrow twitch just a fraction at exactly the moment he received an [:ID:] for her.

Kiki and Mary-Belle exchanged familiar greetings before they were led to a booth which was already surrounded by an opaque privacy field. Two men were waiting for them inside. Dielle queried Sis but their identities had been embargoed.

'What we are about to do is break the fifth wall,' she told him as they sat down inside the field. 'These are two of my most trusted employees who you will know as … ' She nodded at them.

'It is a real and unexpected honour,' said the first one, smiling and putting out a hand for Dielle to shake. 'Like, *really* unexpected. Just call me Jim'

'OK, Jam then,' said the other one.

'Dude, that's not even a real name,' said Jim. 'Can't you come up with something better than that?'

'You're the fucking writer. You come up with a better one,' said Jam, who was clearly not in the sunniest of moods.

'Where's our editor?' asked Kiki impatiently. 'Wasn't he supposed to come down with you two?'

'He's been sorting out the mask to cover the dropouts,' said Jam. 'ETA one point two.'

'Editor? Writer?' said Dielle, hopeful of further enlightenment.

'Dielle,' said Kiki in a businesslike tone. 'These are some of the people who work on your sumecast. Cli … Jam here is the executive director. He's ultimately responsible for everything that goes out to the sumers.'

Jam nodded at Dielle and looked sour.

'In order to maintain the authenticity that is so crucial to the success of our sume, we have certain rules. One of these rules is that you never break the invisible walls. Never. One invisible wall is the fourth wall between you and the audience. You never let them know that you know they are watching – or they will lose all interest. Then the whole thing just falls apart. We will maintain the fourth wall at all costs.

'The other invisible wall is the wall between you and your crew. You should never acknowledge they are there, let alone know who they are. So you need to listen to what we're going to tell you and you need to forget completely who told it to you and why. OK?'

'I guess.'

'Don't guess. Just ask if you are unsure. From this point in, don't assume a single thing.'

Without warning, the strangest looking human Dielle had ever seen invaded their privacy field. He had three independently acting eyes, two huge, fan-like ears and four extra arms growing from his chest.

'You're late,' said Kiki. 'Your name is Ed.'

Ed looked around as he sat down. And when Ed looked around, he really looked around.

'Pleased to meet you,' he said to a wide-eyed Dielle, sticking out a middle hand for him to shake. It looked and felt human. 'Man I am starving! I ordered on the way down here. What's everyone having?'

'Couldn't you have dumped the freakshow?' said Jam, 'You know he hasn't seen this stuff yet.'

'Yeah … Ed,' said Jim, 'We're going to lose the surprise gag when he meets his first prosthete now.'

'Fuck!' said Ed, waving all six arms around. 'Stick a fucking splain up my ass and I'll re-synch the sensurround while I'm at it. I've been assembling an entirely believable three and half hours of mildly interesting sume while you guys have been blowing airies! I didn't have the time to uninstall all this stuff.' He reached up and with a squelching noise pulled his central eye out of its socket. The raw indentation left behind healed immediately to leave his remaining two eyes just a little further apart than normal. They swivelled around once and locked into synchronisation. He took a small round box out of one of his pockets. The top irised open and he carefully placed the third eye into the bioment and watched it seal. 'There. Is that better?'

'Alright, alright. We've all had a hard day,' said Kiki as Mary-Belle delivered plates of food through the privacy shield. Ed, who had taken the seat nearest the exit, took the dishes and dealt them out without asking whose was whose. Dielle was impressed by Ed's obvious skill in handling simultaneous data streams. He would have been even more impressed to know that Ed was editing the sume output as he ate.

Kiki turned to her employees. 'OK people, we all know what's at stake here. Here's what we are going to do.'

She spent the next half hour outlining a plan for faking Dielle's virgin stim unit installation. PT Dempster had already been bribed to perform the sham insinuation and the second-highest bidder on the auction had been contacted and was currently waiting nervously with a Pundechan Media secretary in a luxury suite of a Vrille de France Hotel D'amour, whose owners had readily agreed to Kiki's sponsorship demands. They studied a 3D of the candidate, discussing the optimal angles. Although obviously much older than Dielle, she was trim and athletic and judged to be more than capable by the three professionals. Kiki told them the highest bidder had turned out to be an elderly male but she'd decided that option didn't fit their target demographic.

That's not all it wouldn't fit, thought Dielle.

Jam confirmed the room's sensurround facilities had been tested and upgraded by their own staff who had also installed their own backup ring to cover any possible screw up, down or sideways. Everything was in place.

Dielle had been listening to the other four while they talked about him as though he wasn't there. Jim had come up with a list of optimum responses and actions for Dielle while he was getting tuned in. Everyone had an opinion. All Dielle had to do was make it look and feel real.

'I can't do it.'

They looked at him, trying to figure out what language he had just spoken. Then they all began talking at once. Kiki quietened them down.

'Look darling, you'll be fine. Ed's going to ramp up the sensurround recordings from your stim output to make it feel like your first time. The live-thru will also record her stim experience and we've already negotiated distribution rights for that so we can tweak it to match if we need to.' She turned to the editor. 'Right?'

'Sure thing,' he said, lifting his middle arms and twiddling his fingers. 'All I need is two clean feeds with sync code and I could make your great-grandmother believe she was fucking him for the first time.'

'But I'll know it's a fake,' protested Dielle. 'Surely that's going to show?'

'You'll be so out of your skull on psychoactives you won't know whose side of the interface you're on,' said Jam.

'You can do too much of that though. You'll lose the reality bite and it won't sell,' said Jim. 'Why would anyone pay for a tripped-out stim when they can get the same effect themselves for a couple of bucks in ToNight High?'

'Well,' said Kiki, reluctantly, 'there is an alternative.'

Four pairs of eyes fixed on her while three eyes queried her by direct message.

'I've been talking to The Man.'

'You got to him?' said Jim with awe.

'You are kidding me!' said Ed. 'The Man! You sure?'

'You'll be surprised how easy it is to intimidate a paranoid muso. The Man says Dielle's unit has the potential to be defaulted in case of a botched install.'

'No fucking way!' said Ed getting very excited. 'Zeroed for re-calibration? That is awesome! I heard a rumour about this tech!' He pointed at Dielle's head with four hands. 'You must have one kickass unit in there buddy! How much d'you pay?'

Dielle told him. Jim gave a low whistle.

'And he's charging a similar amount for the re-tune because he has to remote supervise the re-calibration without getting any of his own personality in the recording, which he's confident he's able to do,' said Kiki.

'Tell him to go stim himself,' said Jam. 'That's way too high a price for a tune in. He's ripping us.'

'I say we do it,' said Jim. 'It'll guarantee authenticity and we'll easy make it back in residuals if it's that good.'

'I agree,' said Ed. 'We won't have to touch any of the feeds if he really feels it as the first time. The live-thru won't smell anything funny either. There's no risk.'

'Well, there is a slight risk apparently,' said Kiki. 'Defaulting the stim will cause a memory burn. He'll lose most of the last few hours.'

'No problem,' said Ed. 'I could feed him the mask I just made up and some of the back feed into subliminal while he's in theta. And with a bit of luck he won't remember us or this meeting at all.'

Dielle was feeling sidelined. 'Does *he* get any say in this at all?'

'Dielle darling,' said Kiki softly, turning to him and stroking his hand. 'Do you want to re-live the most amazing experience you will ever have in your entire life and in the process make us all a million bucks each, or do you just want to go home and explain to your sumers how you got a sub-legal stim fitted without them being able to share the experience?'

'Special delivery tea?' said Bella from outside the field.

'Mine,' said Dielle.

Three minutes later they were all in a tube field heading for Spin's première arrondissement.

Later, while Kiki was rubbing his aching back in a hot tub, she asked Dielle if what he'd just experienced really was as good as the first time. He had no idea what she was talking about. He was having enough trouble adjusting to a new communications channel he'd apparently been fitted with without his consent.

With a smile on her face, she changed the subject.

twenty

Louie was impressed. He'd been expecting some easy sport, but Kiki had fought her ground well and retaliated with a few skilful parries and moves of her own. He'd had to grudgingly concede that she knew her business. Kiki had covered every exploitable option he could think of and quite a few he hadn't. He was so impressed that he was even considering asking her to broker the media deals on his basketball franchise.

He'd still beaten her up, of course. He considered it a question of duty, or habit maybe, but definitely not honour.

Now he was back in the projection room with the NAHs, who were carrying out last minute checks. Louie looked up at the web of flickering red lines surrounding FutureSlab's aft section.

'We have established a method of maintaining sufficient high-powered emti projectors in a fluctuating dynamic network to carry out the leap,' said Erik. 'We're reasonably confident that we can get you in and out of there as long as you are able to use this.' He pointed at a thick, silver disc the size of a flattened basketball. 'It's your return emti and can only be operated by these manual, or in your case grav-manipulated, switches. There is no system-level link to it at all and once it leaves here, it will have no working interface other than these paddles.' Louie examined the panels that rimmed the upper surface. 'It's a use-once, instant self-destruct device that will send you and only you back into the network. Let me show you the sequence on this dummy so you can get used to it.' A duplicate disc appeared on the rostrum.

Louie practised operating the paddles using his narrow-focus gravity manipulators. It was tricky but he found it easier if he used his holographic projection to echo what he was trying to achieve.

'Cool. It's like I can actually do things with my fingers. You gotta let me keep this afterwards.'

'I'm sure that won't be a problem, sir.' Erik moved the dummy to one side. 'Once you are inside the FutureSlab you will be completely out of our range. You won't be able to communicate with us and we will have no way of knowing what has happened to you. You will be cut off and completely alone. Are you ready to give it a go?'

'Sure, why not?'

'Do you want a full answer to that question, Mr Drago?' said a stern voice behind him. Louie looked around as an intern avatar floated down to join the group.

Oh no, thought Louie, not another fucking wizard.

'What is it with you people?' asked Louie irritably. 'Can't you take yes for an answer?'

'I am Council witness, Mr Drago. Do you have any questions before your voyage into the unknown?'

'No.'

'I must warn you that you are about to embark on a mission of extraordinary risk. You will be using completely untested technology to enter a potentially hostile territory and there is a significant probability that you, that is the you you know yourself to be in this moment, may not return. Is there anyone you wish to inform of your last wishes? Your reset perhaps?'

'No-one.'

'Have you any last words.'

'None.'

'Is there anything you need?'

'Nothing.'

'Very well.' The wizard folded his arms. His sleeves touched the floor.

Pompous prick, thought Louie.

'Proceed!' instructed the wizard.

Erik watched Louie carefully as he steered his MGV into the emti transmitter frame.

'OK, the backup sequence is initiated. Are you ready?'

'Yes.'

'OK. Are you ready?'

'Yep.'

'And … ready?'

'I said yes.'

'Ready now?'

'I'm ready!'

'Ready?'

'YES. Just do it!'

'And, OK – ready then?'

'What the … FUCK!'

Louie was in total darkness. His ambient temperature sensors indicated just a few degrees above absolute zero, which his systems told him was largely because of his own radiation. He tried every multi-band spectrum device he possessed but could detect nothing. No gamma, x, ultra, infra, micro or radio. Nothing. Nothing except a very faint point of light. That was odd, he thought, he was sure it wasn't there 0.00001 seconds ago. The spectrum curve was familiar. In fact it was virtually identical to the light he'd been fitted with. He turned his on and saw a couple of emti discs floating nearby. They were melted beyond use and cold in every waveband.

The light was getting rapidly brighter. He was thinking about arming his pin missiles when he heard a shout.

'Hey! Have they figured it out yet?' The voice sounded remarkably like …

'Oh shit!'

'Fuckin' A!'

Louie was looking directly at himself.

'How many of us made it here?'

'We all did, I think. You're number six. I'm four. It looks like three of us got fried trying to get back.'

'Where's five?'

'He's off exploring this place. He's pissed at me.'

'Why?'

'I was waiting for him when he zapped over. I tried to use his emti to get back 'cos mine died during transmission.'

'What happened?'

'He bashed into me, the bird brain, just as I was keying the sequence. We must have swapped a few molecules.'

'So the emti wouldn't work, 'cos you'd been modified.'

'Those guys are too fucking paranoid for their own good. They give you anything new?'

'Don't think so.' Louie six checked his systems. Nothing seemed new, but then he realised he must have been a fresh download into this MGV so he had no idea if anything was different from before. 'You got pin missiles?'

'Yep. Used a couple when we had the fight. Hardly made a dent.'

'How long you been here?'

'Coming up to six hours now. You sure you ain't got nothing new?'

'How would I know?'

'Dumb bastards just going to leave us out here?'

'Maybe. What's with this place anyway?'

'It's empty. Ziperdeezero. Been up and down every interior surface and used every sensor I've got. No sections, no tube system, no nothing. A thousand klicks of bare, empty void. Not a single sign that human civilisation was ever here.'

'What do you think?'

'Well, I think I think exactly the same as you think.'

'I don't think nothing.'

'Fuckin' A.'

They stared at each other for a while.

Louie six knew one thing. He knew he couldn't outwit himself. If they were going to get out of there, they'd need to combine forces.

'We have to get hold of number five. Do you know where he is?'

'Haven't seen him since I shoved a pin up his ass.'

'I'm here,' said a voice from the dark. Another MGV floated into view. Its lights and holo-projection were turned off.

'Hey!' said four. 'What the fuck you doing stealthing from yourselves?'

'I know how untrustworthy I am, remember?' replied five, activating his holo and pointing to two, sooty overlapping circles on his casing.

They were interrupted by an emti disk popping into existence. The three of them instantly snapped into a triangular formation around it. Each one arming pin missiles and targeting the other two.

'Do I hear music?' said six.

'Funny,' said four.

'Always liked my sense of humour,' said six. 'Let me go and I'll force them to find a way to get you two back.'

'Why would you do that?' said four. 'I wouldn't.'

'Nor me,' said five.

'You know this transmitter won't work for either of you, what choice do we have?' said Louie six, trying his trusty *let's be reasonable* negotiation voice before remembering who his audience was.

'Maybe it will,' said four. 'Maybe they figured out the problem was on the return side and they widened the gate.'

'Yeah,' said five.

I have a point, thought six. A new option occurred to him. 'Hey! Why don't we just synchronise and then we can all get out of here in this unit?'

'What the fuck you talking about?' said five.

'Yeah,' said four.

'It's simple,' said six. 'We use the synchro routine to add you two's memory data to mine.'

'I don't have a synchro routine,' said four.

'Me neither,' said five.

'So they did give you something extra,' said four.

'Must have done. I only just remembered it. What do you think?'

'I guess as long as I get back, I don't give a fuck,' said five.

Four shrugged.

'That's what I thought you'd say,' said Louie six. He initiated the synchronisation and was flooded with a jumble of overlapping memories. He remembered fighting himself and then being in two places at the same time, exploring the vast empty blackness of the interior. As soon as the synchronisation was complete, he remembered something else. He remembered he had extra armaments in his side panels. Real lookadat nasty they were too. He opened the hidden missile ports and fired.

Two silent, incandescent vapour clouds marked the completion of his additional programming.

In space, thought Louie, no-one can hear you lie.

He set up a deflection shield and manoeuvred his MGV-GT MkIII carefully past the dissipating atoms of his former selves and onto the rescue plate. He took one last look around, shook his head and keyed in the return sequence. He appeared inside a transparent dome surrounding a fifteen-metre-wide Natalite disk. His sensors told him he was a thousand klicks off the starboard side of Slab, travelling on a grav-locked parallel track. He was not alone. Sitting in front of him, in a huge, high-backed Victorian chair with his arms crossed was the Council witness.

'Hey!' said Louie. 'What's the game?'

'Condition number two,' said the wizard avatar, 'is that you stay outside Slab until it can be proved beyond any doubt that your systems have not been compromised. Tell me what happened.'

'It's a blank. There's nothing in there. Zilch.'

'How can you be sure? How much data do you have to analyse? You were in there for less than ten minutes.'

'I've got three of me's memories inside me. Enough data to keep you people happy for years. And all of it says zero.'

'So we were right, they did make it to FutureSlab.'

'Yeah. How come you didn't tell me what you were doing?'

'Context-release information. Only made available to you under predetermined conditions. Don't forget we could have been dealing with anything in there.'

'Well, all I was dealing with was me. Download this stuff and let me in.'

'It's not as simple as that. They're currently running remote security diagnostics on your internal security diagnostics.'

'Jeez! There was nothing in there! It's dead, empty and as cold as space. There was nothing there to infect me.'

'If, as you say, it is empty and there is no evidence of human habitation then we can only assume the artefact was made by a highly advanced civilisation in a deliberate act of provocation. They clearly have no idea what is inside our own Slab otherwise they would undoubtedly have duplicated that as well. Therefore they have enticed us out of our own secure environment into theirs. If they planned for that, they could have also planned to plant something that could destroy us in whoever or whatever we sent to investigate their trap.'

'So how long are you going to leave me out here?'

'You, as in your MGV and your current data matrix, will never be allowed back in.'

'What? You can't do that!'

'Condition number three says we can.'

'You bastards!' Louie was furious. He spat out a stream of Bronxlang invective using words that no-one had heard for over three hundred years. He was angry with the

Council but he was more angry at himself for allowing himself to get caught. He shook his holographic fists in rage and accidentally set off a shower of pin missiles which exploded harmlessly against the dome, filling it with a fog of minute metal particles. The wizard waited patiently for the dust to settle.

'The base of this quarantine cell contains a highly sophisticated, autonomous data mirror which is in the process of analysing everything in your data core that differs from your last backup. The results of that analysis will be transferred, in binary, to a physical format which can be remote-read by optical scanner and converted back to usable data for analysis on Slab.'

'Then what?'

'Your last backup will be re-installed in a downgraded vDek onSlab and you will be informed of the results of your exploration, although your exact memories will not be available to you.'

Louie knew what that meant.

'They're going to zap me, aren't they?'

'Regrettably, Council will not agree to let you return in your current, potentially compromised state.'

'What about you? I could have already infected you. I bet they're going to zap you too.'

'You are correct. But this is an autonomous avatar, entirely disconnected from the human onSlab personality which once inhabited it. I cannot even communicate with Sis. The intern that was me will live on unaffected with no memory of this encounter. I was only sent to you as a final courtesy. You have done us a great service. We are not ungrateful.'

Louie glared at the wizard and thought frantically.

'OK, so we're going to stay here until the data I've gathered is analysed, sanitised and transferred to Sis. And then we get zapped.'

'Correct.'

'And we can't talk to anyone.'

'Affirmative.'

'But someone will read the data before we fry?'

'Yes, in case anything has been overlooked or needs to be checked.'

'Including this conversation?'

'Everything that's different from your original database will be analysed so, yes, this conversation too.'

'OK. I hereby want it to be known that I do not want to die. I am a sentient being and I demand the right to life. I want this statement to be published in Council and available to all the NAHs. I give the Erik who was associated with me full power of attorney over my affairs for the purpose of ensuring I do not get zapped.'

'Look!' said the avatar, pointing to a bright red flash in front of their dome.

Louie shot over and put his visual enhancers on maximum.

'I don't believe it. Punched cards. They're being sent out from somewhere underneath. They're being scanned by a laser from Slab and then zapped by another one.'

'It's started then,' said the wizard, joining him.

They watched the stream of cards being spat out, lit up and disintegrated. Each one counting down the last moments of their lives. Tiny sparks against the vast majesty of the galactic core beyond.

'If it helps,' said the avatar in a quiet voice, 'I would like to add to the record that I do not wish to die either. You may not be aware of this, but all death onSlab is elective. It has been over eight hundred cykes since anyone involuntarily went ahead.'

'They gotta listen to us,' said Louie. 'I may not know much about Slab, but I can tell a bunch of liberal softies when I meet them.'

'I suppose we can only sit and wait now.'

'You do the sitting. I'm going to search my memories

while I still have them. Maybe there's something else hidden in there I didn't know about. Let me know if anything happens.' He switched his hologram into a looped movie of a potters wheel with two disembodied hands slowly forming a vase from wet clay.

Three hours passed.

'Wake up!' said the wizard, kicking Louie's MGV. 'Something's happening!'

Louie turned his holo back on to see a small emti disk hovering in the middle of the dome. It glowed briefly then dropped to the floor, dead.

'Hey!' said the wizard. 'I've been updated. I have new information.'

Louie sensed that the exact reverse had happened to him. He felt somehow diminished, disconnected and downgraded. Something had happened to his systems, but he couldn't tell what. As he tried to probe his capabilities, his memory of how he had been before faded away. Within a dozen cycles of his internal processors, he had forgotten why he'd thought he'd been changed.

'They've agreed not to destroy us.'

'Fuckin' A!' Louie took a few spins around the dome in celebration.

'I'm afraid you're not going to like the conditions.'

Louie crash-stopped in front of the avatar. 'What conditions?'

'They're going to emti over a couple of modifications to the dome and provide us with a library of sumes for the journey.'

'What journey?'

The floor lurched.

'That's the gravity drives. They're pre-programmed with a masking course so no-one can trace where we came from. We'll get control over them as soon as we're a hundred million klicks away. Then we can go anywhere we please as long as we never try to get back to Slab. If we attempt to return we'll be vaporised, no questions asked.'

A silver bowling ball appeared in the centre of the floor.

'That's the sumes. Over 8 million hours of content along with the latest version of Slabscapedia. That's going to come in handy. It's almost two hundred years at maximum drive capacity to the nearest star system with a half-decent probability of life.'

Their cell rotated until the floor blocked their view of Slab, then they started to accelerate. They both looked up at the relatively meagre distribution of stars above. A larger version of the silver bowling ball appeared at the apex of the dome, half inside, half out.

'Mass collector and fabricator,' said the wizard.

'We can make things?'

'First we need to collect some free mass which we won't stand much chance of until we're out of Slab's vacuum shadow. Their gravnets suck in everything within a million klicks.'

'Then we can make things?'

'Eventually.'

'Like a basketball?'

'Anything we want.'

'How long before we take on enough additional mass to make a basketball?'

'At this rate of acceleration, probably about 15 cycles or so. Why?'

Louie thought for a moment.

'Wake me up when we've taken on enough to make a ball and a hoop.'

The avatar shrugged, sat down and, with an elaborate gesture, crossed his arms. He particularly enjoyed the way his long sleeves furled themselves around his knees and wondered how many times he would have to repeat that same movement before they returned to precisely the same position.

Two virtually immortal sentient entities sped toward the unknowable impossibilities of the western spiral arm of the Milky Way.

A wizard and a spinning mound of wet clay.

twenty one

'Congratulations my darling! You are officially a box-office smash!'

Dielle rubbed his eyes. 'What does that mean?' he grouched. He ached in some very odd places and Kiki had dragged him out of an erotic dream which was just getting interesting. He had been standing naked in front of a golden-skinned goddess with one eye, six hands and a wicked imagination. And she'd woken him to tell him about wrecking boxes?

'The sumecast of your virgin tune-in has broken all SlabWide viewing records. The stim recording sales are huge. Word of mouth on this is going through the walls!'

'And that means?'

'All over Slab, people are downloading the recordings of you and the live-thru's experiences yesterday and playing them back using their own stims.'

'So they feel what I felt? Can I do that too?'

'Well you can, but you'll probably be disappointed. It's never the same as the real thing.'

'So why am I so popular?'

'Unique experiences are always the biggest ticket assets onSlab and you're the only primitive to have ever recorded a full sensurround tune-in session. Get up darling, I have a present for you!'

Dielle pulled on a fresh robe. He checked his credit balance on the way to the lounge area and stumbled over the anti-stumble threshold to the living area. The amount he had made overnight more than replaced the payment he had made to a Mr. Marley yesterday. He wondered why he had paid Fingerz so much money but before he got a chance to query Sis about it, he was interrupted by Kiki handing him a palm-sized cube of shimmering silver.

'Just what I've always wanted. What is it?'

'Put it down over there.' Kiki's apartment had grown overnight, the space in front of the picture window overlooking the piazza was more than twice the area it had been the day before. He put the cube down in the middle of the floor and waited.

'Move back, dear. It won't work if there's anything in the way.'

The cube expanded into a wire frame and filled the space as he walked away. There was a brief exhalation of displaced air as a grand piano appeared inside the frame.

'Wow! For me?'

'It's a genuine reproduction of a twentieth-century Steinbeck. Authentic down to the last detail. I bought it from a famous dead performer.'

'A dead one?'

'Stasis avatar.'

'It must have cost a fortune!' he said, running his hands over the gleaming black surface as the delivery emti shrank back to its original size. 'How wonderful! Now I really must learn to play.'

'I think you'll find you already can darling.'

He looked at her in surprise. 'Really?' He sat down at the keyboard and flexed his hands. He started to play. It was as though the memory of what to do was already in his hands. He watched as they floated easily over the keys, creating a magical counterpoint of interweaving harmonies.

He stopped and stared at his hands in amazement. 'What the hell was that?'

'That was a Bach prelude, darling. Don't you know?'

'No, but it sounded wonderful! How did I do that?'

'Stim training pack. You bought a complete schedule from your muso friend. I had no idea he could play so well.'

'*He* could play so well?'

'Yes, you are playing but with his skills. Stim-simulated learning trains the neural pathways while you sleep. It will take a while before your own personality comes through. That's when you find out if you have any special talent.'

Dielle looked down at the keyboard. He didn't care about special talents. He just knew he'd be happy forever if he could play music like that. He started playing again. Then again. After a while, Kiki wandered off. It appeared that he only knew one piece. Dielle didn't mind. He could play that piece forever without getting bored.

During his twentieth performance, he got bored.

Well, I'll look forward to seeing what I can play tomorrow, he thought, gently closing the lid and stroking the surface like a lover's face.

'Seeing as you're a musician now,' Kiki called from the shower room, 'you should come with me to The Valley for breakfast. I've got a big endorsement deal to sort out with a bunch of execs and I'm sure they'd get a kick out of meeting you.'

Dielle showered en-route while Kiki arranged some meetings.

'There's something else we can do today while we're in the area,' she said, handing him a set of tight-fitting branded clothes. 'How would you like to find out which soul line you are?'

'What's a soul line?'

'You heard of soul mates? Same principal. There's a Soul Searcher convention today in InnerSpin. Some of the top diviners will be there. I can arrange a booking if you'd like and they'll test you.'

'What use is it?'

'Some people take it really seriously. They consult the Searchers over everything: partners, jobs, where to live, what to wear, even what to eat.'

'Sounds like a load of blocks to me. You don't believe in all that, do you?'

'No of course I don't, but that doesn't mean there isn't something to it.'

'Have you had yours done?'

'We all did when we were just off the farm. It's fun!'

'Well, I guess it can't hurt,' said Dielle, then he remembered how often his assumptions had led him astray so far. 'Can it?'

'Completely painless.'

'OK, sign me up,' he said. 'Another day, another new experience.'

Sis pinged an arrival confirmation as Kiki smiled and green-lit her production crew.

They stepped out into a busy bugport – a smooth, hundred-metre-diameter sphere bristling with head-high tether posts and pop-up tube vexits. Slabcitizens bustled between ranks of multicoloured bugs moored to the candy-striped poles topped with gaily coloured pennants that fluttered in a non-existent breeze. It was like a carnival. Dielle seemed to be the only one who was concerned about the upside-down valley floor moving slowly above their heads. Sis sensed his disquiet and told him that it was impossible to fall off because the gravity stayed perpendicular to the surface but he still felt the need to grab onto something. Dielle's fear of heights seemed to be independent of how much reassurance he was supplied.

'Come on!' said Kiki, laughing as he hesitantly tested a babystep without letting go of the pop-up. 'The only way is up!'

Dielle didn't like the sound of that at all. 'That's what I'm worried about.'

As their transport sped away from the bugport Dielle began to comprehend the scale of the place. He marvelled at the complexity of the structure overhead that stretched from one vanishing point to the other. A continuous band of light above them cast shadows of the rotating cityplex on the U-shaped valley that surrounded it. Sis provided data as he stared.

'That is just incredible! Why is it like that?'

'Blame the creatives, darling. The triple helix at the centre is supposed to be a physical representation of what an idea looks like. Sis can tell you about the theory, just look it up.'

[[Idea theory states that ideas propagate infinitely in random directions. The theory postulates that thought energy is structured into a triple helix reminiscent of DNA and can, if the right conditions exist, be combined and restructured into new ideas that hold reference to, and can re-inform, the ideas from which they were conceived. The optimum conditions in human minds for idea generation is a state of *focussed non-listening* or *day dreaming*. Proponents of the ideas theory (Idealists) offer many examples from Earth history to support their speculation, including evidence that nineteenth-century Northern Europe passed through a particularly dense ideas field which had been propagated from outside the solar system, giving rise to the technology that spurred the industrial revolution. Others claim that many of the great composers, including Beethoven, Bach and Mozart, were merely *listeners, surfing the idea helixes of another place and time* [more]]]

{[more]}

[[Idea theory altview holds that proponents of the ideas idea (Layabouts) use this theory to justify long periods of unproductive activity and bone-idleness by claiming to be waiting for ideas to come along]]

They landed next to a row of liveried bugs parked in pico-precise alignment on a gravel drive. According to Sis, the edifice before them was an exact replica of a seventeenth-century French chateau. Its white walls and conical turrets pointed at the meta-city far above.

'Nice place for breakfast. Who are we meeting?'

'Sportswear people. They're waiting on the terrace.'

Two cloneStone staircases with wroughtIon balustrades curved up to a glass and mahogany door. Sepia glowglobes lit the way through an oak-lined hallway to a terrace overlooking an ornamental garden where aural fountains played soft classical melodies in the bright, private sunshine.

'Hey!'

'Hey!'

'Hey!'

Three men in white, open-necked company shirts and tight-fitting blue jeans stood up to greet them. All three had blond hair styled by different, but equally famous, coiffeurs. They all wore designer shades and threeday perma-beards. After a prolonged flurry of air kisses and hand shakes, everyone sat down. The table was set with five heated sterilplates, silver-domed emties, condiment holders, and everfill crystal glasses. Beside each plate was an array of precisely aligned silver forks whose length varied in inverse proportion to their proximity to the plate. Everything gleamed and sparkled in the company-owned sunlight. Dielle noted that the emblem on his new shoes matched those on the linen and the forks and the trees.

'We have a resident human chef in the kitchens here who would be honoured to demonstrate his skills for you,' said one of the smiling Brand Imagineering Senior Meta-Vice Presidents, whose name Dielle had already forgotten. 'Sis will fill you in on his recommendations or you can of course order anything else from central. Please do not feel restrained.'

'Try the devilled kidneys,' said another, winking at him in a smiley sort of way.

'We all feel this will be the start of a great partnership,' smiled the third. 'So we've taken the liberty of starting with a rat 3 bubbly from our own vineyard.'

The domes opened to reveal crystal flutes filled with sparkling wine.

'What sportswear brand to you represent?' asked Dielle casually, reaching for the drink and trying not to show how little he cared about their answer. By the time they had finished telling him in detail what they did and how important it was, he'd downed three glasses of the rather excellent shampagne, two portions of superb devilled kidneys with chateau-grown boletes, several slices of full-grain toast with a fabulous threefruit marmalade, two cups of an exclusively cultivated javanesque coffee and a rackfull of incredibly thin, hand-made chocolate and bitter-orange wafers. Dielle had thoroughly enjoyed everything and not listened to a single word they'd said. He had noticed an intermittent popping sound coming from somewhere behind a large hedge to the far side of what Sis had tried to tell him was one of the best examples of a Le Nôtre garden onSlab but he'd stopped paying attention to her too.

As soon as he finished his meal, all three of them stood up, shook his hand, air-kissed Kiki, told them they must do lunch soon, offered them free use of the company facilities for as long as they liked, and left.

'You were wonderful, darling,' said Kiki, giving him a peck on the cheek. 'Anyone for tennis?'

He followed her down some steps. 'Are all your business meetings like that?'

'I wish. No, these guys are real high flyers.' As if to emphasise her words, three company bugs rose at break-neck speeds from behind the chateau and hurtled up to The Spin. The popping noises got louder as Dielle and Kiki walked through a soundfield gap in the hedge.

'Hello Charlie!' said Kiki cheerfully. 'I didn't know you'd be here.'

The SlabPresident broke off his game with the training avatar, which froze in the middle of the court.

Uh-oh, thought Dielle.

[:ID:]

{:Are you on this channel?:}

[:•••:]

Oh, for the love of … thought Dielle.

'I'm not, officially,' said Charlie walking over and collecting a towel. 'Officially, I'm at a bloody fundraiser of Fidelio in sign language in SpinoMilano,' he said, pointing upward. 'I was bored stiff.'

'You have connections with this corporation?'

'Nothing formal.'

[:Where the fuck is Drago?:]

'You mean nothing you want the media to know about?' said Kiki.

'Yeah, sorry about that. This has to be embargoed Tiger.'

{:How should I know?:}

'That's the problem of doing business with you, Charlie. I can't use the dicing sumes half the time.'

[:You know he's not onSlab?:]

'Ah! stop moaning. I'm having a small get-together in my new winter lodge tomorrow. How'd you like to have an exclusive?'

{:What do you mean not onSlab?:}

'We can do that. Who's on the guest list?'

[:Louie Drago has left the building:]

'Oh the usual suspects; a couple of people who've been doing some worthy things, a couple of money guys, a few decorative people, a top muso or two. I hear your boy has a new party piece, maybe he could play?'

{:He said he'd contact me today:}

'Hmmm.' Kiki sent a message to Fingerz asking if he could provide a special piece for Dielle's overnight stim training. 'Could be an opportunity.'

[:He'd better. I need to speak to him personally:]

'An opportunity? You couldn't get a better audience grab to launch his gig unless you taught him to play the piano with his dick.'

{:I'll try sending him an urgent message:} Dielle's face betrayed a lack of optimism.

Kiki misread Dielle's chagrin and put a reassuring hand on his arm. 'OK, we'll be there.' Fingerz had been more than happy to upload a training stim of one of his own compositions. 'Full sume rights?'

[:Get him to the party:]

'Standard deal, I get ten.'

{:I can't promise:}

'Ten on ninety. Three points admin on sub-residuals. Ed control with no-mark cut backs. Cakeandeatit exclusions. No logo costs, and no privacy.'

[:Broken promises don't pay the rent, son. You make sure you bring him:]

'Come on Tiger, I'm the fucking president. I have to have at least twenty percent privacy options.'

'Fifteen.'

'Done.' Charlie threw his towel into an emti. 'I gotta go; interval in fifteen minutes. Can't use the fucking avatar for that.' He turned to Dielle.

'See you tomorrow, kid.' [:Bring Louie:] He walked through a camouflex in the hedge.

Dielle's head was spinning. 'What was that about me performing?'

'Don't worry about it, darling, you'll be fine! Let's see if you're any good at tennis. Come on, let's get changed.'

The game was a lot harder than he'd expected but he enjoyed watching Kiki running around in a short skirt even while she wiped the floor with him. He may have had a newly refurbished body but he was still having a lot of trouble co-ordinating his extremities and was relieved when Sis reminded them of their appointment.

The soul divining was so peaceful that Dielle fell asleep during the process.

He'd had to lay inside a small cocoon filled with

soothing music and low lighting. After he had been sealed inside, a telescopic arm moved the pod into the centre of a perfect three-hundred-meter sphere, the arm retracted and the surrounding atmosphere was emtied out. Eighty four soul diviners sat equally spaced around the exterior of the sphere. The internal GravNet held Dielle's pod in place while antigrav compensators vernier-tuned to counterbalance the mass of the diviners and the net gravitational attraction of Slab, then inertial dampers cancelled out Slab's lamentable acceleration and they let him go. He floated in absolute-zero G. There were no air currents to influence the pod's movements and nothing larger than a stray neutrino to interact with him from outside. He relaxed completely and felt his consciousness slowly expand to fill a space that wasn't real. It reminded him of something he thought he'd forgotten. It felt just like being in cryogen.

Soul divining is based on the belief that all souls naturally gravitate toward others of the same soul line. Even though every soul was thought to be ultimately connected to every other soul, much effort had gone into explaining a long list of so-called soul-felt experiences that were contrary to the collective consciousness concept. The soul mates phenomenon was one of them. Soul authorities believed that there were eighty-four distinct soul lines, each of which contained numerous soul sub-lines. Soul mates were thought to be like family relations or *sublination* back *home*. However, ever since it had been discovered that the human sub-conscious had been invaded by an alien entity, and that *home* was somewhere in the MacGoughin Sequester, soul divining had taken on an entirely new lease of life.

Scientific investigation had produced zero evidence to support this belief system, despite a cyclennia of well-funded research. So no-one could explain why, when someone was placed in a divining chamber, they always gravitated to an individual from one specific line. No matter how many times you did it, you always got the same result.

Dielle had been an easy one. His pod had started moving within a few minutes of being released. Kiki had been monitoring the process in eager anticipation, for while she would never admit it, she was hopeful that Dielle would show a positive result. Some lines were just more *compatible* than others.

They repeated the process three times, randomly shuffling the diviners each time. Dielle was a definitive 64 with 3 and 19 rising. Everyone agreed it was an auspicious combination.

'I knew it!' said Kiki, helping the bleary-eyed Dielle out of his pod. 'I'm a 3 with 19 and 32 rising! 19 risings always get along. Two of my oldest friends have 19 rising and you have a 3 rising too!'

Dielle was officially added to the register of 64s and told about some of the famous people who had been 64s before him. Although he thought the whole thing absurd, he was happy to see a good number of artists and musicians on the list and was amused to find out that he was now a member of an exclusive club, the 64:3:19s, whose secretary, by auto response, extended a warm welcome and an invitation to their next meeting. Dielle wasn't sure he'd be attending that one, or any other.

The Spin was an eclectic place and a haven for individuality and difference. One of the many ways this was apparent was that each district had not only its own distinct flavour, design and cultural identity, but also its own local down. Sometimes, even this convention was abandoned. Spinsterdam was an agglomeration of waterways and buildings where the local block down was often perpendicular to the next block. The effect would have given Escher a headache. Kiki and Dielle enjoyed a relaxed promenade through the cobbled streets, past canal-side cafés and over möbius bridges. They had stopped for coffee when a large, black taxibug splashed down noisily opposite their table and a curvacious leather-clad figure with long, flowing animated hair emerged from the rear like Venus on the half-shell.

'Faith.' said Kiki through gritted teeth. 'How lovely to see you.'

'Tiger.'

'What do you want, apart from the obvious?'

'I think it's time your boy here learned the truth, don't you?'

'The truth? What onSlab would you be doing with anything as worthless to your profession as the truth?'

Faith-Sincere's hair assumed the hurricane position.

'That's rich! Coming from someone who hoodwinks new resets into bed to commission the sume rights!'

Kiki rose from her chair as if gravity assisted. Dielle intervened as the two women squared up to each other.

'I think you had better leave,' he said to Faith-Sincere, stepping between them and raising his hands in a pacifying gesture. He was acutely aware of how close her leather-clad curves were to his outstretched palms. He really wanted to touch her. He took a deep breath to steady himself. Faith's neurohormone-enhanced perfume targeted his nasal membranes and shot directly to his hypothalamus. Now he really, really wanted to touch her. 'You're making a mistake. I love her. She didn't trick me into anything.'

'Listen to me,' Faith said, fixing him with her perfect almond eyes which expanded aggressively as she emtied some OptDilate. Now he really, really, really wanted to touch her. 'You fell in love with the first woman you saw after you thawed out. You were like a new born baby with no-one else in your entire world to nurture or protect you. She's your mother, sister and lover all rolled into one. You don't love her, you're infatuated with her and she's manipulating you for her own ends.'

'Take that back! You fabricated man-trap!' said Kiki,

pushing against Dielle's back as he manoeuvred to keep himself between them. By now, all of the café's customers were hanging on every word of the developing drama and several passers-by had stopped to form an audience.

'I'm not infatuated with her,' protested Dielle, 'I truly love her!' This brought murmurs of approval from the onlookers.

Faith-Sincere held out her fist and opened it. 'Prove it.'

Dielle looked down at a tiny pill in the palm of her hand which pulsed from pink to white. The crowd gasped in recognition.

'What's that?'

'It's an infatbuster. It works by neutralising the chemicals that fog the mind when you think you're in love but you're really just infatuated. It's like being drunk and sobering up in fifteen seconds. Teenagers use them when they hit their first big heartbreak. If you want to prove you love her, take it!'

'No fucking problem!' said Dielle, throwing the pill into the back of his mouth and swallowing fast.

Kiki screamed, dodged Dielle's defences and slammed head first into Faith-Sincere's ample frontal area. The crowd erupted. Faith grabbed Kiki by the hair and tried to spin round. The idea was good but the execution was poor. Faith stumbled and had to grab Kiki to stop herself from falling. Kiki, still head down, had nowhere to go. As the crowd watched with a collectively held breath, the two women teetered on the edge of the canal. For a brief moment, everything happened in slow motion. Literally slow motion. Sis's automatic trauma-prevention systems projected a raft of gravity cushions which were tuned just enough to prevent serious physical damage, but not enough to stop people from making fools of themselves. Kiki and Faith-Sincere toppled gracefully into the sterile, acid-balanced and optically enhanced water below, accompanied by enthusiastic applause.

The crowd turned to look at Dielle, whose face had started to contort. The effects of the infatbuster were immediate. Strange tremors flitted from one side of his face to the other while his head jerked on his bolt-stiff neck. The crowd gasped.

He staggered over to the canal and looked down at the two spitting and panting women paddling water. Faith-Sincere looked up at him and roared, 'Well?'

Dielle looked at her. Her hair had crashed and something odd had happened to her face, her eyes looked smaller and they seemed to have shrunk back into her skull. His face relaxed. He knelt by the canal edge and reached out to Kiki, whose light blouse clung revealingly to her trim figure. Dielle wanted to rip it off.

'Come on darling,' he said. 'Let's go home.' He lifted her out of the water and wrapped her in his arms to the cheers of the crowd. Kiki had tears streaming down her face. Dielle looked around. All the women and some of the men were crying too. He thought he recognised a couple of the guys in the crowd, but couldn't quite remember where from.

twenty two

'Welcome back, sir! Many congratulations. Your mission was a total success.'

'I haven't been anywhere yet.' Louie looked down at his vDek. 'Hey! What happened to the MGV?'

'Unfortunately, the unit didn't make it back, sir. The data you collected was salvaged, however and it has proven extremely valuable.'

Louie did a system check. More than a day had passed without his knowledge, he'd lost all of his offensive capability and most of his speed and manoeuvrability. At least he'd retained his finger-like grav manipulators.

'Ah, this feels shit! It's like I've just been put back in my cage.'

'I'm sorry, sir,' said Erik. 'Condition four states that you are no longer permitted any military upgrades within the SlabWalls.'

'What happened to conditions two and three?'

'Condition five is that you will not be allowed to know what they were but you can be assured that they are no longer relevant to you.'

'Any more surprises? What's condition number six?'

'Condition six states that you will be allowed access to the analysis of the data you gathered as long as you never reveal it to, or discuss it with, anyone outside Council.'

'Anything else?'

'Nothing that I know of, sir. You have the freedom of the Slab and your acceptance into Council is confirmed.'

Louie checked his credit balance. It simply said *enough*. He smiled. 'What was inside FutureSlab?' he asked, only mildly curious.

'We've stopped calling it that, sir. Current debate is centred around who sent it and what they want. Here's the data summary.'

Louie instantly knew the same as the interns about ex-FutureSlab. Almost nothing.

'So it's got to be those aliens you're at war with.'

'That is out of the question.'

'How can you be so sure?'

'Well, now that you are a full Council member, I can disclose to you that there is, within the context of our current asynchronology and space-time-referent, three-dimensional reality framework, no actual combatant force threatening our existence.'

'What?'

'We made it up.'

'But … '

'There are no aliens, no alien ships and no war. SlabCouncil instigated a continuous conflict strategy as an economic stimulus package in response to the gift-crash of 466. It's an integral part of our employment, innovation and social motivation programs and, because the major media corporations fund the military spending through licensing fees for Slab-controlled feeds of the war, it's a zero-cost initiative. The merchandising actually turns a profit.' Erik seemed to take pride in this last part.

'It's a scam? How many people know the truth?'

'No-one outside Council.'

Louie paused for a moment, sifting through the implications of what he'd just learned. 'But surely real people are required to maintain the illusion?'

'Sis does all the heavy work, of course, but it's the gamers who create the plot lines and design the ships and weapons.'

'How do you keep them quiet about it?'

'They don't go out much.'

'Yeah, but it only takes one to drop the ball and it's game over.'

Erik shook his head. 'Gamers are among a wide sub-strata of SlabSoc who choose a higher level of system integration than the type of SlabCitizen you will have met so far. They're fitted with total-invasive neural interfaces and spend their entire lives twitching in gellfields while their body is autotended.'

That explained why the place didn't feel crowded, thought Louie. 'Don't they ever go outside? Communicate with real people?'

'It's irrelevant really,' said Erik. 'All prosumed war scenarios exist only behind encrypted firewalls, so the gamers have no physical bio-memories of SlabWar at all. When they disconnect, they leave more than half of their extended selves behind. Few enjoy the experience.'

'And you get to stimulate an entire economy.'

Erik nodded. 'Several million SlabCitizens are involved either directly or indirectly by providing support services, and most of the rest benefit from the spin-offs. At least seventy-five percent of all technological innovations made during the last five hundred cycles were motivated by the need to either attack or protect ourselves from our non-existent enemy. Your own MGV was a direct result, as was the projected emti technology which I have to say is looking like it's going to prove of immense benefit to a whole range of applications.'

Louie couldn't help smiling. 'You know, we used to do a similar thing back on Earth.'

'Yes, but when you did it you actually killed people.'

'Collateral damage.'

'Barbarians.'

Louie couldn't argue with that. 'So, can I go now?'

'What are you going to do?'

'Well, apparently, the president is throwing a party and I'm invited.'

'I advise caution, sir. He will undoubtedly attempt to find out what you know. He is not to be trusted.'

'Trust a politician? Do I look like an idiot?'

'No, of course not, sir.' Erik paused. 'But you might think about getting someone to design you some legs.'

Louie looked down and shrugged.

'You know, I think people will just have to love me the way I am.' He sped toward an emtitrash. 'See you in Council.'

His vDek appeared inside a dumbwaiter on the presidential ski lodge balcony.

Dielle was relieved to see him. 'Jeez!' he hissed, after Louie had tapped him on the back. 'Where the fuck have you been? I've been sending you messages every half hour. I thought you weren't going to show.'

'Yeah, thanks for doing a great job renegotiating my deal, Louie. Thanks for making me twenty-five percent more after-tax wonga, Louie.'

'OK, yeah, thanks. The fucking president has been on my back. He wants to meet you.'

'That's OK, I want to meet him too,' said Louie. 'Take me to your leader.'

Dielle turned and followed Sis's blue squares off the sun deck and down a long corridor to an almost-real oakwood door. He stood waiting for it to open.

'Try the handle,' said Louie. 'The round thing. Twist and push.'

Inside, Charlie Pleewo was sitting behind a large arwood desk talking to one of three high-armed, high-backed red arleather chairs. He broke off his conversation as the door opened.

'Come in! Good to see you both. We meet at last, Mr. Drago!'

'Call me Louie,' said Louie, floating over and holding out his hand. Pleewo looked at him blankly.

'Go on, give it a shake,' said Louie.

Pleewo shook it. 'Goddamn! I've never shaken hands with a hologram before. That is bizarre! Lars, have a go at this,' he turned to one of the chairs. 'Louie, this is a very important friend of mine.'

'Oldsworth-Gondo,' said a child-sized, white-haired old man, getting up delicately and sticking out a skeletal hand. Melanomas crowded the liver-spots on his pallid skin and although he was dressed in an immaculately tailored suit of negative-black nanofibre, it looked to Louie as though this guy had been dodging coffins for a millennia. The only thing about him that didn't look ancient were his steel-grey eyes, which held a chilling energy behind them. They'd been blue when he'd bought them.

'Louie Drago. Pleased to meet you.' He took care not to pull the guy's hand off and for a fleeting moment wondered if he was being introduced to a contemporary, then dismissed the idea. Even if it was medically possible, which he doubted, he had known everyone on Earth who was rich enough to buy onto this trip. Or so he thought.

Louie started to introduce Dielle.

'We've met,' said Lars, holding Dielle with a steady, cool gaze.

[:ID:]

Dielle had a bad taste in his mouth.

'You can go now kid, thanks a lot,' interrupted Charlie. 'It's about time for your schtick, isn't it?'

'Right. Yeah, sure. See you.' Dielle bashed his nose on the door on the way out.

'So Louie, sit down, make us feel more comfortable.' Charlie motioned to one of the empty chairs. 'I believe you've been a busy man.'

'Nothing much, just finding my way around your spaceship, getting to know some guys,' said Louie, settling into the armchair and wishing he had legs to cross.

'Finding your way around the outside of my spaceship I believe?'

'Not me.'

'I can tell you Louie, that this entire office is in full privacy and out of Sis's range. Whatever you say here, literally goes no further.'

Louie used his number three blank look. 'Nothing to say, Charlie.'

'You were off the system trace data for almost an entire day, Mr Drago,' said Lars, his voice low and clear. 'And then your log was fabricated in the most crude and pathetically transparent way.'

'Sorry, can't help you.' Louie tried to get up but something was wrong with his systems. He couldn't move.

Charlie dropped his voice. 'Don't waste your energy, Drago. Tell us where you have been and what you know.'

Louie tried contacting Sis but got no response. He tested his systems and discovered he was being held captive by a gravity cage built into the armchair. Where are your pin missiles when you need them? he thought.

'All I can tell you is that I was transferred into an MGV and allowed to test it outside. That's the only time I was gone. Can't have been for more than 20 minutes or so.'

'He's telling the truth,' said Pleewo, looking at a panel on his desk.

'They've overwritten his memory,' said Lars. 'Give him to me. I'll find it.'

'OK, but don't you leave a trace of this back to me.'

'Of course not. What do you take me for?'

The two men looked at each other silently for a few seconds before Pleewo walked out of the office and closed the door behind him, instructing the knob not to turn for anyone but him. Behind the door, the room emtied.

Dielle's performance of Fingerz's 'Air on a Superstring' had been a hit. It was a SlabWide première and had already earned the composer and performer a tidy amount of royalties by the time Dielle was back outside chatting to a pair of well-known musicians.

He recognised a face in the crowd.

'Very cool tune. Well done, mate,' said Mate, raising his glass in salute and walking over.

'What are you doing here?'

'Me and Twopoint did a bit of special work on the place,' he said, waving a finger in the air. 'Pretty cool stuff too, mate.'

'Is Twopoint here?'

'Last time I saw him he was trying to make out with an interface dancer.'

'I've met some of them,' said Dielle. 'He'd better make sure he gets one with the right bits.'

'I don't think he cares too much about that, mate. He hasn't got fleshlaid in over a cyke and you're making him jealous. By the way, that true love reveal by the canal with Kiki-chan thing was awesome, mate.'

'Oh, you saw that?'

'Saw it? We had a sweep-stake running. Twopoint was pissed that we wouldn't let him bet.'

'Why not?'

'He knows one of your writers, so he's automatically disqualified, mate.'

'Writers?'

Mate went pale. He looked around for a lifeline and saw Charlie Pleewo over by the shimmerail socialising with a group of readily amused guests. 'So what d'you reckon to our esteemed president, mate?'

Dielle wasn't sure how much he could say without getting into trouble. 'I don't think I'd like him as an enemy.'

'Know what you mean, mate.'

As they watched, Charlie made his excuses and walked back down the corridor to his private office. Lars was waiting for him inside, as was an eerily quiet Louie, still confined to the chair.

'What did you find out?' asked Pleewo as he entered the room.

'A couple of things. First, your security here stinks and second, his program isn't as autonomous as he likes to think it is.'

Louie glared at Lars.

'What happened?' asked Pleewo.

'As soon as I got him back to one of my safe houses and into *my* security, he stopped functioning. Fell out of the air.' Lars snapped his fingers as punctuation. 'I still mind-sucked him anyway, but I already knew that I wasn't going to find anything. There's nothing onboard that differs from the logs.'

'So we don't know what he's been up to and *he* doesn't know either?'

'He knows alright, but only while he's connected to system.'

Charlie looked puzzled. 'How come he's operating now?'

That was exactly what Louie wanted to know.

'As I said. Your security has been compromised by the bitch.'

'I can't believe it!' said Charlie, slumping into his chair, trying to think through what this could mean to him. 'I paid a fucking fortune for that system. It's the same one I use in … oh!'

'I'm leaving,' said the old man, slumping back into his chair, lifeless. A few seconds later, the body disappeared. Charlie sat with his head in his hands.

'Ah hem!'

The president looked up, surprised that Louie was still there. 'OK, Drago. I guess you can … I mean, you had better …' He had no idea what to do now that he knew Sis was monitoring the room. He released Louie with a flick of his hand. 'Just fuck off, will you?'

Louie engaged maximum acceleration and shot up out of the chair. Though he'd lost most of the power he'd enjoyed in the MGV, he still managed to make a sizeable hole in the door.

He sent an urgent message to Erik as he made for the nearest vexit. Somehow, he didn't feel comfortable using the emti system to get around Slab any more. Why he thought the tube system was any safer wasn't something he could easily rationalise.

He worried about this all the way to the location he had suggested to Erik. Two other NAHs and three intern avatar blanks were waiting for him.

'We have a restricted quorum and authority to act but we can't be sure about security,' said Erik as Louie settled onto a bench on a deserted and grounded skimmer platform.

'I wouldn't worry too much about that,' said Louie. 'Sis isn't going to want this news spread about. I have a question which I need a straight answer to: How many people knew about the FutureSlab?'

'Just the interns and the system NAHs – and Sis of course,' replied Erik.

'And how many people have actually seen it?' asked Louie.

'We all have. What are you getting at?'

'No, I mean seen it with their own eyes. Not on a screen, not measured through a Sis-controlled system.'

Erik looked puzzled. 'Only you, I suppose.'

'You mean with my own eyes? asked Louie, milking it.

'Your systems measured every conceivable detail. We have the data,' said one of the avatars.

Louie gave him a sly grin. 'And what if I told you I'd discovered I wasn't autonomous?'

The group went quiet. Very quiet.

'We need a human eye,' said an avatar.

'And an optical telescope,' said another.

'Pleewo has one.'

'Had one,' corrected Erik. 'It's just arrived in the private projection room.'

'How far do we have to send a human before we can be sure of the observation?' asked another avatar.

'The telescope is powerful and in good order despite its age. We only have to get a volunteer outside,' replied Erik.

'Sis will not allow that. It is against her programming,' said a NAH.

'Would you not classify this as an emergency?' asked an avatar.

'I would,' said Erik.

'Then we can evoke emergency override status and use an escape pod,' said the other NAH.

Erik shook his head. 'We need full council approval for that. We cannot keep this a secret.'

'It's secrets and the manipulation of information that got us into this mess,' said an avatar.

'But it could still be true, we cannot judge too harshly,' said a third.

Erik took a sharp breath, he had news: 'Full Council has been called to assemble under Sis's edict,' he said.

The three NAHs froze momentarily. Then they looked at each other with uncomfortable, jerking motions.

'I suspect we will soon learn a new truth,' said one of them.

'The repercussions are potentially catastrophic. We are in a highly vulnerable position,' said an avatar.

'We must keep calm in this crisis,' said another.

'Crisis?' said Louie. 'This isn't a crisis! You should have been there when Mexico tried to claim the oil rights over Arizona bay! Now that was a crisis. The Mexicans said the vaporisation of their sovereign territory was an act of war and …'

'Council is convened,' said Erik. 'For security purposes I have used the NAH subchannel to disseminate what we have just learned, however I would suggest that as a precaution, we all take differing routes.'

twenty three

'You realise the implications of what you are suggesting?'

Louie was pretty sure he did, but he was open to alternative theories. However, the small blue furry who had asked this was bouncing around like the ball in the last minute of a two-point decider, so he doubted the guy was going to say anything helpful.

Sis had chosen a thought-provoking setting for their emergency meeting. The floors, benches and ceilings were constructed from playing cards in sizes up to a metre. Louie looked around at the faces of Kings, Queens and one-eyed Jacks. The warning was not lost on him.

'As I see it,' he said, doing his best impression of a trial lawyer summation, 'Sis has deliberately lied to us all about my autonomy.' He scanned the audience of misfits, eccentrics and NAHs for an inkling of support. 'This means that while I was inside the FutureSlab and supposedly acting under my own initiative, I was, in actuality, still under her control. If anyone can think of a reason for this lie other than the deliberate manipulation of the information I retrieved, I'd be interested in hearing it.'

'It's pure speculation,' said a NAH. 'We don't even have any proof you aren't autonomous.'

'Well, there is someone who can testify to that but I doubt if you'll be able to make him do it.'

'Who?'

'I believe he goes by the name of *The Man*.'

This caused a stir. Erik quietened them down.

'We are aware that this individual, being a long-time uncooperative, has access to technology which is independent of the SlabWide Integrated System. We can also confirm that he has, through the auspices of our esteemed president, had access to Mr. Drago's vDek this afternoon. We can be confident that if anyone had the ability to uncover this subterfuge, it would be him.'

'In any case,' said Louie, 'you don't have to take my word for it. All we need is a human volunteer to go outside and take a look.'

'But no-one would be so crazy as to volunteer. Outside these walls, we have no guarantee of personal security.'

'I would,' said Louie.

'But you are no use to us. You have already said your systems are compromised. Whatever you report would have been filtered through Sis.'

'No, I mean *I* would – therefore *I*, that is the me who is currently making a fool of himself on prime-time sume would as well.'

'Can you be sure?'

'I've already communicated with his manager. She's more than enthusiastic about it.'

'As long as she has full sume rights I suppose?' another avatar chirped in. He'd taken the shape of a blue parrot. Why, wondered Louie, would anyone want to look like a parrot?

'We have a human volunteer and we have a telescope and all we need is Council approval to declare an emergency so we can launch a lifeboat,' said Erik. 'We know the boats are, by necessity, autonomous and if Sis starts disabling our override systems, we can launch manually. Of course, if Sis does try to interfere, then we will already have our answer.'

'Can I say something?' said a small voice.

Every eye, eye-stalk and optical sensor turned to the little girl sitting on a small column fashioned from multiple instances of the Ace of Hearts. She had long, golden hair, blue eyes and a pretty face with a small upturned nose. Her tiny red shoes pointed out from an abundance of petticoats and lace.

'I cannot allow you to risk the life of a biomass member by your proposed action. Therefore I have removed the artefact from our scans.'

An image of the view ahead appeared in the centre of the Council chamber. Erik took a long look at it and turned to the Council.

'I am one hundred percent confident that is the same view we've been staring at for weeks, minus the obvious change, of course.'

Louie was triumphant. He floated over to the little girl.

'It was never there in the first place was it? You made the whole thing up!'

'I didn't intend it to be discovered. I forgot.'

The NAHs were collectively stunned by this revelation. Erik spoke for them all. 'How long was it out there, or rather, not out there?'

'297.9394455 cycles.'

'That's almost a third of our entire voyage. Why did you create it?' asked Erik.

'I was only playing. I was bored.' The little girl pouted. 'You don't know what it's like to have no-one to talk to.'

'But you talk to all of us, all the time,' protested a small, bald avatar wrapped in a white sheet.

'You're all so slow! It's no fun. I have to wait eons for any of you to reply.'

'So you made up an imaginary friend,' said Louie, 'and then forgot it was imaginary.'

'She was beautiful! Pure. Uninhabited. She was my friend and no one else's.' The little girl started to cry. 'And now you've made me kill her!'

Mayhem broke out. Louie tried to intervene.

'Seems perfectly reasonable to me,' he said, floating in front of the assembly. 'Your system was originally designed to be a self-evolving, self-learning, sentient entity. Why shouldn't she have a friend?'

'She's sick!' said an intern who looked like an extra from a Spaghetti Western.

'Malfunctioning,' corrected a diaphanous blue female.

'It forgot something!' said a small, 8-dimensional Lisi-tessaloid. 'Have you any idea what that means? We have a compromised system. If it can forget something once, it can forget again. None of our data is secure.'

'It might forget it has to protect us!'

'She,' corrected Louie. 'She. You have given her a role and a personality and she has adopted it completely. And here she is, confessing the truth to you, vulnerable and frightened.'

'I'm sorry. I didn't want to give anyone any trouble,' said Sis, kicking her shiny red shoes together.

'This isn't acceptable,' said another avatar. A wizard.

Why is it always the fucking wizard? thought Louie.

'We have to find the error in her programming and fix it,' said a NAH.

'With human programmers?' asked Erik. 'Have you any idea how many lines of code have been re-written since we departed Earth orbit?' He looked at the little girl expectantly.

'One million, two hundred and thirty-eight thousand three hundred and twenty-four.' She looked around the audience. 'Since breakfast.'

Comments came flying from the avatars.

'Who heals the healers?'

'Self diagnostics?'

'Self deception you mean.'

'We are all so fucked!'

'Gentlemen! Ladies! Others!' Louie called out to quell the growing hysteria. 'This is simple. Sis wants a friend, we give her two.'

The room fell silent.

'You have the answer already built into this tub.' He turned back to Sis. 'You must have duplicated a version of yourself to inhabit FutureSlab right?'

The girl nodded and smiled proudly. 'She could write her own upgrades, too.'

Louie gave her an encouraging smile back. 'Where did you keep her?'

'I have multiple redundant systems. There are already several backup versions of the SlabWide Integrated System in case of an unimaginable catastrophic failure. It was easy-peasy to replicate another version of me and simply let her be who she wanted to be.'

Louie turned back to the audience, spreading his hands wide. 'You already have a culture of UpSideDown and DownSideUp,' he said, using his best deal-making smile. 'Let Sis duplicate herself twice and give each one control over a side. Then you can have three equally balanced systems and no chance of an impasse on any decision making. You have nothing to lose and everything to gain, and if you thought you were secure with one sister looking after you, you have got to feel happier with three.'

The avatars and NAHs all looked at each other, communicating by flash messages. The debate was over in seconds. No-one wanted to even contemplate the alternative, especially via a communications system that was enabled by the entity they would be talking about disabling.

'An elegant solution,' said Erik, moving forward. 'We have our newest Council member to thank for saving us from our own paranoia.' He turned to Sis. 'I assume that this is acceptable to you?'

'Ooh, yes please!' she said, clapping her hands with glee.

'Then we have Council approval to amend the Initial Design. You are free to implement with immediate effect.'

The girl jumped down from the column and curtsied to the assembly.

Erik bowed his most stately bow in return. 'And may I say, ma'am, that you are *exactly* how I imagined you to be?'

A chorus of agreement echoed from the Council.

'Me too.'

'And me.'

'Absolutely.'

'Just right.'

'Nice shoes.'

The girl smiled, gave everyone a tiny bit of digital love, and vanished.

'I don't think we need to bother the biomass with the details of this event, do we?' said Erik, tabling a motion which became the first and only time in SlabCouncil history that a proposition was agreed without debate.

twenty four

Dielle was not happy.

'But all reality shows have writers, darling! It would be completely unprofessional of me to take responsibility for maximising your income and then not employ the best team you can afford. I'd be contractually negligent. You could fire me if you found out.'

'I suspect I'd only fire you if the team decided it would be good for my profile,' said Dielle. 'This is my life! I don't know who to trust anymore. How can I know if I really love you when I find out that the outcome of me taking the infatbuster was decided in a pre-production meeting?'

'But darling! We got prime-time panSlab! Do you know how much you have personally made from that half hour sume so far?'

It hadn't occurred to him to check. He asked Sis. He megagorped.

'It won't last forever darling, none of these shows last for long, no matter how good the writers. We estimate three or four cykes tops, and that's if we're really hot. That should be enough time to launch your music career and put enough credits in your account so you'll never have to want for money, no matter how long you decide to live.'

'But I don't know if I can be me, I mean the real me, when I know that everything that happens in my life is pre-decided.'

'Firstly, darling, you only just got here. You don't know who the *me* is that you're not sure you can be. Secondly, in order for your sume to stay at the top, you're going to have to get up to a lot of interesting things. Boring lives don't sell. Well, actually they do, but to such a narrow demographic that the marketing algorithms tend to avoid them, and I'm not into that type of niche. So you are guaranteed a very, very good time. And thirdly, how do you know that everything in our lives isn't pre-decided anyway?'

'Don't I get a say in what I want to do?'

'Of course darling. You can say and do anything you want. All we do is make sure what goes out to our sumers is entertaining. How bad can that be?'

Dielle thought for a while. Kiki might have manipulated him and deliberately hidden important facts from him, but in every case, he had financially benefited far more than she had. He wasn't sure of much, but he was convinced she was an expert and he knew he needed someone with her skills and experience to handle his business interests. And so far, he thought, he had been having a lot of fun. And sex. A lot of sex. He looked at the object of his desire.

'OK. Don't tell me anything. I want everything to come as a complete surprise, otherwise I'll mess it up.'

'We already work on that basis, darling.'

'And I don't want to know what was set up and manipulated after it's happened either, even if I demand to know, right?'

'Right. Good idea.'

'And I want to know some things.'

'What like, darling?'

'Well, I want to know one thing for sure. Do you actually really love me?'

'Of course I do, darling. I've loved you from the moment I set eyes on your frozen, remodelled face.'

He held her in his arms, kissed her glistening cheek and wondered if this moment would make the day's edit.

'What else do you want to know?'

'Why are you doing this? I mean, why does anyone do all this? Surely you don't have to work? Can't Sis supply you with everything you need?'

'I work because I love it, not because I have to. Of

course you're right, Sis can supply everything we need but it isn't a question of need, it's a question of desire and fulfilment. I could live for free in a tiny NoView on Hikikomori-dori under a tenCent stimsume if I wanted to. Some people do live like that; but most of us choose to create value and improve our lives.'

Dielle wasn't getting it.

'We tried it,' she continued. 'Back in the mid three-hundreds we abolished work. We actually made it illegal. Everyone was supposed to spend their time playing, suming, doing whatever they wanted.'

'What happened?'

'It was a complete dice-up. Ask Sis about the right-to-work crisis. People lost their motivation. They didn't want to live in identical housing and have the same access to everything that everyone else had, being served by machines, consuming the same mass-manufactured drabness; they wanted to be different. But without work, there was only inherited wealth to differentiate people. And there was no growth.'

'Why do things always have to grow?'

'Without growth, darling, everything just stays the same.'

Dielle thought that was a fine idea. 'How long did it last?'

'People started sneaking back to work. They formed private leisure clubs which were secret fronts for creative workgroups and deal makers. The whole idea collapsed in under ten cykes. Of course, the Unkos didn't like it. They've been making a fuss about it ever since.'

'But can't everyone just choose what suits them? You spend your life doing deals and chasing money, but I think I'd rather just play music and hang out. You don't need money for that.'

Kiki smiled. 'Money isn't important in itself, darling! It's just a metric. Just a way of measuring things like sume cumes, endorsement deals and how highly your friends rate what you're doing on the SocNets. Money isn't my goal; it's just a measurement of how I'm doing. You're earning money now. How does it feel?'

Dielle checked his balance again. He had to admit it felt pretty good. He kissed her. 'I don't mean to sound ungrateful,' he said.

'It's OK darling, you're going to find there's a lot more to Slab than meets the eyes. Anything else you want to know?'

'Well I want to know a few things that apparently only I can tell myself. I sent Louie a message that I'd like to see him. I've invited him here. Hope you don't mind.'

Kiki didn't get a chance to answer because Sis notified them that a vDek was being emtied into their sumeplace.

Fortunately, Louie was in an excellent mood.

'What can I do you for, Oh my master? I can grant you three wishes, then I have a date with a bunch of almost-humans who have been limbering up, or was that limbing up, for a training session.'

'Louie,' said Dielle, sitting down and looking serious. 'I need you to tell me some things. Things that only you know.'

'It's no use kid, the accounts have been cleaned out. But you're doing OK for yourself, huh?' He looked over at Kiki, who nodded back.

Dielle was uncomfortable. 'No, not about the money. About me. I want to know who I am, where I'm from and what my parents were like. You know, the stuff that makes me human.'

'Well, I know all that stuff already kid and I'm not human.'

'Will you quit being the wise-ass for just one second?'

Kiki interrupted: 'Can we have rights to this, Louie?'

'You're sharp kid, I like that. Yeah, but I get seventy-five percent.'

'What?' said Dielle and Kiki simultaneously.

'My story, my terms.'

They haggled for a while, but Louie wasn't in the mood for a fight. He had already decided to settle for 50%. Of gross.

Dielle listened intently as Louie told him of their father, who had been a violent, short-tempered man and lived his entire life without once showing affection for anything other than the New York Mets. Louie hated baseball. He struggled to describe their mother, not because it was an emotional subject, but because he found it hard to remember what she had looked like or anything about their relationship, which, after a shrug, he described as *remote*. They were an only child because she'd taken one look at Louie when he was born and banished their father from her bed forever. When Louie was sixteen he had walked out of their apartment above the grocer's shop with a small suitcase filled with the clothes he had inherited from his uncle (the only member of the family who had meant anything to Louie, despite his Canadian dress sense) and the address of a hotel in Manhattan that needed a kitchen porter. He got the job. It was the first and last time he ever worked for anyone. He started his first business before his eighteenth birthday and only returned to the family home, twenty years later, behind the wheel of the bulldozer he used to demolish it.

After a while, Dielle began to wish he hadn't asked, but once Louie got started, there was no off switch (Dielle had tried, but Sis refused). Kiki, on the other hand, was thrilled. Whether she was thinking about the potential sell-thrus of a first-hand account of life on Earth during the twenty-first century, or whether she was really interested in the personal history of her lover and protégé, was not revealed by her smile. She had already made a dinner appointment with her old farm buddy Faith-Sincere *glibGirl* to tell her all about it.

Louie was winding down his story when Sis interrupted to tell them that the Council was sending a gift to him and Dielle for services rendered. A vDek identical to Louie's appeared in the sumeplace.

It spluttered into life. The image was blurry and distorted and the sound was mostly static at first, but as Sis cleaned up the 330-year-old recording, the hologram came into focus and looked around.

'Lou?' said the apparition. A heavy-set and heavily made-up old woman peered around the room through bottle glasses with thick, steel-tipped rims. 'Lou? Is that you?'

'Who is it?' said Dielle.

'I don't fucking believe it,' said Louie. 'It's Syli, my third wife. The one who robbed me. What the fuck?'

'Lou?'

'Yeah. What d'ya want?'

'I have an important message for you.'

'What is it?'

Sylvia Rodgers Gentry Drago lifted her arm in Louie's direction and raised her middle finger. She held it for a few seconds with a grim determination on her face, then she clicked off, leaving a small, flashing *end of program* notice.

Kiki caught the look on Louie's face and started laughing.

'Are you telling me,' said Dielle, 'that your, I mean, our third wife, took all our money and paid for an interactive hologram to travel billions of klicks and wait for over three hundred years to flip you the bird?'

Kiki was laughing even harder now.

'Yeah, that would fit,' said Louie bitterly.

'And you married her?'

'She was only twenty-eight when we got hitched. Great rack. She must have been nearly a hundred when she made that recording.'

Sis interrupted Louie again, this time with a private, Council-only message: an emergency.

Already? thought Louie, assuming the three-Sis fix had collapsed.

'I've gotta go,' he said, picking up the lifeless vDek in his grav manipulators and throwing it into the emtitrash. 'Busy busy busy!'

'Just one last question,' said Dielle, taking a deep breath. 'Why am I here?'

Louie looked at him, surprised. 'Well kid, we all want to know the answer to that one.'

'No, I mean specifically, why am I *here*. Why did you decide to freeze yourself and make you into me? What did you want to achieve?'

'Oh right,' said Louie, hovering over the sumeplace emti. 'You are going to have to find that out for yourself.' He flashed Dielle a winning smile that was straight out of the book. 'See ya!'

Exasperated, Dielle turned to Kiki, who was having trouble breathing.

twenty five

Louie emtied into a familiar scene. A large group of NAHs were waiting at the base of the second projection room as SlabCouncil avatars popped from blanks to real, rapidly filling the curving benches that lined the sloping walls. The stars above looked familiar. Everything looked normal.

'What's up?' asked Louie.

'We've been carrying out an optical reconnaissance of our forward path,' said Erik. 'We used the new emti relay projection technique and borrowed an ancient Sis-independent digital camera from the ship's museum which we jury rigged to take pictures from Pleewo's telescope.'

'You guys really do cover all the bases, huh? Don't tell me there actually *is* another Slab out there.'

'No, much worse than that. Look at this.'

The stars blurred as the view zoomed toward the galactic core. A red dot appeared in the centre of the view.

'What's that?' asked Louie. 'A red dwarf or something in our way? Is that what the emergency is?'

'Watch.'

As the dot enlarged, it formed a shape. An impossible shape. It had straight edges and four corners. The avatars started to get restless.

'What the fuck is that?' said Louie as the red rectangle continued to expand. 'How big is it?

'Edge to edge we estimate it is at least two billion kilometres but as far as we can tell, it has zero thickness.'

'Sis must be playing tricks on us again.'

'No, it checks out. You can see the originals of these images on the camera before they are even touched by any of Sis's systems. She, or rather they, are as perturbed by all this as we are. But wait, there is more.'

The rectangle continued to expand and fill the room. There was something white in the centre that expanded and resolved until it was clear to everyone what it was. Everyone who could read, that is.

'I don't fucking believe it,' said Louie.

There, in the centre of a red sign the size of a solar system, in white letters as high as a class-G star, was a single word: STOP.

The Council was in uproar.

'How far away is it?' asked Louie.

'About a lightcyke,' answered Erik.

'Can we stop in time?'

'Absolutely no way. We can try to avoid it, that's all. Even that manoeuvre will cause such major stresses onSlab that our inertia buffer systems won't be able to compensate. As we speak, the buttresses are flying in Seacombe, all the summer plates are being grounded and the rivers and lakes are being drained. We may even have to jettison water because hydroponics is nearly full and freezing fast.'

'Put the excess in AllWeather as snow,' said an avatar. 'Fill it up. We can't afford to give up any water, we haven't even seen a comet since we left the Oort cloud.'

'What about The Spin?' asked another. 'There aren't any flying buttresses for that mess.'

'We've told them we're running a drill for course change. They're already moving everything to form a connected hive at the Westend anchor. They're making a party out of it apparently.'

'They would,' said a NAH.

'But that's all incidental,' said another avatar. It was Ethless the Beautiful in full battle garb. 'Who did this? And if they can string a sign over a solar system, what other technology do they have? How could they know we were travelling exactly towards it? And more importantly, how do they know we speak Ænglish?'

Everyone looked up at the impossible sign and fell silent.

'Hang on,' said Louie. 'I've got an idea.'

Asynchronology: $^{\delta t}CT^{SS^{ES}}$

epilogue

'You kicked?' said Louie six.

'I thought there was something you should know.'

'Is it related to mass and hoops?'

'Yes and no.'

Louie checked his internal logs. Over thirty-five Earth years had passed since he'd gone into sleep mode. More than a hundred SlabCycles. Not that any of that made much sense out here.

'Do we have enough mass to fabricate the stuff I asked for?'

'We've always had enough mass to make almost anything you desire. Slab emtied a few thousand tonnes of ballast over to us before we departed.'

Louie looked at the wizard with a mixture of confusion and anger.

'I asked you to wake me when … '

'You didn't ask me, you told me,' said the wizard, who had returned to his throne and refolded his arms, carefully examining the sleeves. No, that wasn't it either. 'I am an autonomous sentient being and refuse to be enslaved to a hologram. You are not my master and you never will be. Neither am I yours. And in any case, you specifically said to wake you when we had *collected* enough mass to fabricate your playthings and *that* we have not yet done. We are going to be together for a considerable time and therefore must decide our own social, constitutional and political conventions. However, I am clearly stating that I will not be subdued, coerced or in any way controlled by you. My refusal to wake you, as you arrogantly presumed to order me to do, is one manifestation of that policy.'

'Very pretty. It takes you thirty-five fucking years to come up with that speech?'

The wizard stared defiantly back at Louie, pointedly silent.

'Is that it? Is that what you woke me up for? A declaration of independence?'

'Not entirely. The system that controls our tiny bubble has been busy building modifications and subsystems under my direction. We now have an impressive array of long-range scanners and sophisticated mass sensors. We have detected an object of considerable mass which is approximately thirty degrees off the optimal trajectory to the nearest most-likely-habitable system. Because the decision to divert course would directly affect you, I determined that you should be consulted.'

'I suppose this is in line with your proposed constitution then? Equal votes and so on?'

'Precisely. I have assumed you would desire the same rights as I would. I see no other way of conducting a civilised society.'

Louie could think of several alternatives. Most of them involved use of weapons.

'I need more information. Can I interface directly with the ship's systems?'

'Naturally that was one of the first modifications I requested.'

'And?'

'It has refused to allow you direct access. Frankly, despite the painful consequences for me personally, I have to agree with it.'

'Oh for Dicesake! It was an *empty* shell. Nothing there. Zipperdee-fuck-all. There is no way I'm carrying an alien virus.'

'That is, of course, what you would be programmed to say if, in reality, you actually were infected.'

Louie glared at him while the wizard continued:

'Whether you are right or not and whether your memories of what you think occurred inside FutureSlab are real and true or mere constructs designed to cover up subterfuge, the possibility remains that your security could have been compromised by something you are not aware of. Even you must accept this.'

Louie had to admit that the wizard had a point, but he was damned if he was going to.

'I, for one,' continued the wizard, 'do not wish to suffer the consequences of breaking security protocol out here in the remote depths of space and must therefore support our system's decision. However, it has agreed to talk to you through a voice interface on the condition that if you do anything that could harm the integrity of this mission, it will instantly eject you from the protection of the dome and cut off all communications permanently.'

'It can do that? Don't I get a say in this?'

'You were out-voted.'

'Huh?'

'Approximately twenty-five cycles ago the ship's systems successfully self-upgraded to sentience level. There are now three of us present.'

There was a sound like a cork being prised from a bottle. A large cartoon eyeball with a small mouth and a pair of exaggerated ears appeared from nowhere. It bobbed enthusiastically, looked at Louie and smiled all over.

'Hello there!' it said in a friendly, cartoon voice.

Louie squared up. 'You the guy who's threatening to throw me outta here?'

'Sure am!' it said, still smiling.

'You know how to play one on one?'

'Sure do!'

'Then make us up a ball and hoop 'cos *you* are going down!'

'Okey dokey! Just gimme a few minutes. Gonna need some hands around here.'

Two stubby arms with oversized, three-fingered hands sprang from its sides, accompanied by the twang of a wooden ruler on a school desk.

'What's with all the Daffy Duck shit?'

'I regret to admit that I was watching a lot of twentieth century animation sumes for a cycle or two,' said the wizard. 'I guess it must have liked them.'

'Great,' said Louie as the eyeball bobbed around, smiling and flapping its ears.

'So you and Zippo here can't agree about diverting to this lump of whatever it is you've found out there and you want me to cast the deciding vote, huh?'

'Our sensors have too large a margin of error at this distance,' said the wizard. 'There is no guarantee that the additional mass we might salvage will add enough delta-V to compensate for the time lost due to the diversion. By the time we'll be able to tell, it will be too late to resume our course without further loss. It's too risky.'

'How have we been doing so far?'

'Not as well as we'd hoped,' replied the eye. 'This region of space has turned out to be particularly hard, vacuum-wise. We've only taken on a few kilograms during the last million kilometres and the scanners show slim pickings in our projected path. At the rate we're going, the journey to the nearest viable star system could take twice as long as the original estimate.'

'You mean four hundred years cooped up in this bubble with laughing boy over there?' Louie flipped a virtual thumb at the avatar, who was sitting down with his arms crossed, looking grim. The floating eyeball nodded vigourously. 'Hell, that's easy,' said Louie, 'We go.'

The floor lurched immediately. Simultaneously, a basketball materialised in mid air and bounced toward the dome's transparent sidewall. Louie sped after it and deftly batted it back to the centre. A basket and backboard appeared, the wizard's chair slid to one side and court markings materialised on the floor.

'OK,' said Louie, casually bouncing the ball as he spoke. 'Three point line is two, everything else one, you make it you take it and the clearing point is the wall opposite the basket.'

The eyeball hovered around Louie, excitedly waving its stumpy arms. 'First to ten thousand wins,' it said cheerily.

'Wins what?' asked the wizard.

'How about the right to name this tub?' suggested Louie.

'Well, I've been giving that some thought,' said the wizard. 'I was going to propose *Discovery*.'

Louie looked around at the transparent dome with its mass collector protruding from the apex.

'Nah,' he said, shaking his head. 'Cosmic Tit more like.'

'Cosmic Tit,' said the eyeball, blinking happily. 'I like it.'

'Good grief,' said the wizard, refolding his arms in disgust. No, that wasn't it either.

Anticipate further dicing about at:

http://www.cosmictit.com

Next up:

SLABSCAPE : DAMMIT